Rye couldn't take her eyes off the remains of her family shop. Villagers wandered past it without a second glance, as if they'd already become numb to the black eye or simply forgotten about it altogether. All except one. A bent figure sifted through the rubble, almost invisible in the shadows of the burned-out frame. Rye watched carefully as he reached down to pick something from the ashes.

A looter! There might not be much left to take, but there was no way she was about to let someone pick through their belongings.

She dodged a foraging piglet as she hurried across the street and ran through the empty, blackened doorframe. Muted afternoon light filtered through the hollow windows, but she could not see anyone in the shadows. Instead, a yellow sheet of parchment nailed to a timber caught her attention. Thanks to her mother's refusal to follow the Laws of Longchance and Quinn's informal lessons, Rye was one of the few village girls who could read.

PROCLAMATION

OF EARL MORNINGWIG LONGCHANCE!

Generous Rewards Offered for the Capture of

Abigail O'Chanter and her Two Offspring!

Wanted for Crimes Against the Shale!

The Luck Uglies
Fork-Tongue Charmers

Paul Durham

Illustrations by Pétur Antonsson

HARPER
An Imprint of HarperCollins*Publishers*

The Luck Uglies: Fork-Tongue Charmers
 For information address HarperCollins Children's Books, a division of HarperCollins Publishers,
195 Broadway, New York, NY 10007.
www.harpercollinschildrens.com

Library of Congress Cataloging-in-Publication Data
Durham, Paul (Paul Joseph), author.
Fork-tongue charmers / Paul Durham ; illustrations by Pétur Antonsson. — First edition.
pages cm. — (The Luck Uglies ; #2)
Summary: "When Rye O'Chanter is declared an outlaw from her own village, she finds herself stuck on a strange remote island. But the island comes to feel much less remote when the battle over the future of the Luck Uglies moves to its shores"— Provided by publisher.
ISBN 978-0-06-227154-9
[1. Monsters—Fiction. 2. Secret societies—Fiction. 3. Adventure and adventurers—Fiction. 4. Fantasy.] I. Pétur Antonsson, illustrator. II. Title.
PZ7.D9337Fo 2015 2014038648
[Fic]—dc23 CIP
AC

Typography by Carla Weise
16 17 18 19 20 OPM 10 9 8 7 6 5 4 3 2 1

First paperback edition, 2016

For my three muses,
who inspire me even when I'm a grump

Contents

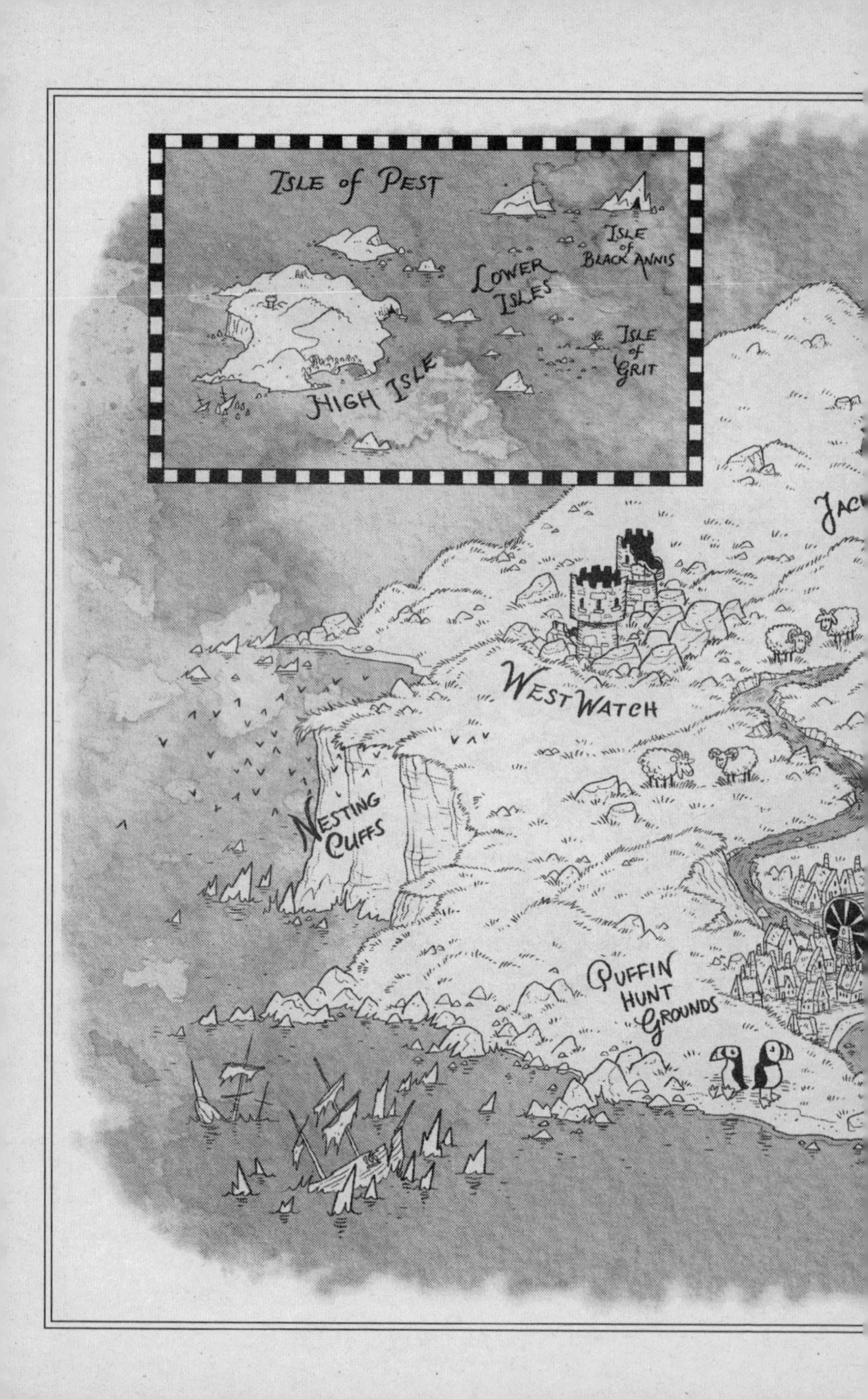

Isle of Pest
Isle of Black Annis
Lower Isles
Isle of Grit
High Isle
West Watch
Nesting Cliffs
Puffin Hunt Grounds

SLE of PEST
HIGH ISLE
THE WAILING CAVE
ONS' PILES
VARLET HOMESTEAD
TARVISH FARM
WALDRON'S FARM
CRUSHED-SHELL PATH
LLAGE WICK
CUTTY HOUSE
GULL ISLAND
N

A Song about Bargains . . .

Come all would-be heroes and join me in song,
And curse the dread outlaws plagued
this Isle for so long.
So take heed my warning, of no favors ask,
Beware the dread outlaws in shadows and masks.
In shadows and masks, in shadows and masks,
Beware the dread outlaws
In shadows and masks.
Our troubles were many, our hopes they were slim.
A dark stranger arrived, he packed
promise with him.
On the grayest of nights a bargain was struck,
What then seemed good fortune turned
black ugly luck.
In shadows and masks, in shadows and masks,
Beware the dread strangers
In shadows and masks.

They'll promise you freedom and all that you dream,
But look past their guise, they're not what they seem.
Your sons and your daughters, in bed safely tuck,
Hold tight what you cherish for that
they shall pluck.
In shadows and masks, in shadows and masks,
Beware the dread scoundrels
In shadows and masks.
My son he now stalks the dark b'yond the sea,
Family forgotten, but what matters to he?
So take heed my warning, of no favors ask,
And curse the Luck Uglies in shadows and masks.
In shadows and masks, in shadows and masks,
Curse the Luck Uglies
In shadows and masks.

—SHADOWS AND MASKS,
From "Songs of Salt and Stout
and Other High Isle Favorites"

Only Trouble Knocks after Dark

It wasn't often that anyone thumped the cottage's rusting iron door knocker after dark, but Rye O'Chanter still never expected to find three twisted, leering faces on the other side. They loomed down at her from behind flurrying snow. Rye knew *what* the masked figures were, if not *who* they were, so perhaps there was no need for alarm. Then again, Luck Uglies had never just shown up on her doorstep before. She took a careful step backward.

Abby O'Chanter joined her, a cloak flung over her

nightdress. She'd already untied her hair ribbon for the night and her dark locks fell loose past her shoulders. In her arms she held the family pet, a regal beast with thick black fur and keen yellow eyes. He was as big as a young child, and as he stretched his long forelegs, he extended sickle-like claws for the benefit of the visitors. Shady could be a ferocious guardian when motivated, which wasn't all that often. Abby combed his luxurious mane with her fingertips and raised an uninviting eyebrow. Rye's mother had never been one to spook easily.

"What is it?" she demanded of the visitors.

The tallest of the three ducked his head under the fresh evergreen garland strung along the doorframe. Shady let out an unexpected rumble from deep inside his throat, the kind he generally reserved for unwelcome denizens of the bogs. Rye saw her mother slip her fingers around his runestone collar in case he decided to misbehave.

The masked figure hesitated, then opted to lean forward without stepping inside. The gnarled leather of a long, beakish nose jutted from under his cowl, so close to Abby's ear it seemed it might jab her. Under Shady's careful watch, the man whispered something that sounded like the rustle of dead leaves. He cocked his head as he spoke, and the mask's hollow black eyes met Rye's own.

The figure leaned back and snow once again settled onto his cloaked shoulders.

"He can't come for her himself?" Abby said, an edge in her voice.

The figure shook his head.

"Come for who?" Rye asked.

Abby ignored her and seemed to bite back harsh words on the tip of her tongue. Instead, she said, "I've got porridge on the fire if you'd care for some."

The masked figure just shook his head again.

"Be off then," Abby said. She didn't seem at all disappointed that they'd declined her invitation.

The figure nodded by way of good-bye and vanished into the shadows of Mud Puddle Lane with his two companions. Rye squinted to see where they went but spied only the flickering lantern lights of their neighbors' cottages. She turned to her mother.

"What is it?" she asked.

"Your father," Abby said. "He's sent for you. You leave to meet him tomorrow."

"But it's finally Silvermas," Rye protested. "*And* the Black Moon. How often does Silvermas fall on a Black Moon?"

Silvermas was Rye's favorite tradition. Where once the holiday was intended to honor deities long forgotten, it had since evolved into a family celebration—a time for one last great feast before the chills and hardship of a long winter. Of course, in practice, Silvermas followed whatever night Good Harper actually happened to arrive in a particular village on his Mud Sleigh. This made for a great amount of speculation and excitement among the children. Rye's mother and the other parents found the suspense to be of less amusement, particularly this year, since it was already early spring and Good Harper was only now making his way to Village Drowning.

The Black Moon—the darkest night of every month—well, that was something else entirely. Villagers locked their doors with the Black Moon's rise, for the men who prowled the night under the moonless sky weren't always so benign. Three of them had just left the O'Chanters' doorstep.

"I don't think your father's timing is a coincidence," Abby said. There was a weight on her face that Rye couldn't quite gauge. "You'll be away for only a day or so."

"He's been gone all winter," Rye mumbled to herself. "Why now?"

It wasn't that Rye didn't want to see her father—she was just getting to know him when he'd abruptly departed to tend to some pressing matters outside the village. He had recently taught her all sorts of useful skills her mother would never approve of—how to shimmy down a drainpipe while blindfolded, how to hide a key under your tongue and still sing an off-color limerick without slurring your words. He'd promised he would see her again as soon as he was able. But all winter she had been looking forward to meeting her friends and trading their Silvermas treats. Folly was usually willing to part with a few caramel pralines, and Rye always convinced Quinn to take the green licorice off her hands. Quinn actually seemed to like green licorice—he was odd like that.

"He wouldn't have called if it wasn't important," Abby said stiffly, then softened. She gently pushed an unruly brown bang out of Rye's eyes. Rye had never been one to fuss over her hair—it was too short to braid but too long to ignore.

"I know you're disappointed, but he's arranged a Silvermas surprise for you. Trust me, I think you'll be pleased."

Rye raised an eager eyebrow.

"You have to wait until tomorrow," Abby said, anticipating her next question.

Abby flashed her a smile, but Rye noticed her mother's hesitation before closing the purple door carved with the shape of a dragonfly. Abby stared down the northernmost end of Mud Puddle Lane, toward the dense pine forest known only as Beyond the Shale. Rye had seen that look before.

"Something in the air?" Rye asked, reaching out to scratch Shady's furry ears. His bushy tail swayed in appreciation.

"Something," was all Abby said, and they went inside for bed.

Morning's first fingers of light had barely cracked the windowsill before Rye and her sister, Lottie, rushed from their room in their nightdresses. The cottage was already warm with the smell of Abby's brown-sugar-and-raisin porridge, but the girls ran straight past their bowls, jostling for position at the cottage door. Lottie had strength beyond her years when there were sweets to be had, and Rye found herself knocked against the doorframe by the compact but determined three-year-old.

For centuries throughout the Shale, in towns large and villages small, residents would fill their shoes with coins and set them out on their doorsteps for Silvermas. Good Harper would then ride the Mud Sleigh through each village and collect the coins while the townspeople slept, to be distributed later to the needy and downtrodden. Good villagers received sweets in return. Bad villagers received a potato or, if they were really awful, mouse droppings. The more coins left, the better the fortunes of the family for the coming year. Woe betide the man, woman, or child who failed to leave at least one miserly bronze bit.

Rye crammed her hand deep into the toe of one oversize boot, then the other. The boots had belonged to Rye's father when he was her age. They were ragged in the heels and probably contributed to her numerous stumbles, but Rye wore them every day. They came in particularly handy on Silvermas—more room for candies. And yet, that morning, they had done no good at all.

"Pigshanks," Rye cursed.

Lottie had already emptied the bulging contents of her shoes and was busy stockpiling treats in her cheeks with the expertise of a chipmunk. She opened her chocolate-filled mouth.

"You said a bad word," she garbled.

"Then you'd better not repeat it," Rye said, holding an empty boot to her eye to get a better look. She couldn't believe that Lottie, of all children, had gotten a full shoe while she had nothing. Not even a potato.

"Wait . . . ," Rye said, finally discovering something deep inside the toe.

She removed a hard, heavy object and examined it in her hand.

"You got coal!" Lottie cackled.

"It's not coal," Rye said, rolling the stone over in her palm. It was the size and shape of a somewhat flattened egg, flawless ebony in color, and smoother than glass, as if polished by centuries of tides. It was also frigid. Instead of warming to her touch, it seemed to draw the heat from her fingers. She'd never seen a stone like it before.

"Rye got coal!" Lottie repeated when their mother appeared behind them. Abby pulled back Lottie's thick red hair so it wouldn't stick to the nougat on her cheeks. "And she said a bad word," Lottie added quickly. She pretended to share a chocolate with Mona Monster, her pink hobgoblin rag doll.

"Maybe that's why she got the coal," Abby said, shooting Rye a look of disapproval.

"It's a *rock*," Rye said glumly. Embarrassed, she tucked it out of sight in her pocket. "Why would Good Harper leave me a rock?" This was shaping up to be the worst Silvermas ever.

"Mistakes happen sometimes, Riley," Abby said. She shifted her leg so that the hem of her dress concealed her own overflowing shoe. It was too late; Rye had already seen it. "One year the Quartermasts' hound got loose and ate all the Silvermas shoes," Abby volunteered. "If that makes you feel any better."

Rye just frowned. It didn't.

"Speaking of which—" Abby began.

"Rye! Lottie!" a voice called. A boy in red long johns hopped on one foot from the cottage three doors down, one boot on and the other in his hands. He was tall and reedy, the sleeves of his undershirt ending well short of his wrists.

"Quinn Quartermast," Abby said, "where in the Shale are your britches? You'll get icicles in your lungs . . . or somewhere worse."

Quinn shrugged and his cheeks turned as red as his long johns. He balanced on one foot and held out a boot full of treats.

"Do you want to trade?" he asked eagerly.

"Rye got coal," Lottie said, examining Quinn's haul with a discerning eye.

"I got a *stone*," Rye clarified. That had a nicer ring to it than *rock*.

"Oh," Quinn said in disappointment, but he quickly put on a happy face for Rye's benefit. "You can have some of mine. I've got plenty of green licorice."

"Thanks, Quinn," Rye said halfheartedly. Lottie turned up her nose at the licorice and pulled her own pile closer.

Rye saw Quinn's eyes suddenly go wide. He blinked hard, as if clearing blurry vision. He pointed to the far end of Mud Puddle Lane. "Is that—" he stammered, awestruck.

Rye and Lottie both turned to look. There, at the farthest end of the frozen dirt lane, was an enormous, weatherworn coach pulled by four heavily muscled draft horses. At their reins was a hefty, gray-bearded man in a wide-brimmed hat the color of a ripe plum. A matching woolly scarf enveloped his neck, its ends draped down to his boots.

Rye looked to her mother, mouth agape.

"You can't say your father doesn't have a flair for surprises," Abby said. There was a tight smirk at the corner of her mouth that told Rye she remained both impressed and exasperated by her father's special brand of flair. "You, my love, are going for a ride on the Mud Sleigh. Now let's get you loaded up before Good Harper finds himself overrun by every child in Drowning."

2
The Mud Sleigh

Never in all of Good Harper Killpenny's many years had the Mud Sleigh been robbed, accosted, or otherwise bothered by bandits or highwaymen. In fact, he rode under the protection of the most fearsome outlaws of all. Thanks to a bargain struck between the Luck Uglies and generations of Good Harpers before him, Killpenny traveled safely without guards, comfortable in the knowledge that a harsh and swift reckoning would befall any opportunist foolish enough to trouble him on his journey.

That was what he told Rye, anyway, as they left Drowning under a clear morning sky. She suspected that this was precisely the reason her father had arranged for her passage on the Mud Sleigh, and the only reason her mother had allowed it. Rye looked back, waved to Abby, Lottie, and Quinn, and examined the contents of the coach. Its hold was loaded up with more gold and silver than a flush noble's treasure hole.

The River Drowning was still frozen over in long stretches, light snow cover transforming it into a wide, smooth roadway. Rye twitched with the excitement of a new adventure as the village's twisted rooftops disappeared behind them, the horses pulling the sleigh along the ice so swiftly that the wind rustled her hair. Soon she was shifting in her seat to get a better view of the Western Woods as they traveled southwest, farther from home than she had ever been before. Eventually, however, all the trees began to look the same. She asked Good Harper four times if they were almost there, until he said something about having a bad ear and stopped responding altogether. She sang a song to pass the time. Rye's voice must have miraculously cured Good Harper's hearing, because he begged her to stop it right away. She sighed and thrust her chin into her hands. It was only midday.

Dusk came early, and by nightfall Rye's boredom had been replaced by a dull anxiety as she huddled under a heavy blanket on top of the driver's box. They had stopped to make camp on the frozen river itself, at a particular bend where Good Harper said they were to wait for Rye's father to come collect her. Rye tried to take comfort in the Mud Sleigh's unblemished history as she listened to howls in the distance. The horses kicked at the ice and shuffled nervously around their camp. These animals must have seen and heard it all in these woods over the years, but tonight something had them spooked.

From his seat next to Rye, Good Harper scratched his beard and popped a cinnamon candy into his mouth. He offered one to Rye, but she just shook her head. It would have been a whole lot nicer if he'd left some for her last night. Good Harper offered her a potato. She turned that down too.

"You've gone quiet," he remarked, which wasn't entirely true. The fact was, Rye could hardly sneak a word in between his own ramblings. After his long months alone on the Mud Sleigh, Good Harper was well-practiced in talking to himself.

"It's a shame," he said with a snort. "Good conversation, or even polite small talk, has become harder and harder to come by."

"I'm sorry, I don't mean to be—"

"The Shale folk have grown stingy," Good Harper

continued, as if he hadn't heard her at all. "Nowadays they fill their shoes out of nothing more than habit. There seems to be no genuine concern for the needy, not even a healthy fear of bad luck. Drowning is the worst of the lot. It's a glorified mud hole with its creeping bogs and notorious forest. Most of its residents barely muster up more than a few token bronze bits, and those who do put out shoes that smell like last month's cheese." He cast her a quick glance. "No offense, by the way."

"None taken," Rye said flatly. That was all true, she had to admit.

"The Earl didn't even invite me to his Silvermas Eve Feast this year," Good Harper grumbled on. "He's got himself a new Constable—can't say I care for him one bit. The wag turned me away at the gates without so much as a carrot for the horses."

Nobody had seen much of Earl Morningwig Longchance all winter—not that anyone was complaining. But Rye had heard he'd enlisted the services of an infamous lawman-for-hire in recent days. The law seldom found its way to Mud Puddle Lane—its residents too poor or unimportant to warrant protection—but Folly said this one had already made some harsh changes in other parts of the village. Rye doubted he could be any worse than his predecessor.

She gazed up at the sky and sighed. Behind the

cloak of the invisible Black Moon, the stars shone like a thousand glowing candles on the Dead Fish Inn's bone chandelier. She wished she was there right now, celebrating Silvermas with Folly and her family. Her thoughts were interrupted by another howl from somewhere across the ice. Good Harper seemed to be paying closer attention to the howls himself.

"Good Harper," Rye said, now that he'd finally fallen silent. "Why did you leave me this? Was I really so terrible this year?" She held out the black stone she had found in her boot.

Good Harper pursed his lips and took the stone between his fingers. "Eh?" he said, examining it closely. "This isn't from me. Someone's playing a joke on you." He huffed and shook his head. "Drowning—those villagers are rotten to the core."

With a flick of his wrist he threw the stone out across the river. Rye heard it hit the ice and skid for a long distance before finally coming to a stop. When she looked out toward where the stone might have settled, she noticed the three distant torches streaking in their direction.

"Over there," she said, and pointed.

"Hmm," Good Harper grunted, and peered out from under the wide brim of his hat.

"What are they?" she asked.

Good Harper rubbed his beard again and sucked his candy. “Can’t say for certain, but they look to be sleds.”

They were in fact three sleds, pulled by teams of enormous black dogs. They came to a halt in the shadows just outside of Good Harper’s camp. The animals’ claws scraped at the ice and their eyes glowed in the torchlight. They snapped and snarled at one another. Angry and distracted, they were too big to be sled dogs. Wolves?

Rye fidgeted in anticipation. A hooded figure stepped off the lead sled and approached. Other cloaked men stayed with their sled teams and shifted in the shadows. She reached back to get the satchel her mother had packed before climbing down to meet her father.

Good Harper placed a hand on Rye’s shoulder before she could get up. “Lass, why don’t you duck inside the coach?”

“Are they not Luck Uglies?” Rye asked, peering at the animals and sled drivers. Although, now that she thought about it, this is not how she would expect her father to greet her.

“It would seem so,” Good Harper said quickly. “I’ll call you out as soon as I know for certain.” He stepped down from the driver’s box. “But,” he added, in a coarse whisper, “if you hear anything amiss, get out and run for the trees. Don't look back."

Rye clambered into the back of the Mud Sleigh as she was told, ignoring the chittering of dozens of caged mice—"treats" for those on Good Harper's naughty list had to come from somewhere. She parted the sleigh's heavy curtain so she could peek through. Good Harper met the cloaked man by the small campfire. Rye could see that he was wearing a mask under his hood.

"Fine evening, neighbor," Good Harper said in an even tone. "That's a most unusual sled team you and your men ride."

"Indeed," the man replied, and looked toward the animals, who erupted into a choir of howls. "The wolves can be quarrelsome, but their size allows them to pull much larger loads than dogs."

The man's voice was a faraway hiss that resonated like an echo from a bottomless well. It wasn't Rye's father's voice. She didn't like it one bit.

"I see," Good Harper said with affected cheer. "And what loads are you carrying that you need such a team?"

"None just yet. But you have quite the heavy cargo in your sleigh. I think I shall need the strength of each and every one of these wolves to haul it."

Rye gripped the curtains with both hands. What was going on here? Good Harper's tone shifted quickly, his voice now stern.

"Neighbor, do you know who I am? This charity is for the needy and downtrodden. The Luck Uglies have ensured my safe passage on these roads for many years, and for that reason I pass no judgment on you or your kind. But I suggest you be on your way in search of a more appropriate mark."

"If it gives you some solace," the man said, "let's just say I am the neediest soul I know. Now step aside."

He placed a firm hand on Good Harper's arm, showing no intention of asking again.

Good Harper gritted his teeth and, to Rye's great surprise, lashed out in anger with an old knotted fist. His blow didn't buckle the marauder, but it knocked his mask to the ice.

The man smiled, revealing the red patchwork seams of his gums. Then he returned the blow. It crumpled Good Harper to his knees.

Without thinking, Rye lurched from inside the coach to help. The assailant towered over the fallen Good Harper and moved as if he might kick him. But Rye's appearance on top of the Mud Sleigh caused him to pause and glance upward. His gaze froze her before she jumped down. Most of the man's ashen white face was shrouded in the shadows of his hood, but she could see that Good Harper's blow had drawn blood from his black lips. He licked the corner of his mouth with his tongue. Rye recoiled when she saw that it was forked like a snake's, the two pink ends dancing over his lips like blind, probing serpents.

Rye darted back inside the coach. She clambered over the mountain of coin purses and kicked aside the mouse cages so she could shove open the back door of the Mud Sleigh. The woods were straight ahead. But as she leaped down, her boots skidded out from under her and she landed hard on the ice. By the time she regained her footing, the fork-tongued man had stepped in front of her, blocking her way to the river's edge. He affixed his mask back over his face.

Rye took a deep breath, her heart pounding. Her mother had told her once: *Walk strong, act like you belong, and no one will be the wiser.* If these were Luck Uglies, she should have nothing to fear. She took a step to her left. The man moved to block her path. She took a step back to the right. He did the same.

"Who are you?" Rye demanded, doing her best to channel her mother's voice.

The reply came from deep inside a hollow. "Names are a precious paint to be shared cautiously. Offer yours first, and I'll tell you mine."

"Rye O'Chanter," she said, forcing herself to stand straight and stare hard at the masked face in front of her.

The man reached forward with a long gloved finger. Before she could flinch, he pulled her hood from her head. He leaned in closer, as if studying her. His mask was scaled armor the texture of an adder's skin, his own eyes just slits behind its red-ringed eyeholes. Unlike all of the other Luck Uglies' masks she had ever seen, this one had no nose. But a gaping maw loomed open, part of a grotesquely distended chin that extended all the way to his chest.

"I've seen you before." He was close enough that she felt his breath when he said it.

"What's *your* name?" she asked sternly, ignoring the knot tightening in her stomach. "Before you do something you'll regret, you should know that my father is a Luck Ugly too."

"Slinister," he said from deep behind his mask. "Now you say it."

"What?" Rye asked, in a retreating voice that was very much *unlike* her mother's.

"You asked me my name and I told you. Now repeat it."

"Slinister," Rye said quietly. If words had taste, this one would have rolled sour off her tongue.

"That's correct," he said. "And yes, I know very well who your father is. In fact, I know him better than you do."

The hollow of his masked mouth was so black and wide it seemed it might swallow her. She took a step away. When he didn't move to follow her, she took another.

"You may go," Slinister said, waving a dismissive hand. "Perhaps we'll have a chance to visit another day."

Rye's steps quickened as she moved along the ice, never taking her eyes off the man named Slinister. She found Good Harper struggling to regain his feet. She grabbed him by the shoulders and helped him up, then hurried him across the frozen river. His plum-colored scarf dragged behind them.

"Remember my name, Rye O'Chanter," Slinister called as he watched her go. She glanced back over her shoulder just once and was relieved that the night now shrouded his fiendish mask.

As Rye and Good Harper took refuge in the safety of the woods, Slinister's cohorts slipped from the shadows and plundered the Mud Sleigh, loading their own sleds with every last gold grommet and silver shim. They unhitched the horses and led them away. Finally, when the sleigh was stripped to nothing more than an empty shell, the looters lit a raging ring of fire around the camp. Their sleds had disappeared far downriver by the time the sleigh broke through the melting ice and sank beneath the frigid water.

Rye and Good Harper huddled under a tall pine. Rye shivered more from the shock than the cold. She couldn't comprehend what had just happened.

"A pox on the Luck Uglies and their bargains," Good Harper muttered. "Mouse droppings for the whole lot of them."

No sooner had he uttered his curse than a specter clad in black leather and fur appeared like a flickering shadow. In the moonless night, Rye could have mistaken it for a massive wolf rising up on its hind legs, but in its hands, two blades glinted in the light from the fire. Rye pressed her back against the tree. There was nowhere to run.

"Come to finish the job?" Good Harper called defiantly.

The shadowy figure loomed for a moment then, stepping forward, violently thrust its swords downward. Rye pinched her eyes tight. She heard the steel sink into something moist. Perhaps she was just too numb to feel their bite. But when she cracked open one eye, fearful of what she might find, she saw both blades embedded in the ground.

The figure pulled off its wolf-pelt hood and clutched her by the shoulders.

"Riley," the man whispered, his familiar gray eyes wide in a face of faded scars. "What in the Shale are you doing out here?"

"Harmless!" Rye exclaimed. She blinked in disbelief. "You tell me—you're the one who sent for me!"

He gently touched her cheek. His hands, like the rest of his body, were etched with tattoos, and while Rye didn't think there was anything magical about the circular patterns on his palms, whenever he did this it seemed to warm her whole body, his night-chilled skin notwithstanding.

"Make no mistake, I'm always glad to see you," he said softly. "But I did nothing of the sort."

Rye shook her head as if she didn't hear him correctly.

"Three Luck Uglies came to our cottage with a message. And here, on the river, there was a man—a Luck Ugly, I thought. He called himself Slinister." She shuddered at the thought of his split tongue. "He said he knows you well."

Harmless's jaw hardened. A darkness seemed to creep through the lines of his scarred face. Rye had only seen brief flashes of that look before, and each time it had unnerved her. Harmless must have sensed her unease, and pulled her close. His embrace and tender tone shielded her from the fire in his eyes as he scanned the burning river.

"Don't fret," he whispered. "We'll sort this out in due course. But right now we must be on our way. I know a safe place to spend the night."

The hour was late by the time Harmless escorted Good Harper to the closest roadhouse on the path back to Drowning. But to Rye's surprise he then led her away from the warmth of the inn. They traveled not to the village but over the edge of a tall bluff and down the jagged coastline. Waves crashed around them as Harmless navigated a rocky shoal that seemed to lead directly into the sea. He stopped only when they reached a mountainous outcropping nestled among the tide pools.

"Here?" Rye asked in disbelief.

Harmless put an arm over her shoulder and waved a hand above him. "Here."

What looked to be a massive sea stack loomed over them. But now, within spitting distance, it became clear that it was nothing of the sort. The battered rocks had been hollowed out, and rising from the waves were two enormous doors. Each the width of a castle's drawbridge, they were wide enough to sail a ship through with the tide out to sea, but would once again become a submersed secret when the water rolled back in. A towering, weatherworn mansion seemed to grow out of the craggy rocks, its crooked gables, twisting turrets, and jumbled archways slinking upward like coral in search of sun.

Rye shot Harmless a wary glance from under the folds of his fur cloak.

"You'll like it. It's a secret—even from the Luck Uglies," he said, appealing to her insatiable curiosity. "We won't stay long. I promise to return you to Drowning in short order."

But as luck would have it, the lingering hand of a stubborn winter delivered one last blow the next morning. And no one, not even Harmless, the High Chieftain of all the Luck Uglies, was going anywhere at all.

3 Grabstone

Rye sat alone on a cold, black rock jutting out from the sea. She counted in her head as she stared at the violent, churning waves. *Two hundred eighty-nine. Two hundred ninety.* Rye hated being alone. She liked waiting even less. But she didn't dare move for fear of slipping on the barnacles and being dragged out by the current.

A dusky brown gull struggled to fly against the wind.

Rye squinted at the bird. It gave her the sudden sense that she'd been in this spot once before, which was odd, since she had never traveled outside of Village Drowning. She shook off the unnerving feeling and resumed her count.

Two hundred ninety-nine. Three hundred. Five minutes now.

A gale sent the gull hurtling off in the wrong direction, and it disappeared into a brightening sky that had been gray with fog and snow since Rye's arrival.

Rye pulled her new seal-leather coat tight at the collar, its thick hood snug over her head and its long hem covering her to the knees. Even in an ocean storm it kept her remarkably warm and dry. The seal whose hide it was made from met no harm. The reclusive northern salt seal was the only mammal in the world known to shed its skin. Harmless had given her this coat as a belated twelfth birthday present. He'd missed that birthday over this past winter, just as he'd missed all the others before it.

Harmless might seem like a strange name for a girl to call her father, but Rye's father was—to put it nicely—an unusual man. Rye hadn't even known that she had a real live father until last autumn. That was when he appeared like a wisp of smoke out of the ancient forest known as Beyond the Shale. He'd been gone for over ten years.

Not everyone had been happy to see him. Harmless

was a Luck Ugly. An outlaw so notorious that he and all of his kind had been driven into exile by Earl Morningwig Longchance. But, with Rye's help, Harmless was able to summon the Luck Uglies and once again save Village Drowning. It had been under attack by a fierce clan of Bog Noblins—vile, swamp-creeping beasts who had threatened the lives of the villagers. One would think that such an achievement would have earned a certain degree of appreciation from the Earl, but Longchance's hatred of Harmless only grew. It was Harmless's threat—that the Luck Uglies would be watching—that had kept Longchance at bay ever since.

Rye pulled her knees into her chest to avoid the whitecaps that snapped at her oversize boots like frenzied sharks. Finally, when her count reached *three hundred thirty,* Harmless broke through the surface of the water. He pulled himself onto the rock and refilled his lungs with a great gulp of air. His long dark hair was tied into a wet knot atop his head. The leather-and-tortoiseshell goggles over his eyes made him look like a bug-eyed flounder. Where the skin of his bare chest and arms wasn't etched in the green ink of faded tattoos, it flamed pink from the cold. He dropped a heavy bag at her feet.

"How long was I down?" he asked with an expectant smile.

"About five and a half minutes?" Rye said.

Harmless frowned at himself. "Poor showing. I made it six the dive before." He threw a heavy cloak over his shoulders and clasped on a runestone necklace that matched the chokers Rye and the rest of her family wore around their necks.

"Well," Rye said, picking her numb fingernails, "I did lose track of my count once or twice."

"Nonetheless, it was quite productive," he said, brightening.

He reached inside the bag and retrieved a strange black object, holding it carefully between his thumb and forefinger. It was the size of an ordinary stone, flat on the bottom, but with long, sharp spines jutting out in all directions.

"What is that?" Rye said, and reached out to touch it.

"Careful. This is a midnight sea urchin," he said with delight. "The most toxic creature in the northern oceans—one prick of its spine is enough to fell a draft horse. They make excellent darts."

Rye pulled her hand back warily.

"It also happens to be our lunch."

He unsheathed a sharp knife and cut open the bottom of the sea urchin. Rye peeked inside the shell. It looked like something Lottie might have expelled from her nose.

"Would you care for the first one?"

"Um, no, thank you."

"No worries, plenty for later," he said, and slurped the creature up from its shell. He wiped his mouth with the back of his hand, carefully placed the prickly remains of the first sea urchin into the bag, and removed another.

Rye stared out at the churning waves around them. She couldn't see more than ten yards in the swirl of snow, fog, and ocean spray.

"Harmless, aren't you cold?" Rye asked.

"Spring is finally in the air," he said cheerily, eating the second sea urchin. "And the tide's on its way out. Our path back to the house will soon be clear."

Rye saw nothing but an impenetrable blanket of fog that consumed the earlier hints of sunlight.

"There's always a path, Riley, you just need the courage to take the first step." Harmless pointed into the fog. "Look, you can see the top of the first rock right there. Follow me."

Harmless skipped across the slick rocks as if they were a well-worn trail through a meadow. Rye had improved with practice over the past few days, but the slippery brown seaweed still pulled her boots out from under her with the slightest falter.

A staircase rose from the waves, ending at a landing high above their heads. Scowling, barnacle-pocked faces loomed over them as they carefully climbed the hand-carved steps, the mansion's walls sculpted into the shapes of hungry sea monsters, wailing hags, and nautical gargoyles lifelike enough to put a scare into even the hardiest seafarer.

This was where her father had brought Rye after rescuing her from the woods. The place he kept secret—even from the Luck Uglies.

Harmless called it Grabstone.

They ate at the large table by the main fireplace, surrounded on all sides by salt-sprayed windows and sweeping views of the sea. One window was cracked open, and a rather frosty-looking rook peered in from the ledge, sleet accumulating on its inky black wings.

"Have the rooks brought any word from Mama?" Rye asked.

"Nothing yet," Harmless said. He broke off a crust of bread from their loaf and dangled his hand out over the ledge. The bird eagerly took it from his fingers with its long, gray beak. "Don't be too troubled by it, though. I wouldn't be eager to fly in these winds either."

Harmless had sent word of their whereabouts to her mother by way of a rook, much the way Rye and Folly used pigeons to convey messages back home. But even after several days and two more birds, there had been no reply.

"And what about *him*?" Rye asked.

In addition to carrying handwritten notes, Rye had seen the clever rooks communicate with Harmless in other ways. Occasionally they brought him what looked to be random nesting items: a scrap of leather, or piece of fishing line. But from them Harmless could glean distant comings and goings.

"Slinister masks his movements well," Harmless said, and Rye tried not to cringe at the mention of his name. "But I suspect that, like everyone else, he and his allies hunkered down somewhere to ride out this storm."

Harmless had explained to Rye that while Slinister was in fact a Luck Ugly, he was a man who harbored radically different notions than her father. They had once been fast friends, but a rift had grown between them over some matter Harmless didn't elaborate upon. Slinister became the leader of a small but ruthless faction of Luck Uglies called the Fork-Tongue Charmers. They masked themselves in ghoulish white ash and blackened their eyes and lips with soot. Their name came from their gruesome custom of splitting their own tongues as a display of commitment. The disfigurement symbolized a pledge that could not be easily undone.

Harmless must have noticed the lingering look of concern on Rye's face as she fidgeted with her spoon.

"I won't lie to you, Riley. Slinister is a dangerous man, one haunted by wounds of the past. Even his name is an old jeer that he's embraced and now wears defiantly. I am sorry that you ever had the misfortune of meeting him, and I'm afraid that I'm to blame for that. I'd heard the Fork-Tongue Charmers planned mischief for Silvermas—under cover of a Black Moon. I had been tracking them for weeks, but obviously I underestimated Slinister. And it turns out, I was an hour too late."

Harmless shook his head, as if still puzzled by his own misstep.

"But why me?" Rye asked. "Why send a false message only to rob Good Harper and leave me freezing in the woods?"

"He lured you onto the Mud Sleigh so that I would find you there," Harmless said. "Slinister wanted to show that he was one step ahead of me. It was wrong of him to use you that way, and I promise he will be held accountable." There was a fleeting hint of darkness in Harmless's tone. "But the message was a forewarning meant for me, and you are in no jeopardy."

"How can you be sure?" she asked. She remembered Slinister's parting words. *Perhaps they would have a chance to visit again.*

"We have rules—unwritten but understood—not unlike the House Rules your mother raised you with," Harmless explained. *"Answer the Call. My Brother's*

Promise Is My Own. Say Little, Reveal Less. Lay No Hand on Children of Friend or Foe. Those are just a few. Sadly, ours don't rhyme as cleverly as your mother's," he added with a smirk. "But the consequences of ignoring them are, shall we say, severe. No Luck Ugly would break them."

"You realize it wasn't so long ago that I broke every one of Mama's House Rules?" Rye muttered. And besides, she thought, if Harmless was so confident, why did he feel the need to bring her here to Grabstone?

"You mustn't worry, Riley," he said reassuringly. "I knew that calling the Luck Uglies back to Drowning after all these years would bring with it certain . . . complications. Ten years is a long time for men of independent spirit to be apart. But the Fork-Tongue Charmers are still Luck Uglies. *Once a Luck Ugly, Always a Luck Ugly, Until the Day You Take Your Last Breath.* That is perhaps the most important rule of all. And as brothers, we will settle our differences in our own way."

"And what way is that?" she asked.

Harmless pushed himself up from the table and bowed his head.

"More often than not," he said solemnly, "by way of a dance challenge."

"Harmless . . . ," Rye said, pursing her lips and crossing her arms.

"It's true," he said, and did a few steps of jig so

poorly it made Rye blush. "And if that doesn't resolve it, we have a baking contest. The man who serves the best dumplings wins."

"Then you're doomed," Rye said with a laugh, swirling her spoon in his homemade stew—a medley of sea urchins and other slimy things that crawled out of tide pools.

Harmless smiled and turned to look out the windows.

"There's another blow coming in," he commented, and Rye sensed he was happy to change the subject.

Rye reached out and snatched the rest of the bread while Harmless studied the approaching storm. She hid it in the folds of her shirt.

"Can we watch it from the Bellwether?" she asked. The Bellwether was the room nestled in Grabstone's tallest turret—a chamber sealed shut at all times behind a door so bare it didn't even have a latch or keyhole. Harmless had told her it was off-limits.

"You're nothing if not persistent, Riley, but no." He looked back at her. "When I bartered for Grabstone, the Bellwether wasn't part of the arrangement. And you know I never break a deal."

Harmless was always negotiating bargains of one sort or another. He didn't seem eager to explain who Grabstone belonged to before or what he had to trade to get a whole house, either. Well, the whole house except the Bellwether. Harmless seemed to do a lot of things other people might describe as dishonest—but breaking deals wasn't one of them.

Rye shrugged and belched loudly after finishing the pungent stew.

"You're welcome," Harmless said. He burped too, and they both laughed.

Harmless had once told Rye that, in some cultures, a loud belch was how you thanked your host for a good meal. She and Lottie had eagerly adopted the custom. Their mother had not been pleased.

Rye climbed the stairs to her room. Grabstone was built tall and narrow. Instead of halls there were stairways—a great number of them. The bedchambers were situated in the tallest tower, beyond the reach of even the highest waves. This high up, she could hear the wooden timbers straining against the wind.

Pausing briefly at her own door, she continued up the last flight of dark steps. They ended at the Bellwether. No one—not even Harmless—was allowed in there, and yet Rye had heard footsteps on the floorboards overhead. On her first night at Grabstone, she saw shadows under the crack of her door. When she jumped from the covers and threw open the latch, the stairway was empty. Rye wasn't persuaded by Harmless's suggestion that it must be rats.

Seeing strange things in the dark didn't frighten her anymore. Not seeing them—that was still the scary part.

Rye removed the leftover bread from her shirt, crouched down, and carefully placed it at the base of the Bellwether's formidable door. Only a small glass peephole adorned its stark face. She peeked over her shoulder to make sure Harmless wasn't coming, then pushed up on her toes, craned her neck, and was just barely able to press her eye against the circlet of glass. The distorted lens revealed nothing but cloudy shapes, as it had when she'd tried this before. Rye struggled to stay on her tiptoes, wishing she was an inch taller.

An earsplitting noise rattled the entire tower and Rye leaped back.

Thunder.

She could tell the clouds had opened up, and a fierce, freezing sleet pounded the roof. Rye climbed back down the stairs to her room. The sky danced with light outside her window. Lightning bounced from cloud to cloud. Snow lightning was considered bad luck. The worst kind.

Rye sifted through a pile of unusual trinkets until she found her bronze-and-leather spyglass. Grabstone was full of oddities and minor treasures, the likes of which she had never seen before. Harmless had little use for them and Rye had already collected the most interesting ones here in her room. Rye squinted at the thin band of rocks and sand that stretched from below her window to the beaches and cliffs. Grabstone was connected to the shore by a treacherous shoal jagged enough to sink ships and thwart the curious who might attempt to venture there by foot. Normally, pipers, gulls, and the occasional seal inhabited the shoal, but that day only waves and sleet battered its rocks.

Then Rye jolted in surprise. There *was* something out there. A light?

She lifted her spyglass for a closer look. It was indeed a light—a lantern. It bounced and bobbed, pausing as waves hit, moving forward quickly but clumsily through an afternoon that was now as dark as night. Rye held her breath. *Who would be out in this storm*? Another wave and the little light seemed to topple to the ground. Whoever was carrying it slowly regained their footing. Then, one final wave crested over the entire shoal, making it disappear beneath the sea for just a moment, and the little light went out entirely.

Rye rushed down the stairs. She found Harmless in a small sitting room, its windows thrown open. He snoozed in a hammock strung to the beams of the house, the howling winds from the sea strong enough to rock him gently back and forth.

She shook him awake, the hammock now bouncing like a ship in a squall. He blinked away the sleep.

"Someone's trying to reach us," Rye said. "There is—well, there was—a light. Out on the shoal."

"Hmm," Harmless said, "I'm certainly not expecting anyone. Don't worry, the rocks make quick work of uninvited guests."

He folded his hands back on his stomach.

"Harmless, someone's in trouble," Rye said.

"Indeed. The sea is a more ferocious watchdog than the most ill-tempered hound."

Rye shook his arm.

"Harmless, isn't there only one person in the whole world who could know where we are?" she asked urgently.

Harmless furrowed a brow. He was beginning to understand.

That person was Rye's mother. She wouldn't venture out to Grabstone unless it was of dire importance. And she wouldn't stand a chance out on the shoal in that storm.

4 Messages Undelivered

Harmless tried to make Rye promise not to follow him out onto the shoal. Even if a wave dashed him against the rocks he wanted her to stay put—at least until the storm blew over. Rye had just frowned. Surely Harmless had gotten to know her well enough to realize she couldn't promise *that*.

He'd been gone nearly thirty minutes when she finally threw caution to the wind and gathered the supplies she imagined she might need for an ocean rescue—a lantern, a coil of rope, a flask of hot stew.

Fair Warning, her mother's knife that had once bitten the hand of Morningwig Longchance himself, was sheathed inside her boot, although the fiercest thing Rye had ever done with the blade was shuck an oyster. Icy rain slashed her face as she stepped onto the slick stone steps, but she stopped abruptly as a drenched figure emerged from the fog.

It was Harmless, a shivering body in a sleet-crusted cloak dangling from his arms. Rye was shocked to see that it wasn't her mother. It was the body of a girl.

Rye and Harmless huddled by the fire in the entry hall, where Harmless had carefully laid the child. "Were you going on a picnic?" Harmless asked with a smirk, nodding at her flask.

Rye's eyes flared.

"Sorry, a poor time for humor," he said softly. "Your friend is most resourceful. She found a little cove to hole up in and wait out the storm. It was dry . . ." He glanced down at his sopping clothes. "Relatively speaking."

Rye looked at the girl in anticipation.

"Give her a drink of stew," Harmless said. "I'll fetch some dry clothes."

Rye watched for any movement in her friend's face, her white-blond hair frosted to the color of snow, glassy eyes flecked as blue as ice chips.

"Folly," Rye whispered.

Folly's eyes focused at the sound of Rye's voice. Her red cheeks creased into a grin.

"Here, drink," Rye said, and pressed the flask to Folly's purple lips.

She accepted a big mouthful and swallowed it down, her grin turning into a frown.

"Ugh, what is this?"

"Snails, whales, and sea bug tails."

"Really?" Folly said, her eyes now brightening with interest. "Can I take some for an experiment?"

"Of course," Rye said, and smiled at her best friend, the ever-aspiring alchemist. She handed the flask to Folly, who cupped it in her cold hands.

"How did you find us?" Rye asked.

"Your mother was talking to my mum at the inn," Folly said. "She received your message from the rook but was worried that you hadn't replied to hers."

Rye wasn't surprised that Folly had overheard her mother. She suspected her friend must have the biggest ears in Drowning—there was scarcely a story or secret whispered around the Dead Fish Inn that she didn't catch wind of sooner or later. But the fact that Rye and Harmless had missed a message from her mother was more troubling.

"What message?" Rye asked eagerly.

But Folly's cheeks had lost their color after their

brief exchange and she fell silent, her teeth chattering so fiercely she could barely part them long enough to swallow sips of the steaming stew. Only after Folly was good and dry, bundled in blankets and dressed in Rye's extra shirt and leggings, did Harmless and Rye bring her upstairs to the big table by the fire. Harmless busied himself in the pantry. Folly's blue eyes were wide, marveling at the most unusual surroundings.

She took notice of Harmless, who appeared to be wringing the neck of a very recently deceased fish over a tumbler.

"What's he doing?" she whispered to Rye.

"Mackerel oil," Harmless replied from the pantry. Rye had long since discovered that there was little Harmless didn't hear or see.

"Helps keep the mind sharp," he explained, tapping his temple as he examined the cloudy liquid that now filled the glass. "Care for some? I know better than to ask you, Riley."

"Uh, all right," Folly said.

Rye cringed at Folly's mistake. Harmless looked most pleased to bring an extra mug as he joined them at the table.

"So, Folly," Harmless said, "as delighted as we are to have you pay us a visit, I must ask what brings you out here in such foul weather. Riley mentioned a message."

"It looked to be a pleasant day when I left the village this morning. It finally felt like spring," Folly said. She took a sip from the mug Harmless had offered. She gave him a tight-lipped smile, strained to swallow, and politely slid it away. "The weather turned rather suddenly," she rasped.

"Indeed," Harmless said. "A fickle storm this late in the season is not a good omen. But, more important, the message?"

Folly seemed to hesitate. "Mrs. O'Chanter sent a message by rook. Two days ago now. You never received it?"

"No," Harmless said. "The fellow on the ledge turned up yesterday but bore no message. He seems to have had a rough go of it."

Folly swallowed hard. "You heard what happened to the Mud Sleigh? On Silvermas?"

Harmless and Rye exchanged looks, and Harmless nodded to Folly.

"They say it was . . ." Folly began, and peeked over her shoulder out of habit. ". . . the Luck Uglies." She whispered the name, even though she knew very well who and what Harmless was. "After the attack on Good Harper, the Earl's new Constable made some immediate changes. 'Valant' he's called, and from what I've heard, he's not like the other lawmen."

Rye saw Harmless lean forward, listening intently.

"My father says Valant has a long reputation—whatever that means. He doesn't stay in one town for more than a few months. I heard he came from Throcking most recently. He makes the prior constables seem like lambs."

Folly paused, shifting in her seat before continuing.

"Among other things, Valant has . . ." Folly hesitated.

"It's all right, Folly," Harmless said. "You can speak freely."

"He . . ." She looked at Rye with eyes that made Rye's stomach sink. Folly swallowed hard before forcing out her words. "Burned the Willow's Wares."

"What?" Rye shouted in alarm. The Willow's Wares was her mother's shop.

"Your mother and Lottie are fine," Folly added quickly. "There was no one inside."

Rye was dumbstruck. "He . . . how could . . . what about . . ." Her eyes jumped from Folly to Harmless and back again. *"Why?"* She gasped and, for the first time she could remember, found herself speechless.

Harmless sat back without emotion, but Rye could see the gray-flecked stubble of his beard twitch as he tightened his jaw.

"Your mother and Lottie have moved out of your cottage. They've been staying with us at the inn," Folly said. "Just to be safe."

That was a relief, although Rye's ears now burned

red in anger. The Earl had displaced her family once again. It seemed the safest place for the O'Chanters had become the most notorious tavern in the most dangerous part of town.

Rye tried to settle herself. "Did my mother send you here?"

"No. Nobody knows I came." Folly shrugged at Rye's look of disbelief. "I thought you should know."

Rye shook her head, but not without affection. She couldn't hope for a more loyal—and at times more foolhardy—friend.

Rye glanced at Harmless. He rubbed his jaw and pinched the stubbly beard on his chin. Finally, he said simply, "We'll leave with tomorrow's first light, whether it brings sun, snow, or hail. Longchance didn't heed my warning, and now the weight of that decision shall come heavy and swift."

The gravity of Folly's news bore down on her, but Rye put a hand on Folly's arm as she considered her friend's own reckless journey. "Your parents will be worried sick about you."

"It may take them a few days before they even realize I'm gone," Folly said flatly. "They've been a bit distracted lately. Mum's got another one on the way."

Rye raised an eyebrow. "Another what?"

"Another Flood," Folly said.

Rye couldn't believe her ears. Folly was already the youngest of nine children, the rest of them boys. After twelve years, Rye assumed Folly's parents were finally done stocking the inn.

"Folly, I didn't even know she was . . ." Rye's voice trailed off.

"Me neither," Folly said. "She didn't mention anything, so I just assumed she'd put on a few winter pounds to warm her bones. Mum says that after nine children, delivering babies is like cleaning out the wine cellar—an important job you do once a year or so, but not worth fretting about until you finally run out of room."

"Well, that's great news," Rye said, pasting a broad smile across her face. "You're going to be a big sister." Rye knew, as someone who served that same role for a little red-headed firestorm back home, it was no easy task.

"Isn't that great news, Harmless?" Rye coaxed.

Rye's question seemed to pull Harmless from his thoughts. He looked up, his eyes returning from somewhere far away.

"Yes, yes, indeed. Fabulous news, Folly. You'll be an expert in screaming infants and soiled linens in no time I'm sure," he said with a smile.

Rye frowned. That wasn't exactly the type of

encouragement she'd had in mind.

"I need to tend to a few things before morning," Harmless said, pushing himself up from the table. "Folly, make yourself at home. Riley, be sure to pack whatever you wish to take from this place. We won't be returning anytime soon."

Rye's night proved to be a restless one. She was still staring at the timbers above her bed when Folly nudged her. The creaks and groans of Grabstone took some getting used to and must have woken Folly, too.

"Rye," Folly whispered, and nudged her again, harder. "Are you awake?"

"Ouch, Miss Bony Elbow. Yes, I am."

"Do you hear that? Someone's outside."

Rye heard the familiar shuffling in the hallway. A shadow broke the dim crack of light under the bedchamber's door.

"It's just the ghost from the Bellwether," Rye said.

"What?" Folly asked sitting up. "I thought you didn't believe in ghosts anymore."

"Oh, right," Rye said. "In that case it's just a big rat. Try to get some sleep."

"With ghosts and giant rats outside the door?"

"I'll take care of it." Rye said, slipping from under the covers and lighting a candle.

"Where are you going?"

"Shhh," Rye said. "Just watch."

She tiptoed toward the door silently. She reached for the latch without making a sound. But as her fingertips touched it, the shadow disappeared from under the door and there was a creak on the stairs, followed by silence.

Rye opened the door quickly. The stairway was empty.

She looked at Folly over her shoulder. "See?"

Rye carefully climbed the stairs to the Bellwether. Her small candle barely penetrated the shadows, but it was enough to illuminate the landing at the top. The door was shut tight, but the bread she'd left earlier had disappeared, just like the other offerings she'd set out each of the past several nights.

Whatever lurked in the Bellwether, real or imagined, it seemed to be restless too.

5 The Sniggler

Harmless hadn't been exaggerating when he said they would leave at first light, and after their fitful slumber, Rye and Folly found themselves sleepwalking across the shoal and up a rocky beach. Their departure had been hurried, but Rye was careful to stash her spyglass in her pack. She also brought a stout walking stick made of hard black wood that she'd found in Grabstone's assortment of trinkets. It came with a leather sling so she could stow it over her shoulder when she wasn't using it. She found the walking stick particularly useful now as they navigated the uneven stones.

Harmless took notice of it and raised an eyebrow. "Where did you come across that?" he asked.

"In one of the bedchambers. Do you like it?"

"Hmm," Harmless said. Then, after a moment, "Yes, it does seem to suit you."

The light of dawn grazed the dunes as they arrived at the edge of a tall bluff. Rye squinted against the wind as she watched the whitecaps roll into shore, but even though they had just hiked from Grabstone, she couldn't see the shrouded mansion through the morning's mist.

Harmless was busy examining a simple farmer's cart. It was empty and horseless.

"Folly," Harmless inquired, "how did you manage to get out here?"

Folly's shoulders slumped. "There was a horse hitched to that cart yesterday. I guess it got tired of waiting." She sighed and shook her head. "My father's not going to let me leave the inn again for a month."

"I guess we need to find another ride then," Harmless said. "Come on, girls. This way."

They followed Harmless along a narrow sand path that traced the edge of the bluff. Before long they came to a wind-beaten fisherman's shanty that looked to have weathered one too many storms. Behind it was a small, sheltered stable.

"Ah, there we are," Harmless said, and quickly made for the paddock.

"Will we ask the fisherman if we can borrow a horse?" Rye asked, hurrying to keep up.

"I'd hate to trouble him at this hour," Harmless said, a glint in his eye. "But stay here and keep a lookout for him, would you, Folly? Just in case he happens to wake up."

In the stable they found nothing more than a few bales of rotting hay and a sad, gray nag with ribs Rye could count.

Harmless frowned. "Not much of a selection. I guess this old girl will have to do. Riley, set her reins, would you?"

As Rye got to work, Harmless searched the stable and found a farrier's bag. He took a nail and a small hammer, removed a swatch of fabric from his pocket, and nailed it to a post.

"Just in case someone misses her," he said with a wink.

The fabric was cut into the shape of a ragged four-leaf clover—its color black as night.

Rye had seen one like this before. In fact, she had it in her very own pocket at that moment.

It meant a Luck Ugly had promised you a favor. Hers had been given to her by someone other than

Harmless and, at her mother's request, she still hadn't told him about it.

They rode for most of the morning, staying on the hard-packed sand so that the wagon's wheels wouldn't become stuck. Folly snacked on some strips of dried meat as Harmless tended the reins. Rye fidgeted, as she was prone to do when forced into long bouts of inactivity. Harmless seemed to sense it.

"We're taking the back way, but it won't be much longer now," he encouraged. "See, there are the twin culverts."

Rye and Folly looked ahead. From the bluff, fortified on all sides by enormous boulders that looked like they could only have been assembled by giants, were the mouths of two gaping tunnels. Each was wide enough to fit not only their mare and wagon but also an entire fleet of draft horses. Dark and shallow currents flowed and gurgled from the culverts, etching a lattice of scars into the packed beach as they meandered to the sea.

"The twins are restful today," Harmless noted. "When the Great Eel Pond rises too high, this stretch of beach can be impassable."

He must have seen Rye's quizzical look.

"The culverts drain the surrounding waters under, rather than over, the village. Without them, Drowning's name would become quite literal."

As their horse splashed through the runoff, the pungent smell of sewage and salt rot permeated Rye's nose. She tried to peer into the blackness behind the culverts. Rye saw nothing in the darkness, but there, on a rock by the edge of one tunnel, stooped a small, hunch-shouldered man in a heavy cloak. He dangled a hand in the icy runoff. Next to him was a covered pail.

Harmless took note of him too.

"A sniggler," he said, with a hint of curiosity. "Let's bid him good morning."

Rye knew that snigglers fished for eels by thrusting baited hooks into the dark places where the creatures were known to lurk. Eels fetched a good price at Drowning's butcher shops.

Harmless directed the cart toward him.

"Morning, good sir," Harmless called.

The sniggler cast an eye toward them. He pulled his hand from the water and thrust it into the warm folds of his cloak.

"Good day to you, traveler," he croaked in return.

Harmless stopped the cart a short distance from him and flashed a smile.

"How is the day's catch?"

"Fair." The sniggler placed a hand atop the pail. "Quite good actually."

"Really?" Harmless said, jumping down from the farmer's cart. "That's splendid news."

"Yes," the sniggler said with a tight smile. "So good in fact, I was about to call it a morning."

Rye saw the sniggler rise slowly, his shoulders slumped. His bones must have ached from years at the backbreaking work. He picked up his pail.

"I am so glad to have caught you then," Harmless said, taking a step forward. "I do enjoy a fresh eel. Might I buy one or two from you before you are on your way?"

On the cart, Rye exchanged glances with Folly and shrugged her shoulders. Her father seemed to have an insatiable appetite for slimy creatures.

The sniggler stiffened. "I'm afraid these eels are spoken for. The butcher will be expecting me."

Harmless cocked his head. "You can't spare but one? I have silver shims and will pay more than a fair price."

The sniggler eased himself down from the rock onto the sand, his back so stooped that he stood barely taller than Rye. He dragged a foot behind him, the hem of his cloak covered in sand. Rye could tell that he must be lame.

"I'm sorry, but no. I must honor my bargain." He looked Harmless over carefully.

"I can certainly appreciate a man of scruples," Harmless said, and came to a stop a short distance from the sniggler. "But perhaps you will at least allow me to see your catch? For surely these are extraordinary eels."

The sniggler stopped as well. He cast his eyes toward the cart, examining Rye and Folly in a manner that seemed less than friendly.

"I'm but a simple fisher," the sniggler said. "Mine are ordinary saltwater eels. And small ones at that."

"Don't be so modest, sniggler. You must have a magic touch." Harmless looked him hard in the eye. "For the Great Eel Pond was fished dry long ago. It has not been home to eels in my lifetime."

The sniggler hesitated. "Odd luck is in the air," he said, carefully removing the top from the pail. "You may see my catch," he went on, reaching inside. "But take care. They bite."

The sniggler snatched his hand from the pail and flicked his wrist so fast that Rye hardly saw it. A flash of steel caught the sun and Harmless dropped to all fours like a cat. A thud echoed below her. She looked down. A sharp throwing knife had just missed Harmless's chest and embedded itself in the side of the farmer's cart. A second blade cut through the air. Harmless rolled quickly and it only pierced the tail of his cloak, pinning it to the hard sand.

The sniggler cursed. He shook his own cloak from his shoulders as he stood at full height. He darted toward the culverts at a speed that would put Rye and Folly to shame, his lame leg and bent spine miraculously healed.

Harmless ripped his cloak free and checked on the girls. Finding them unharmed, he eyed the culverts. The sniggler had already disappeared inside.

"He's a scout," Harmless said. "For who I don't know. But my gut tells me we must make it to the village before him."

Harmless reached back over his shoulders. Two short swords appeared in his hands.

"Ride that way," he said, pointing the tip of a blade down the shoreline. "It will bring you straight to Drowning. But stay clear of the main gate. And, to be safe, don't take the hole in the wall."

Rye knew exactly what he meant. Mud Puddle Lane ended at a crumbled hole in the village's protective wall. Harmless wanted her to stay away from the cottage.

He pointed the other blade toward the culverts. "I'll follow our friend the sniggler." He flashed a predatory smile. "Perhaps, with luck, I can slow him down."

And with that, Harmless disappeared into the dark mouth of a culvert, the splash of his footsteps trailing behind him.

6
A Village Drowning

Rye and Folly abandoned their horse and cart at a farm near the village limits, and were able to slip into Drowning along a well-worn cow path. They blended in among some farmers taking their skinny, winter-weary livestock to market.

"We'll want to move quickly through the streets," Folly was saying as they splintered off from the pack. "The Constable and the Earl's men have been stopping villagers for questioning ever since Silvermas. Considering who your father is, I don't think we'll have the right answers."

"And what about the Shambles?" Rye asked. The Shambles was the part of the village where Folly and her family lived. "Will soldiers be there too?"

"The Shambles still keeps its own order—or disorder," Folly said with a touch of pride. "No constable or soldier dares to go there. Just as it's always been."

Drowning rose up around them as they walked briskly through the neighborhood called Old Salt Cross. The day turned balmy as winter finally surrendered, the spring snow mashed into mud on the cobblestones under the traffic of boots, hooves, and wheels of horse-carts. Rye and Folly kept to the middle of the roads like the others, wary of sharp-toothed icicles that dripped from the eaves and rooftops, promising a wicked braining for anyone caught underneath one at the wrong time. The faces of the villagers were dour and they seemed to go about their daily chores with little cheer. As Folly had warned, the Earl's soldiers were conspicuous and plentiful, stationed at every corner, and ever-watchful with suspicious eyes.

Rye spotted a huntsman loping past with what looked to be bundles of withered black leaves in each hand. Upon closer inspection, she was stunned to see that they were the feathers of a dozen black birds the man carried by their lifeless feet.

Rye grasped Folly's arm. "What's he doing with those rooks?"

"Off to the butcher's I'd guess," Folly said without stopping. "The Earl's put a bounty on them . . . a bronze bit per pound. Rook pie's sure to become a village staple."

Maybe that was what happened to her mother's message, Rye thought, chewing her lip. A bounty on rats she might understand, but one on rooks—the Luck Uglies' messengers—that seemed like more than just coincidence.

Rye didn't have a chance to ask anything else before she was interrupted by the sound of a jingling bell coming their way. She looked to find its source, expecting a donkey or perhaps a farmer's cow, but instead a woman hurried by them with a small child in her arms.

The woman wore a locked, iron-framed mask over her face. A metal bar stretched between her teeth like a bridle. Between her cheeks, the branks were fashioned into a long pointed nose like that of a mole, and the bell dangled at the end. The woman's eyes caught Rye's for an instant, then dropped to the street in shame as she passed.

Rye heard the mocking jeers and laughter of two nearby soldiers. She stopped to gawk in disbelief. Folly clutched her by the sleeve and pulled her forward before the soldiers took notice.

"What is that? What have they done to her?" Rye demanded.

"It's called a Shrew's Bridle," Folly said quietly. "For women accused of speaking ill of Earl Longchance. Men stand to fare much worse."

Rye's ears began to burn. "Let me guess, the new Constable's doing."

Folly just nodded. "He seems fond of harsh devices."

Rye was still simmering when Folly headed for the shortcut to Dread Captain's Way. Rye held her back and insisted that they take Market Street instead.

"It will be crawling with soldiers," Folly pointed out. "Trust me, Rye, you don't want to go there."

"Yes, Folly, I really do."

Folly sighed. "Fine, we'll stop and get Quinn. He should be at his father's shop. Keep an eye out for the feral hogs, they're extra surly. They've been foraging by the canal since yesterday, so it's best to stay out of the back alley."

The winding cobblestones of Market Street were as busy as ever, clogged with merchants, villagers, and soldiers. They hadn't made it more than a block when Rye realized that this was not ordinary midday traffic. Rather, the crowd seemed to bottleneck at Market Street's widest point, the mass of bodies so thick that Rye and Folly could only inch forward.

Rye stood on her toes for a better view. An elaborate pillory had been erected in the middle of Market

Street—an iron cage atop a raised wooden platform. It must have been built in the past few days—she'd never seen it before. Fortunately, the stocks and shackles inside the cage were empty. Above the pillory a black-and-blue banner fluttered in the breeze. She knew the emblem well.

An eel-like hagfish coiled around a clenched fist. The crest of the House of Longchance.

"The new Constable's doing," Rye said matter-of-factly.

"They're calling it the Shame Pole," Folly explained. "I'm just glad there's no one in the cage."

A small procession pushed through the crowd on foot. Three soldiers in black-and-blue tartan and a teenage boy who looked to be a squire took positions at the pillory's base. A lean, broad-shouldered man, garbed not in Longchance tartan but in a fine black vest, climbed the steps. He wore a thin leather war helmet fitted snug on his head, and on top of that sat a rather handsome crimson hat shaped like a stovepipe. No mustache covered his lip, but thick, golden hair burst from his jaw, his beard waxed into five elaborately curled points like hairy fingers beckoning. Coiled on his belt was what looked to be a multi-tailed whip made of knotted red cord, and in his fist was a length of chain. Collared at its end, an enormous, mottled gray dog followed him on long haunches.

The man wore an unexpected, almost pleasant, smile on his face as he addressed the assembled villagers. His hard-edged eyes did not match his smile.

"Constable Valant," Rye said, under her breath. He looked more like a sellsword than a lawman.

Folly nodded.

"Residents," the new Constable called out, in a voice that was strong but silky. "As you can see, our Shame Pole is now complete."

Valant waved a hand at the open cage door and empty shackles. His tone of appreciation quickly darkened. "But today it remains unoccupied. That tells me you have been less than forthcoming with me." He cast an accusing glare out at the crowd.

The teenage squire puffed out his chest and flared his narrow-set eyes, doing his best to mimic the Constable's severe gaze.

"I expect each of you to remain ever-vigilant by bringing me information on those who break the Laws of Longchance or otherwise seek to do harm to our most honorable Earl," he continued. "To help you do your part, hear this list of villagers who have committed crimes against Drowning and the House of Longchance. Provide me with their whereabouts so they may serve their time on the pole, and may their lingering shame help guide their future deeds."

The squire handed Valant a parchment scroll, which

he unfurled nearly to his feet. The Constable cleared his throat and hooked a thumb in his belt as he began to read.

"Emmitt Adams—guilty of touching the Earl's cloak while it was being mended at the tailor. Three hours on the Shame Pole." As he called out the names, his words fogged the chilly air like the smoldering breath of a dragon. "Sarah Barley—guilty of sticking out her tongue at Lady Malydia Longchance in the noble schoolyard. Sentenced to a vigorous tongue-scrubbing by way of a horse brush and two hours on the Shame Pole."

Villagers began to return to their toils while Constable Valant worked through the long list of minor offenses and their excessive penalties. Rye's ears reddened in frustration—it seemed the Earl had emerged from his winter slumber even pettier than before. As the crowd thinned, Rye scanned the familiar Market Street shop fronts: the butcher shop, the fishmonger's stall, the coffin maker's, and Quartermast's blacksmith shop, among others. But one shop was now very different. Rye felt a lump in her throat as she stared at the husk of scorched brick and timbers. The Willow's Wares, or what was left of it, was no longer a colorful standout among Market Street's weathered gray facades. Rather, it was a charred skeleton—a permanent pillory.

"Jameson Daw," Constable Valant was calling out from his list. "Guilty of public drunkenness and uttering untruths about the House of Longchance. Repeat offender. Sentenced to five stripes at the thrashing stump and eight hours on the Shame Pole!"

Rye looked over her shoulder at the Constable—the man responsible for doing this. Her ears had turned as crimson as his hat.

Folly seemed to want to say something, but just bit her lip. She put a hand on Rye's shoulder.

"We should go," Folly said after a moment. "I'll find Quinn, then we'll get out of here."

She darted across the street to Quartermast's, but Rye couldn't take her eyes off the remains of her family shop. Villagers wandered past it without a second glance, as if they'd already become numb to the black eye or simply forgotten about it altogether. All except one. A bent figure sifted through the rubble, almost invisible in the shadows of the burned-out frame. Rye watched carefully as he reached down to pick something from the ashes.

A looter! There might not be much left to take, but there was no way she was about to let someone pick through their belongings.

She dodged a foraging piglet as she hurried across the street and ran through the empty, blackened doorframe. Muted afternoon light filtered through the hollow windows, but she could not see anyone in the shadows. Instead, a yellow sheet of parchment nailed to a timber caught her attention. Thanks to her mother's refusal to follow the Laws of Longchance and Quinn's informal lessons, Rye was one of the few village girls who could read.

PROCLAMATION
OF EARL MORNINGWIG LONGCHANCE!
Generous Rewards Offered for the Capture of
Abigail O'Chanter and her Two Offspring!
Wanted for Crimes Against the Shale!

The proclamation included a drawing of her mother, with pouty lips and evil, smoldering eyes; a small, wild-haired girl with a ferocious look on her face; and someone who appeared to be a rather skinny, unkempt boy. Why did they always think she was a boy?

Rye's blood ran cold. She was officially a fugitive, but why? Had the Earl decided to goad Harmless by targeting his family? She pulled the hood of her coat tight around her head and peeked out nervously at the villagers wandering past. When she was sure no one was looking, she tore the parchment from the post, crumpled it into a ball, and stuffed it into her pocket.

The sound of nearby activity caught Rye's ear. Skipping over the rubble, she crouched and hid behind the remains of a brick wall at the back of the shop. She heard hooves on cobblestones. Snorts. She peeked over the wall where she could see straight into the back alley behind the Willow's Wares. It was just several large hogs rooting through the refuse with their long snouts.

Rye breathed a sigh of relief. She pulled the parchment from her pocket, unfolded it, and read the proclamation again.

"You shouldn't be here," a stern voice said behind her.

Rye spun around to find the man she'd spotted rummaging through the shop, a scorched tin box tucked under his arm. From under his hood, long inky-black hair framed his sharp-edged face. He studied Rye with pale blue eyes the color of robins' eggs and couldn't conceal a hint of a smile at the corner of his thin lips.

"In fact," he added, "this is the very last place you should be."

7 Scales and Swine

"Bramble?" Rye asked in disbelief.

The man lowered his hood. "It's good to see you again, niece," he answered warmly.

Bramble Cutty was her mother's brother. That made him Rye's uncle, of course. Not that she really knew him at all. They'd met ever so briefly the prior autumn, and it was quite some time before her mother got around to telling Rye who Bramble actually was.

Bramble also happened to be the Luck Ugly who had given her the black swatch of fabric that she kept in her pocket. The Ragged Clover.

A furry head with round, dark eyes popped out from the folds of Bramble's cloak. Rye leaped back. The small black monkey shrieked and bared its teeth. She knew him, too. The little ape had never been particularly pleasant to her.

"Quiet, Shortstraw," Bramble hissed, and stuffed the monkey's face back under his cloak with a shove of his palm.

"He's not fond of the cold," he explained. "Makes him ill-tempered."

Bramble handed the charred tin box to Rye. "This is for your mother if you see her before I do. It's all I could find."

Rye ran her fingertips over it, turning them black with soot. She slipped the box inside her coat.

"Tell me, Riley," Bramble said, "what are you doing back in Drowning?"

Rye looked up at the burned beams and rafters around them. The lump returned to her throat. "Folly told us about . . . this."

Bramble nodded gravely. "Well, now you've seen it for yourself. Abby's been in quite a twist, as you can imagine. It's a brazen gesture on the part of Longchance and his Constable—especially given the warning he's under."

Rye vividly remembered the warning Harmless had given Morningwig Longchance. She'd been there in the courtyard of Longchance Keep along with the small band of masked Luck Uglies. Harmless spared Longchance's life but promised that the Luck Uglies would be watching—and he would show no such restraint if Longchance were to ever trouble his family again. The Earl had either forgotten the warning—or no longer feared it. Had the new Constable emboldened him, or were the Luck Uglies too preoccupied with their own differences to be bothered?

"And where in the Shale is your father?" Bramble asked. "Surely he hasn't sent you back here alone?"

Rye told Bramble of the sniggler and Harmless's pursuit into the culverts. Bramble's face darkened.

"That man would drop everything for the thrill of the hunt," Bramble muttered, then seemed to catch himself. "Not a problem, though. I'll see you to the Dead Fish myself."

It wasn't the first time she had heard Bramble express frustration with her father.

"Bramble," Rye said, lowering her voice out of habit, "what do you know about Slinister and the Fork-Tongue Charmers? Have they been heard from since the attack on the Mud Sleigh?"

Bramble narrowed an eye. "These are complicated times," he said, in a manner that seemed dismissive of her question. "I won't miss Silvermas anyway. I've gotten one too many potatoes . . . and mouse turds . . . in my boots."

Whether Bramble missed Silvermas wasn't exactly her point.

Bramble cast his attention to something over her shoulder. Rye turned to see Folly and Quinn stepping through the debris, hurrying toward them.

"There you are," Folly said, and then paused at the sight of Bramble. "And . . . hello."

"Greetings young Flood," Bramble said. "Floppy is it?"

"Folly."

"That's right. Hard to sort out your lot with all the names."

Folly frowned.

"You're back," Quinn called to Rye, his kind face bright. "When I heard about the Mud Sleigh I was . . ."

He pursed his lips tight as if grasping for the words, then simply threw his long arms around her. She awkwardly accepted his hug. He had a steel helmet tucked under his elbow. It poked Rye in the ribs.

"Sorry," he said. "I smithed this one myself," he added proudly. "Or started it anyway."

"You're the blacksmith's boy, no?" Bramble asked.

Quinn nodded. He lived alone with his father, Angus, the blacksmith, and always did his best to please him. That sometimes made him a bit of a rule follower like his father, but, for the most part, Rye and Folly had broken him of that bad habit.

"It's not the worst work I've seen," Bramble commented. "But your hands may be better suited to the quill than the forge."

Quinn looked at his blackened hands and sighed in agreement. All of his fingers were swollen, bandaged, or both.

"Enough chatter then. Let's be on our way to the inn," Bramble declared, casting a wary eye around them. "Before the villagers begin to wonder what's so interesting in here."

"I'm coming too," Quinn said eagerly.

"We'll split up and meet at Mutineer's Alley. I'll go first—I'm most likely to draw attention coming out of this place. You three wait a few moments then head out after me. Just try to look like nosy little scamps. Can you manage that?"

Bramble looked them over. They just blinked back at him.

"Perfect," he said.

Bramble pulled his hood over his head, climbed through an empty window frame, then paused and looked back at them. "Step lively and stay inconspicuous," he warned, before disappearing.

Rye, Folly, and Quinn waited for several minutes,

then pulled their hoods tight and ventured out onto Market Street.

The Constable was still reading from his list. "James Whitlow. Guilty of fouling the Earl's private privy at the Silvermas Eve Feast. Fine of ten silver shims and one hour on the Shame Pole."

"We missed you at Silvermas," Quinn whispered as they moved quickly down the cobblestones.

"Yes, we should talk about that," Rye said with a frown. "Next year, let's save our coins and buy our own candy—"

Rye stopped abruptly. The Constable's words had caught her ear from the pillory.

"And now for the most egregious offenders," he said, running his finger down the length of the scroll. "Abigail O'Chanter," he read. "Guilty of trafficking in stolen goods, harboring known criminals, and conspiracy to commit treason. Punishment is seizure and destruction of the guilty's property and imprisonment in the dungeons of Longchance Keep for not less than . . ."

Rye's head instantly flushed with a rage so great she couldn't hear the rest of his words. Someone whispered to her to ignore it, to keep on moving. She thought it might be Quinn. They were in front of the fishmonger's stall. Rye thrust her bare hand into the trough of ice and pulled out a stiff, frozen mackerel by its tail. She couldn't feel the cold.

Rye marched toward the pillory. Someone else grabbed at her arm. It might have been Folly. The Constable had moved on to the next name on the list.

"Harriet Wilson. Guilty of—"

Rye flung the fish. It knocked the parchment scroll from the Constable's grasp and bounced off his leather vest before landing at his feet. He considered his empty hand with surprise, then glowered out at the crowd. The soldiers and the squire looked her way as well. The Constable's dog growled and strained at its leash.

Suddenly Rye was aware of her surroundings again and found herself backpedaling away from the Shame Pole. She bumped hard into two bodies. It was Quinn and Folly, who had caught up with her a moment too late.

"Tell me you didn't just hit the Constable with a fish," Quinn said as he carefully eased his helmet over his head.

Rye looked at the shimmering scales stuck to her palm. "I didn't just hit the Constable with a fish," she replied.

The squire spotted Rye and pointed. The three soldiers leaped down from the pillory.

"Scatter!" Rye yelled, and the three friends did just that. Growing up together on Drowning's winding streets, they'd practiced this many times before.

Rye darted down one end of Market Street while Folly and Quinn tore off in different directions. Rye pushed past a merchant and nearly ran headlong into a cow's rump before glancing back over her shoulder. She saw Folly's head of white-blond hair sprinting safely down a narrow lane. But she was shocked to see that all three soldiers had taken off in pursuit of Quinn. That wasn't how it was supposed to work. The soldiers should have split up to chase each of them. There wasn't a man in Drowning the children couldn't outmaneuver individually but, once outnumbered, things could get tricky. She saw Quinn's wobbly helmet disappear down the alley near the remains of the Willow's Wares. The soldiers had left him with no other option.

"Pigshanks," Rye cursed. She knew the alley dead-ended at the canal. With three soldiers behind him, Quinn would be trapped. She changed course and ran back for him.

Rye turned the corner at full speed and skidded to a stop. She found just what she had feared. The three soldiers stood menacingly in the middle of the alleyway. Quinn had pulled up at the far end, where its cobbles met the foul-smelling canal that drained swill from the village to the river. The shallow water was filled with more pigs than Rye could count, their heads rooted up to their ears in the runoff. Each looked heavier than a full grown man. Quinn glanced from the soldiers to the pigs and back again, weighing an impossible decision.

Rye looked around the alleyway. A young piglet snuffled about, having wandered off from the rest of the animals. It sniffed something interesting on her boots. She reached down and scooped him up in her arms. He oinked and squirmed but didn't seem overly alarmed.

"Sorry, little fella," Rye whispered in the piglet's ear, then gave him the gentlest pinch on the tail.

The piglet squealed as if jabbed by a butcher's blade and lurched to free itself from her grasp. The sows pulled their snouts from the murky water and grunted in reply. A soldier looked back at Rye and the little pig.

"Quinn! Get out of the way!" she called, and set the piglet down. It ran back toward its mother, on the opposite side of Quinn and the soldiers.

Quinn knew exactly what was about to happen—village children were taught early never to get between a sow and her young. He darted to the side of the alley out of the pigs' path, pressing himself against a building. The soldiers weren't as quick, and they found an army of wet, angry hogs bearing down on them with their tusks.

Rye and Quinn didn't stop to catch their breath until they'd made it to where Bramble was waiting at Dread Captain's Way. Shortstraw had climbed out from his hiding spot in Bramble's cloak and now perched on his shoulder, his furry arms crossed impatiently.

Folly arrived just behind them. "There you are," she said, gasping for breath.

Quinn struggled to remove his helmet.

"What happened back there?" Bramble demanded. He grabbed Quinn's helmet and yanked it off with a pop. Quinn rubbed the red welt it had left across his forehead.

"Rye hit the Constable with a fish," Folly said.

Bramble looked at Rye in disbelief and shook his head. "Perhaps we need to discuss the meaning of inconspicuous."

They followed him to an obscure flight of carved stone steps tucked under a crumbling archway. It was called Mutineer's Alley. No guards or gate blocked their path, but everyone in Drowning knew where those steps led. And it was no place for the unwelcome.

Rye glanced over her shoulder as they started down. No soldiers followed, but someone was standing in the shadows of the backstreet she and Quinn had taken to reach Dread Captain's Way. She thought it looked like the Constable's squire.

Bramble nudged her with an elbow. "A fish, eh?"

Rye shrugged sheepishly.

"That's my niece," he said with a wink.

She looked back again, but the squire, if he had been there at all, was now gone.

At the bottom of a deep embankment, below the village itself, sat the Shambles. Its black-market shops, grog houses, and gambling dens had grown up like persistent weeds on the damp edges of the village, until eventually the Earl had stopped trying to pluck them. The Laws of Longchance weren't enforced here. The Shambles was not a safe place for allies of the Earl.

Shortstraw chittered happily as they worked their way down Little Water Street, the snail trail of a dirt road that traced the banks of River Drowning. Dinghies bobbed at the docks. In the distance, where the mouth of the river met the sea, Rye could see the tall mast of an anchored schooner silhouetted against the sky. Rye was sure the invisible eyes of the Shambles were on them, but their faces were familiar here.

At the end of the street, a four-story inn squatted in the shadow of the great arched bridge that spanned the river's narrowest point. Overhead, a black banner with a white fishbone logo snapped in the wind. The thick iron doors of the Dead Fish Inn rose above them like portals to a castle, and they always struck Rye as more suited to withstanding a siege than welcoming guests. But at that moment, there was no place she would rather be.

8 Where Nobody Knows Your Name

The air was stale with stout and sailor sweat, which made perfect sense since a small fleet of grog-swigging boatmen had congregated at the center of the inn. They'd pushed aside the tables and chairs and huddled in a large circle around two blindfolded, bare-knuckled combatants. The men traded wild, flailing punches over the cheers and groans of the onlookers.

Folly's two oldest brothers, the twins Fitz and Flint, leaned against a heavy beam and watched with interest from under their manes of white-blond hair. The twins, each massive individually, had been born conjoined at the hip, giving them the formidable aura of a two-headed giant. Their matching glowers and otherworldly appearance assured even the surliest patrons of the Dead Fish behaved themselves.

So it was that Rye, her uncle, and her friends arrived relatively unnoticed. Rye pulled her hood from her head and the inn's roaring fireplaces immediately warmed her chilled cheeks. A woman bustled past, balancing a full serving tray of empty glasses on her round belly with one hand. She paused at the sight of the children, blinked in disbelief, and abruptly dropped her tray onto a table. The woman's hair was as white-blond as Folly's except for a single streak of silver that she pushed behind her ear.

"Riley O'Chanter!" Faye Flood exclaimed. "What in the Shale are you doing here?"

Before Rye could answer, Folly's mother threw her arms around her and pressed her tight. Faye's stomach was as hard as a melon and, when she saw the look of concern on Rye's face, she waved it off.

"Don't worry about my little shelf," she said, rattling her fingers on her belly. "Flood babies are a hardy lot. More important, how did you get here?"

Folly jumped in excitedly. "I went to find her. There was a storm—"

"Rat in the jacks! There you are, Folly," Faye interrupted. "I've hardly seen you the past two days, love. Your chores are piling up."

Folly's face fell.

"We've got freebooters in port," Faye continued, with a nod to the crowd of sailors circling the brawlers. "There are bar rags and linens in need of washing. You can play with your friends after you've finished."

Folly frowned at Rye with a look that said *I told you*, and slumped off.

"As for you, Riley dear, Abby is around here somewhere." Faye glanced about.

But Rye's gaze had already found her. Her mother's face seemed even more lined with worry than it had just days before, but to Rye she was still the most beautiful woman in the whole village. Rye felt her eyes well up with tears.

Abby opened her arms wide. Rye stepped forward and buried her face in her mother's shoulder. She didn't let go for a long while.

Rye started to ask questions, but Abby just pressed her head back to her shoulder and held her close. Once Rye had settled, Abby eased her toward the Mermaid's Nook, the secluded corner of the inn that housed Rye's favorite table. Rye set her walking stick on the carved tabletop and sat down.

"Mama," Rye said finally, "the Willow's Wares?"

"Don't give it another thought," Abby said quietly. "It was just a building. No more than brick and wood. What's important is that we are all safe now."

"Are we?" Rye asked.

"Of course," Abby said.

"But we were attacked this morning."

Rye explained their encounter with the sniggler and detailed the Constable's announcement on Market Street. Abby listened intently.

"And this," Rye added, unfurling the crumpled parchment in her pocket.

Abby looked over the Earl's proclamation. Rye watched her mother's grim face. Abby was silent.

Finally, Abby spoke. "Do I always look that cross?" She arched a playful eyebrow.

"Sometimes," Rye said, but she was not calmed by her mother's jest. "The Earl is searching for us," she said matter-of-factly.

Abby nodded. "It seems so. Not that he'll find us easily." She gave Rye just a hint of a knowing grin. "No one here knows our names."

The correct answer when asked about someone's identity at the Dead Fish Inn was always, *Who? Never heard of him*. Abby tossed the parchment into the roaring fireplace.

"But why come after us now?" Rye asked. "Does he believe this new Constable will protect him?"

Abby shook her head gravely. "That I don't know. But if Longchance seeks trouble hard enough he's sure to find it sooner or later. I expect your father will be here shortly. When he arrives . . . he, your uncle, the others . . . will be certain the matter is addressed."

Rye looked across the inn to where Bramble had joined two men at the bar. They sat casually over numerous empty mugs, their mud-caked boots tapping on the rungs of their stools. But Rye sensed a wariness in their constantly shifting eyes, like hungry predators watchful for their next mark.

"Bramble told me to give you this," Rye said, remembering the battered box. She took it from her coat and handed it to Abby.

"Did you look inside?" Abby asked as she pried apart the bent clasp. She opened it a crack.

"No," Rye said, shaking her head, and was surprised to realize that, for once, her curiosity hadn't gotten the better of her. "What's in there?"

"Memories," Abby said. A warm thought seemed to cross her mind.

Abby removed a small metal object from the box. It was a hair clip in the shape of a dragonfly, its silver so tarnished it was almost black.

"Someone gave this to me long ago, but it seems you could best use it now," she said. She pushed Rye's unruly hair from her eyes and clipped it back. "Much better."

Quinn arrived and placed two mugs of plum cider on the table along with his handmade helmet. His eyes widened and he stared slack-jawed at the realistic, life-size mermaid carved into the tabletop. Abby strategically slid the helmet across the table to afford the mermaid some degree of modesty.

Bramble joined them with goblets for himself and Abby. "What do you have here?" he asked Rye, examining her hand staff on the table. "May I see it?"

"My walking stick? Sure."

Bramble felt its heft in his hands. He squinted and examined its polished features.

"A walking stick, you say?" He sounded amused. "This, my dear niece, is a High Isle cudgel. Made from the hardest blackthorn ever felled. I haven't seen one in years."

Abby raised an eyebrow.

"Like a club?" Quinn asked.

"Yes, like a club," Bramble said. "But nastier."

With two lightning-quick strikes, he brought the cudgel down against Quinn's helmet on the table. Rye, Abby, and Quinn all jumped at the sound. Shortstraw fled under a chair. The rest of the inn hardly noticed.

The steel crown of the helmet was crushed as if pummeled by a boulder. Rye was relieved nobody's head was in it.

Bramble chuckled and handed the cudgel back to Rye. "This is a rare find. Guard it closely until you learn how to use it."

Quinn stared at his bashed handiwork.

"Apologies, Quinn," Bramble said. "I'll buy you another."

Rye noticed Quinn's fallen face and didn't think that cost was the point.

"Your uncle and I need to discuss a few matters," Abby said to Rye while shooting Bramble a reproachful look. It always amazed Rye how a glare from her mother could give pause to even the most dangerous of men. "Why don't you and Quinn go find your sister? She's made herself quite at home here, so I can't say where she is . . . in trouble, no doubt."

There was a heavy thud in Rye's lap, and a warm furry mass stretched across her like a blanket.

"Shady!" Rye hugged him around his thick neck.

"Obviously someone else has missed you too," Abby said. "He's taken a liking to the inn himself. The twins guard the door well, so he's stopped trying to escape."

Shady's kind were known as Gloaming Beasts—mysterious catlike creatures who could go years hiding in plain sight. Rye had always taken him for a simple house pet. That is, until he revealed his true nature by helping Harmless thwart a clan of ruthless Bog Noblins. Gloaming Beasts were the bog monsters' only natural predator. They were also renowned for their wanderlust, which was why Abby kept him under lock and key.

Rye set him on the floor and she and Quinn headed off to find Lottie. Shady snaked in and out of Rye's gait as she walked, rubbing his back against her legs.

The freebooters were still hard at the grog and their gambling.

"Round six!" barked a man at the center of the crowd.

His thick hair was the color of steel and tied into a ponytail that stretched down his back. One eyelid sagged at half mast, a hollow, empty socket peeking out from under it. He held six fingers in the air.

"Get your bets in now," he shouted. Gold grommets and silver shims began to change hands. "All right, spin the lads six times apiece!"

Leathery hands grabbed each blindfolded fighter and began to turn them in circles.

"Wait!" he called out, and Rye started in alarm.

The ringleader pinched his dead eye shut and used

the other to examine Rye, Quinn, and Shady.

"What's going on around here? I've never seen so many children or animals in one tavern," he grumbled. "And not one looks to be of the edible sort. Animal or child."

Rye took a step back.

"Sorry," she said. "I'm looking for a little girl."

"Is Fletcher Flood running an orphanage now?"

"She has red hair. Carries a pink rag doll wherever she goes. She's loud—"

"Wait a moment. Pickle?" he asked.

"No, her name's Lottie," Rye began, "although I can see why someone might—"

"Yes, yes, Pickle. You know her?" the man asked.

"Er, yes," Rye said, shocked. "She's my sister."

"Why didn't you say so? In that case, come, come." He waved a hand. "Out of the way, you deck rats."

As the sailors moved aside, Rye spotted the three-year-old on the shoulders of a hulking brute at the back of the crowd, her perch giving her a bird's-eye view of the fighting. Lottie's face beamed when she spotted Rye, and she slapped the sailor on his bald head with Mona Monster until he lowered her to the floor.

Lottie rushed forward and threw her arms around Rye's waist with such force she nearly knocked her down. Rye kissed Lottie on her tuft of hair that always smelled like straw and syrup drippings, and for a moment it brought her back to the bed they shared on Mud Puddle Lane.

Lottie pulled herself away and demanded, "Come," tugging Rye by the sleeve to be sure there was no misunderstanding.

She picked up a wire birdcage and hurried to the Mermaid's Nook, placing it on the table with Abby and Bramble.

"My baby blue dragon," Lottie announced proudly as she opened its little door and reached inside.

Rye and Quinn exchanged curious glances.

"Lottie was very proud to finally learn to use her chamber pot," Abby explained. "So for Silvermas we got her this . . . a baby blue dragon. As promised."

Lottie extended both hands. "Newtie!" she proclaimed.

A rather small speckled lizard cocked its head and looked up at them. It seemed perfectly at ease in her hands.

"It's so little," Rye said.

"And brown," Quinn added.

"Him's just a *baby*," Lottie said with a roll of her eyes, as if she'd explained this a dozen times already.

"Yes, Riley," Abby said, nudging her gently. "It's just a baby."

"He no be blue until he's *older*," Lottie explained.

"Oh, of course," Rye said.

"*Much* older," Abby clarified.

Shady licked his lips at the sight of the little creature.

"No, no, Shady," Lottie said crossly, shaking a finger. "Mice good. Newtie—no eat him."

"Where did you find such a handsome dragon?" Rye said, looking at their mother and playing along. She had to admit, she'd never seen a lizard quite like this one in the bogs. He seemed to glisten in the light and had folds of skin, like fins, under each of his front legs.

"Your uncle came across him. He's always had a strange fascination with exotic pets."

"I bartered for him in Throcking," Bramble said proudly. "The merchant had all sorts of interesting things. Scorpions, snapping turtles, razor eels. But your mother's instructions were quite specific. This little fellow was the only, er . . . dragon . . . he had."

"To be honest," he whispered as an aside, "he seemed happy to be rid of it. Threw it in for free with two pelts and a flagon of ale."

"Suppertime," Lottie said, carefully setting Newtie on the table and digging into her pocket. She dumped onto the table a fistful of hard-shelled brown objects that looked like burnt pecans, until they scuttled in different directions on hairy legs. Shortstraw screeched and fled.

"He's afraid of roaches," Bramble explained with a shrug.

Newtie sprang to life. He cocked his head from side to side, puffing out his chest eagerly, on alert. A sail-like crest flared up from the ridge of his back and along his curled tail as he darted forward, snatching each roach with a long pink tongue until they were all gone. He crunched the bugs contentedly in his jaws.

"Lottie, where did you get those?" Abby asked in exasperation.

"The kitchen," Lottie said, and seemed genuinely surprised by the fuss.

Quinn frowned. "I think I'll be heading home for supper now."

Rye watched the lizard swallow its feast. "At least he'll never go hungry around here."

That night the cook prepared calf's-head soup and Fletcher Flood grilled a boar on the spit over the fireplace. Rye ate with her family in the Mermaid's Nook. She fished through her soup with her spoon, making sure she didn't end up with an eye. Abby cut boar into bite-size chunks for Lottie while frowning at Shortstraw, who was sitting on the table and scratching his hindquarters.

"You'll have to excuse him," Bramble said. "The fleas have made him ill-mannered."

Bramble stabbed a slab of pork with the tip of a

sharp knife and ate it from the blade.

Lottie grabbed a cutting knife to do the same, banging it down with such force it nearly cracked the plate.

"Lottie," Abby yelled, and snatched it from her hands before she put it in her mouth.

Rye sat back and stifled a giggle.

A louder sound caught all of their attention. The great iron doors of the inn creaked open. Fitz and Flint stepped from their post to block the way but eased aside as several broad-shouldered men in dark cloaks filed in.

Rye sat up in her chair and tried to make out their faces. A man followed briskly behind them and pulled his hood from his head. His keen eyes scanned the inn, and Rye saw the relief pass over his face once he'd spotted her. He headed for the Mermaid's Nook quickly. Rye watched to see whether the men he'd arrived with would follow, but in the time it took her to blink they had already disappeared. In that fleeting instant it was as if the shadows of the Dead Fish Inn had swallowed them whole.

"Harmless!" Lottie called.

"And so the High Chieftain has finally arrived," Bramble muttered, and slumped back into his chair, a tankard in his hands.

Harmless smiled and placed a hand on Rye's shoulder, then stepped over and patted the crown of Lottie's head with affection. His eyes fell on Abby, and Rye's parents looked at each other with a degree of fondness that she couldn't quite gauge. Even after all that had happened since his return to Drowning, they still hadn't dwelled under the same roof in more than ten years.

"It's a great relief to see you all," he said. "Even you, Bramble."

Bramble raised his drink in greeting and then pressed it back to his lips, withdrawing behind it like a mask.

Abby pushed aside the folds of Harmless's cloak where he had kept a hand pressed to his ribs.

"You're hurt," she said, in the matter-of-fact manner she used when she didn't want to cause alarm.

He waved her off and flashed a grin for Rye and Lottie, although Rye noticed that he sat down gingerly. "Just a scratch," he said, and lifted a spoon to dip into Abby's soup. It emerged with an eye. "My lucky day," he said, and slurped it up.

"Riley told us about the attack this morning," Abby said. "Who was it?"

"It was hardly an attack," Harmless replied, dismissing the notion. "Codger was a lookout. He would have simply fled if I hadn't pressed the issue."

"Codger?" Bramble asked, leaning forward.

Harmless nodded grimly. "I didn't recognize him

until it was almost too late."

Bramble's pale blue eyes were grave. "Did you—"

"I spared him when I realized he was a brother, although he's in no condition to trouble anyone soon."

"Codger's always been a follower," Bramble grumbled. "An underling. He'd never raise a hand to you acting alone."

"He refused to reveal who he answers to, but it is not difficult to guess. He and Slinister will have their time of reckoning in due course."

Rye cringed at the mention of the Fork-Tongue Charmer.

"But Longchance comes first," Harmless said. He glanced at Abby, Rye, and Lottie, then his eyes fell on Bramble and he spoke quietly. "Tomorrow we visit Longchance Keep."

Rye shifted in her chair. Harmless leaned in closer to her uncle. He flashed a narrow smile, and she barely heard the words slip through his clenched teeth.

"Tonight we find out who will join us."

It was late in the evening when a motley band of musicians took up the pipes, fiddle, and tin whistle. High overhead, the sun-bleached skeleton of a long-extinct sea monster hung from the rafters by anchor chain, its bones now home to hundreds of candles that bathed the inn in light. Some of the more daring village maidens had ventured out to the Shambles to dance, donning the colorful dresses they couldn't wear anywhere else in Drowning.

Abby had already carried Lottie up to bed, and Rye was losing the battle with her drooping eyelids despite trying to stay awake to hear more about Harmless's plans to ride on Longchance Keep. But Harmless and Bramble had parted ways after supper, and if there were other Luck Uglies at the inn they'd disappeared like spiders into the cracks of the walls.

Rye reluctantly dragged herself upstairs to Folly's room. She was so tired that she hardly noticed the steady stream of men headed in the other direction—disappearing down the steps to the wine cellar of the Dead Fish Inn.

9

Thorn Quill's

Rye dreamed of her mother's bumbleberry pie. She was just about to dig into its warm berries, a dollop of sweet cream piled on top, when a shuffling sound jarred her ears.

She awoke disoriented, uncertain of where she was. She hoped it might be her cozy bed on Mud Puddle Lane, then remembered the creaking floorboards of Grabstone's Bellwether. But instead she found herself huddled in blankets on the floor, staring at pickled insects, dried swamp blooms, and a wedge of ancient cheese, all housed in multicolored bottles. It was Folly's shelf of makeshift potions. The hollow sockets of a tiny skull stared back at her from among the bottles—the Alchemist's Bone, a charm Harmless gave to Folly to help her with her experiments.

Rye sighed and rolled over. It was never easy to fall back to sleep with all of the inn's nocturnal noises.

Then she heard it again. Something moving in the room. She propped herself up on an elbow. Folly was sprawled in her bed, mouth agape, fast asleep after her long day of chores. The door to the room was cracked open and a sliver of hallway candlelight streamed across the floor. Rye sat up and blinked away the sleep.

A hooded figure stooped over Folly's dresser, rummaging through Rye's things.

"Hey!" Rye called. "Get out of there."

At first she thought it might be Fallow, Folly's youngest brother, who always took great delight in snooping on them. But then the prowler glanced over his shoulder, hastily tucked something under his arm, and disappeared out the door. It was the coat Harmless had given her.

A thief!

Rye sprang from the blankets and leaped into her boots. Her spyglass, Fair Warning, and her other belongings remained on the dresser. She grabbed her walking stick and sling—if it really was a cudgel, maybe she'd use it to teach the thief a lesson. She considered waking Folly, but after a second glance at her drooling, slumbering friend, didn't bother. She ran to the hall and saw the thief dart into a guest room at the end of the hallway, shutting the door behind him.

Rye didn't stop to call for help. She didn't think the entire inn would appreciate being woken over a stolen coat—surely it wasn't the worst offense commited inside these walls. Instead she rushed to the guest room and flung the door open, cudgel in hand, only to find it empty. A rope ladder, not unlike the one Rye and Folly used to sneak in and out of Folly's room, dangled out the open window. She hesitated but a moment, then slung the cudgel over her shoulder and started down the ladder.

Rye landed hard in the alleyway behind the inn. The cold night air hit her and, for a moment, shocked her back to her senses. The Shambles was no place for anyone to be caught alone after dark, and yet here she stood shivering in the shadows of its ramshackle flophouses. But then she spied the hem of the thief's cloak as he turned the corner at the end of the alleyway. Her ears reddened and she continued her pursuit.

The thief turned onto Little Water Street, and by the time Rye made it to the packed-dirt road, the night air was eerily still. The lanterns and candles had been put out in most of the windows. The black river flowed silent. Rye heard a door close. There was a faint glow farther down the road. She recognized the shop but had never been inside.

Rye carefully approached Thorn Quill's. Through the fogged glass window, she could see a roaring fire in the fireplace. The hand-scrawled sign hung in the window advised her to THINK TWICE. Rye did, then summoned her courage and pushed open the door.

The blast of heat inside the shop hit her so hard she had to take a step back. There was a sour smell to the place—familiar but unpleasant—a faint scent of the bogs. A man lay on his side atop a table with his back to her, the collar of his shirt loosened and one arm free from its sleeve. The shop was quiet except for the tap-tap-tapping of metal and wood instruments. The man held aside an elaborate braid in his fist so that he could be tattooed on the back of his neck—his shoulders already covered in green-black designs so realistic that his skin seemed to writhe like scales. Thorn Quill himself huddled over his subject, firmly striking what looked like a hairbrush over his subject's skin with a small wooden mallet. The process must have been extraordinarily painful, but the man on the table didn't flinch.

Thorn Quill turned on his stool, his bloodshot

eyes peering back at Rye from under his stringy gray hair. He continued to work bare-sleeved in the sweltering shop, his own skeletal arms so darkened with ink work that it looked as if he'd dipped them in tar.

"Come for a pinch, lass?" he asked, raising his wooden tool. What she thought was a hairbrush was more like a tiny rake spiked with rows of razor-sharp animal teeth. He checked over her shoulder. "All by your lonesome are ya? You're a bit on the young side, but we won't tell if you don't. Maybe a nice hummingbird, or a buttercup?"

He smiled a black-toothed grin. For a moment Rye felt very small standing there in her nightdress, the pink scars on her knees peeking out over the tops of her oversize boots. But she ignored his jab.

"Maybe I'll have one of those," she said dryly, giving it right back to him. "What is it?"

She couldn't make out the design on the other man's inflamed skin. What looked like an upside-down tree trunk stretched down his neck and upper spine, forking into two thick, curved branches that curled back up to his shoulder blades.

"The marks are a secret between the artist and his canvas," Thorn Quill said. "Let's just say you need to earn a patch like this. And when the color fades, you need to earn it once again."

Rye looked around the small studio. Several cloaks

hung in a corner and tapestries draped from the low rafters depicted Thorn Quill's more impressive designs. Shelves lined the walls, overflowing with bottles, ink, and various plants needed to make the dyes. Several wharf rats chittered in a large cage in the corner. Rye hoped they were pets and not ingredients.

She glanced again to the cloaks hanging on their hooks. There was a coat there too. A familiar one.

"Did someone else come in here?" she asked hesitantly. "A few moments ago?"

"Look around. I assure you I'm not hiding anyone under the table." Thorn Quill thrust a dirty thumb toward the crooked door at the rear of the shop. A darkened room lay behind it. "Check the storeroom if you'd like."

There was no way Rye was about to head back into that room. Besides, she'd already found what she was looking for.

"My mistake," she said.

If Rye had more time, she might have taken greater notice of the tattoo on the man's upper back. What could be mistaken for an upside down tree was in fact a serpent's tongue, its forked ends curling back like branches. At the tip of each end was a black four-leaf clover.

But the oppressive heat of the place and Thorn

Quill's words had made Rye uneasy, and she was now eager to leave.

"I'll be going now," she said, and made sure Thorn Quill saw her start for the door.

"Come back any time," Thorn Quill said without enthusiasm. He returned his eyes to his work and dabbed the man's fresh wounds with a scarlet-stained rag.

As soon as he looked down, Rye darted for the cloaks, quickly snatching her coat from its hook. She would have been outside before Thorn Quill could rise to his feet, but as she rushed to go she found her path blocked. A teenage boy of about sixteen stood in front of the door. Had he slipped silently from the back room? The boy flipped over the parchment sign in the window so that the words MOVE ALONG now faced the street. His narrow-set eyes regarded her curiously, but without kindness.

Rye glared back toward Thorn Quill to demand an explanation, and found the man with the tattooed neck pushing himself up from the table. When he turned and faced her, she almost fell backward into the fire.

Slinister's red-rimmed eyes bore down on her from behind his mask.

10
Spidercreep

"My father and the Luck Uglies are here in the Shambles," Rye said quickly, stepping as far away from Slinister as the small space would allow. "They're at the Dead Fish Inn right now. Surely you know there's little they don't see. If you harm me"—she glared at the boy and Thorn Quill, too—"you'll have more than a girl and an old man in the woods to reckon with this time."

"I know very well who is in Drowning, Rye O'Chanter," Slinister said from deep behind his mask, an edge of amusement in his voice. "But the Luck Uglies aren't watching the streets of the Shambles. They've gathered below it, in a place called the Spoke, and right now they're engaged in critical discussions that cannot be disturbed. So, at the moment, there's nobody here to reckon with me at all. Except for you."

Rye knew all about the Spoke, the secret tunnel system that lay beneath the village streets. In fact, not so long ago Rye herself had unlocked a thick, shackled door housed deep within its bowels. It had allowed the Luck Uglies access to the Spoke once again from the forest Beyond the Shale. Harmless had warned her that there might be unintended consequences. Rye suspected she was staring at one of those consequences right now.

"Thorn Quill," Slinister said, "why don't you step in back while I speak with the girl."

Thorn Quill's eyes darted to the darkened doorway. "With that . . . ?" His voice trailed off. "Think I'll take a stroll outside instead." He threw a cloak over his shoulders, took a briar pipe from the mantle, and stepped out onto Little Water Street, easing the door shut behind him.

Rye considered rushing after him, but Slinister, and now the boy, watched her carefully. The boy struck Rye as familiar, but she couldn't recall where she had seen him.

"You were in my room," Rye said to Slinister. "Why did you steal my coat?" She shook it at him in her fist.

"That was Hyde, my young friend here," Slinister replied. "Although I *did* send him. And he wasn't trying to steal your coat. If he was, you would have never heard him at all."

Hyde grinned proudly, revealing the tips of his teeth.

"Please . . . put it on," Slinister said. "Unless you prefer thrashing about the Shambles in your nightdress."

Rye carefully slipped her arms into the sleeves of her coat, adjusting her cudgel back in place over her shoulder. "You lured me here," she said. "Why? To hurt me? To hurt Harmless?"

"If I meant to hurt you, Hyde would have smothered you with a pillow. And you'd still be dreaming now and forevermore."

Rye's skin crawled under her coat.

"I know you're a Fork-Tongue Charmer," she said, doing her best to ignore the sensation. "Harmless's enemy. An enemy of the Luck Uglies themselves."

"And yet, how much do you *really* know?" Slinister asked, stepping closer. Rye inched away but her back found the wall. "What has the High Chieftain—the man you call Harmless—told you about the Fork-Tongue Charmers? That we are malicious? Evil?" Close to her now, he seemed to sense her discomfort. He paused for a moment, then stepped away.

"For that matter, what has he actually told you about the Luck Uglies? Do you really know any more now than when he first returned to Drowning?"

"I know the Luck Uglies honored their bargain with Longchance to save the village from the Bog Noblins. That Longchance broke that bargain and lied to the villagers to be sure they turned against them. And I know there are codes you all live by—"

"How little you know of him—your own father," Slinister interrupted, and Rye thought she heard pity laced in his voice.

"I know him well enough," Rye said, her ears reddening. "He said you were friends once. But you have differences. Clearly you can't let go of them."

"Differences?" Slinister picked up Thorn Quill's nasty little tool. "Let me share something he surely did not. Your father took something I cherished long ago and hid it away." He paused and fingered the sharpened animal teeth. "No matter how much I begged and pleaded, he refused to tell me where it was. Even with the Luck Uglies scattered in the wind for ten long years, he's kept it secret from me."

Rye furrowed her brow. Harmless had hinted at many of the things he'd done. It certainly wasn't impossible that he'd taken something that belonged to someone else. In fact, she had the sense he'd made a habit out of it at one time.

"What was it?" she asked.

Slinister looked down at the tool, pressing it hard into his thumb. "Something I have never seen nor touched but that made me who I am. Something that remains mine and only mine, whether I live or die, and that even the High Chieftain cannot deny."

Rye shook her head. "I'm not very good at riddles."

Slinister put the rake of teeth down on the table with a hard bang.

Rye jumped. "I'm not trying to be cheeky! I'm really bad at them."

"There's a tempest coming to Drowning, Rye O'Chanter. I brought you here to speak with you before it swallows you, your father, and the entire village whole. Before that happens, you will help me find what the High Chieftain has taken."

"I think we can bear one more storm," Rye said. "Winter won't last forever." She didn't mention that she had no idea what sorts of things Harmless had taken over the years, nor any idea where he'd put them.

There was a chittering in the corner. The rats in the cage scuttled about fearfully. Hyde poked a finger at them. Rye's chest tightened with a sudden realization.

"You," she said accusingly. She now recognized

him as the boy who had watched her and her friends flee down Mutineer's Alley. "You're the Constable's squire!"

"Hyde is very cunning," Slinister explained. "He doesn't speak much, but he's proven to be a capable chameleon. He is my extra eyes and ears, and helps me keep abreast of Longchance's actions."

Rye's temper flared. Had Slinister known the Constable intended to burn the Willow's Wares? If so, that made him as guilty as Valant and Longchance themselves.

There was a scuffling somewhere in the darkness behind the storeroom's entryway. Rye heard what sounded like the jangling of chains. Both Slinister and Hyde looked toward the noise. Had they imprisoned someone?

"Hyde, feed him before he gets too restless," Slinister said. Hyde picked up the rats' cage with both hands and Slinister took his place between Rye and the front door.

"Who's back there?" Rye asked.

Slinister turned to Rye. "Never mind that. The night is short and you need not share his fate. I'll ask you one question and, depending on how you answer, I'll allow you to leave this place."

Rye just stared into the chasm of Slinister's masked

mouth. Did her fate really hang on the answer to another riddle?

"Just one," he repeated and raised his index finger. "Are you ready?"

Rye shook her head, but Slinister asked anyway. "Where does your father hide his darkest secrets?"

Rye opened her mouth but had nothing to say. The truth was, she knew very little about her father or his secrets. She had hoped that would change after he'd returned to Village Drowning, but the tapestry of Harmless's past had proven to be difficult to unravel.

She felt Slinister's eyes studying her carefully. "You were right," she said quietly. "I know little of him."

"I'll share a secret," Slinister offered. "I told you I've seen you before. But not in the way you might expect. I have dreamed of a place I've long sought. And in that dream, I saw you there. Why, I do not know." Slinister leaned in, his voice more menacing. Rye recoiled. "But I *do* know there is more you're not telling me."

Rye's skin turned cold despite the oppressive heat of the shop. Surely she couldn't help what Slinister dreamed about. She summoned her courage and stepped forward to leave just as Hyde approached, balancing the cage of rats in his arms.

"Not yet," Slinister scolded, signaling for her to stop.

Rye forced herself to find Slinister's eyes behind the red-ringed slits of his mask. "My father keeps his darkest secrets to himself," she said, and remembered Harmless's words at Grabstone. "He says little . . . and reveals less."

Slinister cocked his head and, without seeing his face, Rye couldn't tell if he was angry or impressed by her reference to one of the Luck Uglies' own codes.

But Rye didn't waste a moment to find out. With all of her strength she gave Hyde a hard shove, knocking him into a shelf and sending the cage tumbling to the floor. Slinister wasn't so easily surprised and made his broad frame wide, blocking the shop's front door. Rye turned and ran the only place she could—through the doorway to the storeroom.

The dimly lit room was even more cluttered than the shop itself, but she saw no sign of Slinister's prisoner. She looked desperately for a door or window to exit, and when one didn't present itself, she scanned the overflowing shelves for something she might hurl at her pursuers. Rye spotted the sharp tools of Thorn Quill's trade just as Slinister appeared in the doorway. She moved to grab them, but the floor disappeared beneath her and she felt herself plummet briefly into darkness before hard, unforgiving earth greeted her backside.

Rye blinked rapidly, trying to force her eyes to adjust to the gloom. Faint candlelight from the storeroom above illuminated the square hole through which she'd fallen. The dirt around her smelled earthy and organic. Fumbling with her fingers, she grasped one of the many orb-shaped objects that surrounded her and lifted it to her nose. It smelled like an onion. She sniffed another. A beet. She had fallen into a root cellar. But there was another, more pungent smell, stronger than it was in the shop—the bogs.

She scrambled to her feet. Slinister and Hyde would surely be down here in an instant. Their silhouettes hovered over the hole and blocked out the candlelight above. But to Rye's surprise she could still see, her surroundings dimly illuminated by a bluish glow. A rattle of chains stopped her in her tracks. She spotted something stirring in the shadows in front of her.

Rye craned her neck downward.

"It can't be . . ." Rye gasped out loud.

A dull blue glow emanated from the runestone choker around her neck.

Rye's runestones were a warning. They glowed blue to alert their wearer whenever a Bog Noblin was near. More important, they were a warning to the Bog Noblins themselves. Long ago, Harmless and the Luck Uglies had declared that the greatest of harm would come to any Bog Noblin who trifled with the bearer of the runes. Rye had seen firsthand how effective those stones could be. They had saved her more than once.

A shape shifted in the shadows. In the pale glow of her choker, she saw a vaguely human form crouched with its back to her. Its skin, waterlogged and gray, hung in folds from its sinewy frame. She could count the bony ridges of its spine. The musty cellar air was thick with the bogs. The sickly looking thing was no bigger than Rye.

A Bog Noblin could never fit down here, she told herself. The beasts were enormous, taller than a full-grown man and twice as thick.

But when it turned to face her, there was no room for doubt. Like all of its kind, the weight of the mire had flattened the Bog Noblin's head and elongated its toothy jaws, and the acidic waters had tanned its coarse hair and beard into rust-orange ropes.

A terrible, inhuman wail pierced Rye's ears as it lurched for her. Rye flung herself backward just in time, barely avoiding the creature as it snapped its jaws behind what appeared to be an iron muzzle. It snorted at the air desperately with its piglike nose, straining at the thick collar around its neck and pulling the attached chain to its full length.

"Hyde! Climb down there and unchain Spidercreep!" she heard Slinister call out from above.

Rye scuttled away on her hands and knees. Regaining her feet, she ran to what looked to be the farthest end of the root cellar, desperate to put as much distance as she could between herself and the Bog Noblin. But when she reached out to brace herself for impact against the earthen wall, she was surprised to find that she just kept going, disappearing into an even blacker tunnel. Rye didn't stop to make sense of it; she just kept running as fast as she could. She felt the patter of earth and pebbles on her shoulders like hail. Her boots slapped the loose soil and shallow puddles splashed her bare legs. Rye lost all sense of direction as she ran, bouncing off walls and crashing into what she thought were dead ends only to turn herself around and run some more. Just as the blue glow of her choker began to subside, a hidden root sent her tumbling. She felt the sting of reopened scars as her knees hit the ground.

Rye sat up and pressed her back against the tunnel wall. Now, in absolute darkness, she realized she must be in the Spoke. Its tunnels had been carved out long ago by the Luck Uglies themselves, and Drowning's hidden underbelly still remained a little-known secret. Rye knew there were other entrances and exits throughout the village: abandoned wells, forgotten cemeteries; even the now smoldering basement of the Willow's Wares concealed entryways into the Spoke's catacombs. Thorn Quill's root cellar must have been another.

Rye caught her breath. The glow from her choker

softened and winked out altogether.

She sighed in relief. Now she could sort out how to get back aboveground.

Suddenly the choker flared to life, the glow so intense that it illuminated her face. She heard the scratching and scuffling of rapidly moving footsteps.

Rye knew her weary legs could take her no farther. Reaching over her shoulder, she drew the cudgel from its sling. Her choker should ward off the Bog Noblin once it found her, but Slinister and Hyde would not be similarly deterred. She stood, clutched her choker in her hand, and held it out from her neck.

"Do you see this?" she yelled into the void around her. "Do you see what this is?"

The shadows were silent. Maybe it had.

Then something struck Rye harder than she'd ever been hit before. It took the wind out of her lungs and sent her sprawling onto her back.

Spidercreep pinned her to the ground and perched heavily on her chest. He was snuffling furiously, smelling her. His breath reeked of the sour stench of the bogs.

She struggled desperately as the beast pressed itself against her, pounding her ribs with hard knotted stumps that felt like fists. Knots of rust-orange hair whipped her face. Spidercreep snapped, but she didn't feel his bite, the frame of the muzzle protecting her from his jaws.

Undeterred, he unfurled his long black tongue through the iron bars. Rye pinched her eyes tight as it lapped across her face like a giant snail. Rye yelled and thrust her elbow at his face. It slipped through the muzzle and Spidercreep instantly bit down into the thick leather of her coat. Rye panicked and tried to thrash free, but he held her elbow tight like a dog latched onto a joint of meat.

Desperate, Rye tightened her grip around the cudgel. Swinging her arm up, she bashed Spidercreep in the side of his head. There was a clank of metal and her elbow popped free. Another swing sent Spidercreep flying off her.

Rye sprang to her feet emboldened, her ears burning, and stepped toward the creature to give it one more wallop for good measure. In the light of her choker, she could see Spidercreep cower like a frightened hound. His pathetic whimper made her pause—long enough for him to leap aside and flee into the darkness.

Rye stood at the ready, listening for signs of another attack. But her choker began to fade as the Bog Noblin's retreat took him farther away, until the glow eventually disappeared entirely. There was no sign of Slinister—no footsteps or torchlight. She touched her elbow and felt bare skin. Spidercreep's powerful jaws had ripped away a mouthful of leather, but everything important remained intact.

Her relief lasted but a moment. Now she was alone. And lost. Beneath the ground in absolute darkness.

Rye pulled her coat tight around her cold, damp body and closed her eyes. Although she couldn't dally, she'd allow herself just a moment to catch her breath.

But the darkness of the Spoke soon enveloped her like a tomb. She didn't even realize she'd nodded off until the crawl of fingers on her face jarred her from her sleep.

11
Friends in Low Places

"What are you doing down here, silly?" a voice whispered in Rye's ear.

Rye jolted and lurched away. A lantern flared in front of her. She blinked and shielded her eyes, the lantern's glow burning them after so long in the dark.

"Sorry," the voice said. "The lantern's for you. I don't need it, of course."

Rye peered through the glare. A pale-skinned boy smiled back at her. His black hair hung in dirty strings on either side of his long face. His mismatched eyes flickered in the light. One was brown, the other blue.

"Truitt," she gasped in relief. "How did you find me?"

"I hear everything that happens down here—sooner more often than later."

He extended a hand and helped her to her feet. She hugged her friend. His shoulders were bony, but they gave her comfort. He'd come to visit her on Market Street once over the winter, but she hadn't seen him since.

"I couldn't believe my ears when I heard your voice," he said. "But I was glad to nonetheless. I heard what happened to the Willow's Wares."

"Everything's turned upside down, Truitt. I don't even know where to begin."

"Start with how you found yourself lost in the Spoke," Truitt said. "But tell me as we go—this is not a safe spot." He handed her the lantern. "Follow me."

Truitt led the way through the dark, only occasionally grazing a wall with his fingertips to get his bearings. His feet navigated the tunnel floors without the slightest stumble, and even with the benefit of the lantern and her walking-stick-turned-weapon, Rye struggled to keep up. She always found Truitt's dexterity to be remarkable. He was blind.

Truitt was what the villagers called a link rat—not that Rye would ever call him that unpleasant name ever again. He wasn't much older than Rye, but he'd spent almost his entire life in the Spoke, venturing out into the village after dark to guide travelers by lantern light through its treacherous alleyways in exchange for spare coins. For parentless children, Drowning's streets had always been more dangerous than the tunnels beneath it.

"I was chased down here," Rye explained as they walked. "By a Bog Noblin, but not like one I've ever seen before."

"Are you certain it was a Bog Noblin?" Truitt asked. "Something has been following the link children in the tunnels, Rye. It drags them off and we never see them again. From what we have heard, it is something less than human."

"I'm sure of it," Rye said. "Why these didn't work I have no idea." She fingered her runestones and shook her head. "Could it be they are one and the same?" Rye asked. Perhaps Slinister didn't always keep Spidercreep chained up.

"Whatever it is," Truitt said, "we need to stop it. If the link children aren't safe here, there is no haven for us in all of Drowning."

Rye considered the other possible comings and goings in the Spoke.

"Truitt," she began cautiously, "did you hear anything

else down here? Some sort of gathering maybe?"

"It was a most unusual night," he said over his shoulder. "Once in a Black Moon we'll come across a lost reveler. Or sometimes a child crawling after a stray cat. But last night the tunnels echoed with creepers. Men. They gathered not far from here and stayed until nearly dawn. At times their language was . . . heated."

"Luck Uglies?" Rye whispered, even though they were most certainly alone.

"I couldn't say for certain, but they talked about an assault on Longchance Keep under the cover of darkness."

It had to be the Luck Uglies, Rye thought. Slinister told her they were meeting in the Spoke, and an attack on Longchance Keep sounded like the type of important business that would require their full attention.

"Did they say when? Will it be tonight?" she asked.

Truitt shook his head. "Voices travel far but unclearly in the Spoke. They didn't strike me as the sort of men who would appreciate unwelcome ears. I didn't linger."

Rye hesitated before asking her next question. "Will you warn her?"

Truitt stopped and turned. He knew who she meant. Malydia Longchance. She was the Earl's daughter—and Truitt's twin sister. The Earl had cast Truitt, his own son, into the sewers when he was just an infant because of his blindness. But Malydia lived with her father in Longchance Keep.

"You have good reason to distrust Malydia. She's been nothing but cruel to you, for reasons even I don't understand. But she is not her father, and I won't leave her to his fate if I can help it."

"If you do tell her, Harmless—and the rest of the Luck Uglies—could be in danger," Rye said.

"I haven't spoken with her yet, but I'll drag her into the tunnels if that's what it takes to keep her out of harm's way. As for the Earl," Truitt said, a look of disdain flashing across his normally kind face, "the Luck Uglies can string him up from the highest tower of Longchance Keep if they care to. I won't let her warn *him*."

Truitt pointed overhead, where a dented tin canopy was punctured with dozens of holes. Rye looked up, then down at her chest. Tiny pinpoints of light dotted her filthy coat.

"We're here," he said.

Truitt slid aside the scrap-metal cover and gave Rye a boost so she could climb out of the hole. She squinted in the bright morning light and peeked around the narrow backstreet. The last remnants of winter had melted into deep puddles in the spring air, and several scrawny hens pecked through them in search of worms. Rye heard what sounded like the noise of morning foot traffic, but the footsteps were heavy, metallic. She glanced up. The moss-etched stones of a wall loomed high above her, forming the base of a staircase. The steps were packed with men. Shoulder to shoulder, their black-and-blue tartan flashed everywhere she looked. They held their positions, steel greaves clicking as they shifted nervously. Soldiers!

"Truitt," Rye whispered down into the tunnel. "Where am I?"

"Have you been underground so long you've already lost your bearings?" Truitt called up with a chuckle. "You're in the Shambles."

Indeed, she was at the foot of Mutineer's Alley. Implausible as it seemed, the entryway to the Shambles was filled with Longchance's men.

"Something's going on up here," she said. "There are soldiers—lots of them. Stay in the Spoke. I need to get to the Dead Fish Inn."

"Rye, come back down with me if it's not safe. I can get you there through the wine cellar."

"There's no time for that," Rye said. She was already sliding the tin canopy back into place. "I'll let you know as soon as I find out more about the Bog Noblin," she added quickly, and dropped the scrap metal over the hole, silencing Truitt's protests.

❖ ❖ ❖

Rye hurried along the backstreet where it ran parallel to Little Water Street, then moved to cut across when she was a fair distance away from Mutineer's Alley and the soldiers. But what she saw caused her to stop dead in her tracks.

A much smaller procession of soldiers already marched through the Shambles, snaking their way down Little Water Street. No one had seen a soldier in the Shambles for decades, so it was with great interest that the neighborhood's denizens filtered from the taverns and shops as the procession passed by. They followed them casually in large numbers and, in the process, sealed off the group's return path.

Rye watched closely from an alley. Three soldiers in black-and-blue tartan accompanied the man with the crimson hat and leather helmet—Constable Valant. He clutched a chain leash and his enormous, mottled gray dog trotted alongside him, as if out for a morning stroll. The crowd behind them had grown into the dozens. The faces of the Shambles' residents were hard and grim.

What are they thinking? Rye wondered. Then she caught herself midbreath and crouched even lower into the shadows. The Constable's squire marched along with the procession. His narrow-set eyes darted back at the crowd gathering behind them. Had he led them here? Who was Hyde really deceiving? The Constable, Slinister, or both?

Rye suspected there was only one place they could be walking so purposefully. She'd have to use the back alleys to make it to the Dead Fish Inn before them. She pulled the hood of her coat over her head and thrust her hands into her pockets. Something hard and cold met her hand.

Rye removed the object from her pocket. A smooth stone as black as the Spoke rested in her palm, identical to the one she'd found in her boot on Silvermas. She knew for certain she hadn't put it there herself. Rye dropped it to the ground in surprise and wiped her hands hurriedly, as if its touch alone might taint her.

12
In Shambles

Fitz and Flint stared down at the filthy, mud-streaked street urchin and told her to shove off before she drove away any more customers.

Rye tugged off her hood. "It's me. Let me in!" she said, pushing past them. "You might want to watch the street—trouble's coming." They stuck their thick necks out the iron doors for a closer look.

Rye felt something heavy on her foot. Shady pawed at her knee, his claws snagging the hem of her night-dress. His thick fur bristled at the new scent on her coat, but she didn't stop to pet him. She spotted Folly and Quinn watching her expectantly from a table. Bramble sat with them, alternating bites of an overripe brown pear with Shortstraw. The circles under his eyes were dark, as if his night had been as long as Rye's.

"You're back," Folly said, and wrinkled her nose. "And you're a mess."

"Quinn, what are you doing here?" Rye asked.

"I brought tarts from the bakery," he said with a broad smile. He took a wax-paper bundle from his pocket and unwrapped it excitedly.

"Where's my mother?" Rye said quickly.

Quinn frowned and rewrapped the sweets.

"She's not with you?" Folly asked. "Lottie wanted to take Newtie out for a walk this morning. Your mother went with her to fetch some things from the port shop. You weren't in bed when I woke up—I assumed you'd joined them."

"A *walk*?" Quinn said, shaking his head. "Lottie dotes over that lizard like it's a lamb. She feeds it so much I think it's doubled in size."

"They're in the Shambles?" Rye asked in alarm. "Bramble, I need to talk to Harmless right away."

"I haven't seen him since dawn," Bramble said, picking a tooth. "It was a bit of a brannigan last night—and not the fun kind."

"The Constable's coming," Rye said. "With soldiers. He's here . . . in the Shambles."

Shortstraw broke into a cough that splattered munched pear all over the table.

"You'll have to forgive him," Bramble said, shaking monkey spittle from his hand. "The dry heat from the fireplace gives him coughing fits." He looked at Rye with his pale blue eyes. "Soldiers *here*, you say? In the Shambles? That seems unlikely."

"It's *true*. I saw them myself."

Bramble flashed a skeptical scowl. "You must be mistaken, niece. *Maybe* the Ale-Conner, he's been known to sample the local fare. But no lawman would be brazen enough to come to the inn."

A flicker of light overhead caught everyone's attention.

The skeletal chandelier tottered as a black shape balanced among the bones. Rye saw that it was a rook, the first live one she'd spotted since returning to Drowning. It jabbered and called with its long gray beak.

"That's an unusual signal," Bramble commented to himself. "Around here anyway."

"What is it?" Rye said.

Bramble hesitated. "Soldiers," he finally muttered.

Rye clenched her jaw and stared hard at her uncle. Concern flashed across Bramble's face, but he was calm when he said, "Fuzzy, tell your father."

Folly scowled but hurried off without correcting him.

"I'll see what I can find out," Bramble said, and made for the doors.

Rye pulled on her leggings, sheathed Fair Warning in her boot, and quickly gathered the rest of her belongings before joining Quinn and Folly in a guest room on the second floor. Folly's parents had sent her upstairs, even though she would have preferred to stay below with her brothers. They thrust open the shutters, giving themselves a bird's-eye view of Little Water Street.

Just below them, Constable Valant's procession had reached the inn. The crowd had swelled behind them, and the Shambles' residents now clogged the dirt street, watching quietly with hard eyes. Valant stepped forward. Dwarfed by the inn's iron doors, he removed a glove and rapped politely with his knuckles.

There was a chuckle from the crowd. The doors did not open.

He cleared his throat and rapped again. The doors still did not budge.

"Maybe no one's home!" someone yelled with a laugh.

Valant raised his knuckles a third time, but before he

could knock once more, a door creaked open. The twins Fitz and Flint met Valant at the doorway, their broad shoulders blocking his passage. They stared down at the Constable, who smiled in return. He craned his head to the left to look past Fitz, but Fitz leaned to block his view. He tilted his head to the right, and Flint did the same.

Finally, the Constable said in his silky voice, "Gentlemen, I come in search of drink and good conversation. I understand you have both inside."

The twins said nothing.

"Certainly my coins are as good as any other's, are they not?"

The twins didn't move. Valant just stared back, his grin still fixed upon his face, the waxed points of his peculiar, golden beard bristling like spines from his jaw.

"No dogs," Fitz said finally.

"Ah, of course," Valant said, and handed the leash to Hyde. "My apologies." He took a step forward.

"We mean you," Flint added, with a disdainful flick of his chin.

The soldiers bristled and Rye heard the sound of swords being unsheathed, but Valant signaled them to stand down. Quinn glanced at Folly nervously.

"Breathe easy, everyone," a voice called.

Folly's father squeezed his lanky frame past the

twins and stepped through the doorway. He wiped one hand on his apron and balanced two mugs in his other fist. Fletcher Flood's short hair matched the color of the rest of his family's and he wore the gap-toothed, ever-present grin of an expert barkeep.

"You'll have to excuse my boys' sentiments, Constable," he said. "You see, when they were born, word reached Longchance Keep that the twins were somewhat . . . different . . . from other babies. The Earl at the time seemed convinced that they were monsters, some sort of curse upon the village. He too sent a constable and a group of soldiers—much like yours here—to take them from their cradles. He intended to lock them away in the dungeons . . . or drown them in the river—some unpleasantness I'd rather not recall."

Valant nodded solemnly. "Sounds like an unfortunate misunderstanding."

"Indeed. There were a lot of misunderstandings that day. It was over twenty years ago and, while the twins have no memory of the actual events, they've certainly heard the story. In that respect their memories are quite long."

"Understandable," Valant said.

"My own memory is growing a little rusty," Fletcher continued, and his barkeep's grin fell away. "I can't recall exactly what happened to those soldiers. Their bones hung for a time under the bridge after the ravens picked them clean, but after that, who can say?"

Folly's other six brothers appeared behind Fletcher and the twins. They ranged in age from thirteen to twenty, but even the youngest was built tall and formidably. They all crossed their arms and wore matching glowers. Rye swallowed hard and looked to Folly. She recognized her friend's pinched expression. Folly wasn't frightened for her brothers; she was angry she hadn't been allowed to join them.

"Since those dark days," Fletcher continued, "we've had a rather hard and fast rule about soldiers—or constables—in the establishment."

The growing crowd on Little Water Street watched silently with menacing eyes. The soldiers shifted as the crowd stirred around them.

Fletcher's face lightened as he handed a mug to the Constable, who accepted it cautiously.

"So, while I can offer you a drink," Fletcher said, "you'll understand that any conversation you seek, you'll need to find outside."

Fletcher tipped the mug in a toast, and pressed it to his lips.

"Rules are rules," Valant said with a tight smile his eyes did not mirror. "I will respect them."

Valant took a swig from his mug. His brow furrowed for just a moment.

"Do you like it?" Fletcher asked. "This is just the regular house ale," he said with a nod to his own drink. "But what you have there is our Earl's Special Reserve."

Valant raised an eyebrow. "Special Reserve?"

"Yes. We hate to be wasteful around here. It's a very special blend made at the end of each night by wringing out the mops. You'd be surprised by what gets spilled on the floor."

There were loud howls and guffaws from the crowd.

"On the house," Fletcher added, flashing his wide, gap-toothed grin.

Rye cringed at the thought. She'd seen the floors of the Dead Fish at the end of a long night. Quinn held his breath nervously. Folly beamed.

But the Constable's stare was unflinching. He merely smiled, glared at Fletcher, and lifted his drink in a return toast. Valant pressed the mug to his lips and finished it in three long gulps, wiping his beard with the back of his hand when he was finished.

"Would it surprise *you*, Fletcher Flood, to know I've drunk worse?"

He thrust the mug into Fletcher's palm.

"Thank you for your hospitality," Valant said with a slight bow, his voice as smooth as spider's silk. "It shall be long remembered."

Valant turned on a heel and marched across the dirt road, bumping shoulders and pushing through the crowd without apprehension. The soldiers and Hyde followed, taking up positions on the main wharf.

Valant threw up his hands and announced, in an almost-convincingly sincere voice, "My apologies for the inconvenience, Shamblers, but on the authority of Earl Longchance this port is hereby closed until we've searched the cargo of all boats. It's come to my attention that bootleg goods and contraband may be flowing in and out of these docks."

"Of course bootleg goods flow through the Shambles," Folly said in disbelief. "Everybody in Drowning knows that."

"I don't think this is about black-market spices or smuggled grog," Rye said. "The Constable's sending a message."

"He's about to get himself strung up by his toes in the process," Folly observed.

"I'm not so sure about that," Quinn said, pointing out the window. "Look."

From the window, they could see the village walls at the far end of Little Water Street and the winding steps of Mutineer's Alley. The large troop of soldiers Rye had seen earlier now sprang into motion and began descending into the Shambles. Distracted by the Constable's display, the crowd had congregated in front of the Dead Fish Inn, and now no Shambler stood in their path.

Rye's cheeks flushed with alarm. "We need to warn my mother."

They hurried downstairs and out the doors in search of Abby and Lottie.

By the time they'd made it outside, tensions had quickly escalated. The crowd had become so thick in the street that the friends needed to push their way through. Rye struggled to find any sign of her mother or sister. The angry masses slowly inched toward the dock, as if ready to drive the Constable and the soldiers into the river itself.

At the end of the wharf, one of the soldiers sifted through the contents of some bags and containers waiting to be loaded. Valant eyed the findings before moving onto the next crate.

Rye heard a soldier's voice growl from somewhere amid the crowd near the wharf. She saw signs of a scuffle and heard a young voice protest in anger. The soldier stepped up onto the wharf's wooden planks and carried something to Constable Valant. It was a metal cage. Rye, Folly, and Quinn all froze and looked at one another in alarm.

"What in the Shale do we have here?" Valant said, and unclasped the door.

He plucked out the contents by its tail. It was Newtie.

Valant studied the lizard carefully. Newtie thrashed

as he hung upside down, snapping at the Constable as ferociously as his small mouth could muster.

"A perfect example!" the Constable called out, with a *tsk-tsk* cluck of his tongue. "It is illegal to import reptiles into Drowning. Who knows what havoc unknown species can wreak on our local fish stock?"

Rye fumed. The Constable was grandstanding—it was obvious that her sister's pet was no threat to anything larger than a kitchen roach.

Valant's dog growled excitedly and tugged at the chain leash Hyde had fastened to the end of a pylon.

"We'll dispose of this right now," Valant said, cocking an eye at the dog with a chuckle. "Snack?"

The dog wagged its tail and opened its mouth, canines gleaming. Valant dangled the lizard over its jaws.

Rye gasped.

Newtie flared his sailfin crest at the dog and Valant paused, raising an eyebrow. "*That's* interesting . . ."

"Newtie!" a small but booming voice cried.

Suddenly, Lottie broke free from the masses, rushing down the dock. Valant squinted at the angry red-headed fireball heading his way. Losing interest in the lizard, he flicked it onto the planks of the wharf. Newtie darted away from the dog's snapping jaws.

"No!" Lottie yelled, and running straight forward

without stopping, buried two little fists into the Constable's gut. The unexpected attack actually caused Valant to buckle over and cough.

Lottie rushed past, pursuing Newtie as he scurried down the wharf toward the water. But before she could catch him, she snagged her shoe on an uneven plank and fell hard on her hands and knees. She watched helplessly as Newtie reached the far end of the pier and tumbled over the side, disappearing beneath the black water of the river.

Valant caught his breath and his hand went to the red whip on his belt. Unfurled now, Rye saw that it was a cat-o'-nine-tails.

"You nearly cost my dog its treat, child," Valant said. "Now you'll meet my cat."

Valant raised his arm. Rye felt her heart pound in her chest. But before Rye or anyone else could move to stop him, Valant's head jolted back violently and he stumbled several paces. Rye couldn't comprehend what had happened until Valant regained his balance. His crimson hat sat askew on his head, impaled by the shaft of an arrow that now protruded from low on its crown.

It was at that moment that all of the Constable's composure seemed to fall away, and his eyes turned rabid. He reached up and clutched the arrow by its fletching, pulling it free from the scarred leather war helmet in which the arrowhead was buried. The arrow's tip snagged fabric on the way out, and he examined his fine hat still impaled on the end.

"Not . . . in . . . the . . . HEAD!" he bellowed, his face consumed by an almost inhuman rage.

Rye looked for the archer. It was not one of the sailors or fearsome vagabonds who made the Shambles their home. Instead, Abby O'Chanter stepped forward from the crowd, the smooth curves of a crossbow at her shoulder and her eyes simmering with a rage even hotter than Valant's.

Abby had already nocked another arrow and would have surely buried this one home had Lottie not regained her feet and rushed for her arms. At the same time, the angry mob surged down the pier toward the Constable and his small party of soldiers. Rye heard a vicious bark, followed by screams as Valant's dog was set loose upon the masses. Rye saw Hyde rush to the Constable and point in Abby and Lottie's direction.

A rhythmic thud of metallic drums sounded up and down Little Water Street. When the beat was joined by shouts, Rye realized that they weren't drums at all. Rather, it was the Earl's soldiers, pounding their swords against their shields in unison as they marched down the narrow dirt road from Mutineer's Alley. The Shambles' residents redirected their attention from the Constable to the advancing wall of armored bodies. They huddled together, forming their own tightly packed mob in front of the Dead Fish Inn. Rye, Folly, and Quinn found themselves pressed together so tightly that they couldn't break away. The soldiers came to a halt just past Thorn Quill's shop, leaving a short stretch of vacant dirt between the two factions. They ceased their pounding, and the Shambles fell eerily quiet.

Longchance's men stared out from under their helmets. Shamblers glared back, men and women alike, their faces hard and unrelenting. Blades appeared from inside boots and under dresses. Those who were otherwise unarmed picked up oars, broken bottles, and other makeshift weapons. Rye didn't doubt the Shamblers' ferocity but feared their fate against the more heavily armored troops.

Only then did the first black figure appear, climbing like a serpent from the river itself. Its companions crawled out from under wharfs and shadowy alleys. Beneath hoods, their faces were masked with white ash, their lips and eyes streaked with soot like skeletal eye sockets.

From the rooftops above them, the rest began to descend, dropping themselves like spiders right into the middle of Little Water Street. Rye saw cowls and leering, hook-nosed faces. Flashes of scrap-metal teeth.

The Luck Uglies.

Their leather boots padded silently as they filled the narrow gap between the soldiers and the Shamblers. The folds of the Luck Uglies' cloaks shifted, revealing nimble blades and nail-studded gloves waiting to strike. Rye had never seen the masked outlaws by the light of day; she doubted anyone had. She couldn't tell who they were regarding more cautiously—the soldiers, the Shamblers, or one another.

Then, like a spark to tinder, the first bottle was hurled at Longchance's men from the Shamblers and, as one, they cried out and streamed forward. Soldiers, Shamblers, and Luck Uglies collided in a sprawling, street-wide clash.

Rye lost sight of Quinn but saw Folly get knocked to the ground. She felt herself being swept away, her frame crushed by larger bodies in what had become an uncontrollable riot.

She called out desperately for her friends, but a hand clasped over her mouth. Someone grabbed her roughly by the shoulders and dragged her away.

13
A Losing Hand

Rye found herself on a damp embankment. High overhead, a stone arch of the great bridge that spanned River Drowning blocked out the sun. Chaos roared in her ears. Behind her, the dirt walkway of Little Water Street was a battlefield.

The strong hands on her shoulders went to her head. They were familiar and warm. Harmless seemed to read the concern in her eyes.

"Bramble has your mother and Lottie on their way into the Flats," he said, nodding to where the embankment stretched out from under the bridge and headed away from Little Water Street. That was where the Shambles came to an end, replaced by rolling mudflats where the river flowed into the sea. Villagers called them Slatternly Flats after the worms and mollusks that burrowed there.

"What about Folly and Quinn?" Rye asked.

Harmless tightened his jaw in thought. "The doors of the Dead Fish Inn will hold," he said. "But your friends won't be able to get inside at the moment. I'll bring them with us for now and get them home safe after you're on the ship. Head that way," he indicated, pointing a sword toward the mudflats. "I'll be right behind you."

"What ship?" Rye asked, but Harmless had already rushed back into the conflict on Little Water Street.

Rye looked in the direction of the Flats. The tide was out, and Rye saw the silhouette of a tall-masted schooner bobbing offshore. In the distance, several small shapes had gathered where the waves met the sand. She started toward them, and stopped and turned expectantly when she heard the sound of steps at her back.

It wasn't Harmless. Instead, two men hurried toward her. They wore flowing cloaks, but their hoods hung loose. Their faces were deathly white. Sweat from their brows streaked soot down over their cheekbones like ominous, black tears. Rye noticed the tattoos covering their forearms and ending at the hilts of the swords in their fists.

"It's Bramble's niece," the taller one said, catching his breath. "We're lucky to have found you."

"Yes, Snip, where's your uncle?" the snaggle-toothed one asked.

"There, by the ship I think," she said, raising a finger toward the Flats, then regretting it. She suspected now that these men were Luck Uglies, but there was something particularly unsettling about them.

"Let's all find him together, shall we?" the taller one said.

More footsteps pounded behind them and Rye was relieved to see that it was Harmless with Folly and Quinn in tow. Her friends looked flush, but none the worse for wear.

"Riley," Harmless said in an even tone, "take Folly and Quinn with you." He gestured to the two men. "We have some cleaning up to do. Hurry now." He flicked one sword in the direction he intended, and Quinn and Folly didn't ask any questions. They just hurried to join Rye.

But, to Rye's surprise, the two men extended their arms so the tips of their blades faced Harmless. Harmless did not seem to share her surprise. He stepped forward purposefully, his short swords in each hand pointed to the ground.

He stopped only when each of their blades was within a whisker of his throat.

"I find myself in dark spirits today," Harmless growled. "Choose your next move with great care."

The men glanced at each other, then back to Harmless. Their blades didn't waiver.

"So you've cast your lot with Slinister and the Fork-Tongue Charmers," Harmless said without moving, shifting only his gaze from one to the other. "At least your corpse paint makes you both a little easier on the eyes."

Rye realized now that their faces had been intentionally masked with white ash and soot.

"It's been a long time, High Chieftain," the taller Charmer snarled, ignoring Harmless's barb. "There's a new game afoot. And we've learned to bet on the player with the strongest hand."

"The deck is stacked against you," the other chimed in. "You just don't realize it yet."

Rye saw a look of sadness cross Harmless's face, then his eyes glinted with a wolfish fury.

"I'm afraid you've bet poorly. Now lower your arms, or the only losing hands today . . . will be your own."

Quicker than Rye could blink, the razor edges of Harmless's two blades came to rest under each of the Charmers' sword hands. He pressed them against the skin of their wrists hard enough to show it was no idle threat.

"Care to bet on whose hands are the fastest?" Harmless asked with wry grin. "Or maybe you've forgotten?"

The men glanced at each other with heated eyes, but each took a step back. Harmless eased his blades to his side and circled around the Charmers warily as he joined Rye, Folly, and Quinn.

"We stand aside today because of who you are and what you've done before," the snaggle-toothed Charmer called as Harmless gathered Rye and her friends. "But next time, we'll consider the slate to be wiped clean."

"Then I suggest you spend your final days well," Harmless replied darkly.

The Charmers retreated into the shadows of the bridge. Harmless did not look back at them. He put his arm around Rye's shoulder and a hand on Folly's back, rushing them and Quinn away to the Flats.

Rye glanced over her shoulder once. High atop the bridge, she thought she saw a solitary masked figure in black watching them go with red-rimmed eyes. But when she looked again, he was gone.

A hard-scrabble group of men paced irritably on the sand where they'd beached three wooden longboats. One of the men turned and ran toward them, his pale blue eyes ablaze.

"What happened back there?" Bramble demanded.

"Two of our brothers showed their hands," Harmless said curtly.

Abby rushed forward and joined them, dragging Lottie close behind her. Rye's sister had somehow managed to retrieve Newtie's empty cage from the wharf. She held it sullenly with Mona Monster.

Abby threw her arms around Rye and looked to Harmless for answers. "What now?" she asked, casting her eyes to the boats.

"I was able to make some hasty arrangements for your safe passage on the *Slumgullion*."

He gestured toward the schooner anchored in deeper waters.

"Passage where?" Abby said, her thin black eyebrows sinking low over her eyes.

Harmless hesitated.

"Where, Gray?"

"Pest."

"Pest!" Abby exclaimed, her eyes flaring. "Without asking me?"

Rye tried to make sense out of her parents' hurried words. She knew the Isle of Pest was where her mother and Bramble were raised, but they almost never spoke of it. Abby had not returned to Pest since leaving well before Rye was born. For all Rye knew, it might have been on the other side of the world.

"Perhaps if you hadn't buried an arrow in the Constable's hat I would have had time to explore other options," Harmless was saying to Abby.

"Yes, you'll have to forgive me," Abby retorted. "Impulsiveness is normally your domain. But you may have noticed your youngest daughter was about to learn a painful lesson about lawmen and their egos."

Harmless rubbed his chin. "She does seem to display a rather aggressive disdain for authority figures."

"I wonder where that might come from," Abby said, without a hint of uncertainty in her voice.

"We're leaving Drowning?" Rye asked urgently.

If her parents heard her at all, they didn't bother to reply.

"Yes, I wonder too," Harmless responded hotly. "What are you doing carrying your crossbow openly?"

"Surely you've heard," Abby said, throwing her arms in the air. "I'm a wanted criminal now. I thought I should dress the part."

"Why are we leaving Drowning?" Rye yelled, stepping between them.

Harmless and Abby broke off from their jabs. Her father's face softened.

"It can be no coincidence that the Earl's soldiers marched into the Shambles on the very day we were set to ride on Longchance Keep. This is no ordinary constable. He has no fear of the Luck Uglies. And after months of licking his wounded pride, it seems Longchance has grown similarly emboldened."

"But why must we flee? Can't we go—" Rye caught herself, and was careful not to say Grabstone. "Somewhere else?"

"If the Shambles is no longer safe, then nowhere in the Shale is. I already know that two of our kind have betrayed their brothers. For now, it's best that you go somewhere even Luck Uglies no longer tread." His eyes narrowed. "Until I know which Luck Uglies I can trust, we cannot trust any of them."

Although Rye's mother's face was hard, she offered no objection to what Harmless was saying.

"Except one," Harmless added, looking over to Abby. "You know where to find him," he told her quietly.

"No offense taken by the way," Bramble muttered out the side of his mouth.

"And Slinister?" Rye asked. "I saw him again last night—at Thorn Quill's. He was with the Constable's squire," she added quickly, before her mother could erupt at her disclosure.

Harmless looked surprised, then even more resolved.

"Whatever Slinister's intentions may be," Harmless said after a long pause, "he's the last person who would align himself with the Earl and his Constable. Beyond that, his intentions remain murky, which is all the more reason to get you to Pest. I'll be better able to address both the Earl and the Fork-Tongue Charmers knowing that there's an ocean between you."

"He says you have something—" Rye began, but was interrupted.

"Gray!" a voice called from the shoreline. "It's now or never. I'm not waiting for a kiss good-bye from the Earl's men."

Rye recognized the voice as belonging to a man from the Dead Fish Inn. It was the one-eyed freebooter she'd seen the day before.

"You must be off," Harmless said to Abby. "Captain Dent hoists the colors of a freebooter. He swears no allegiance to the Earl, nor to me, but we share—shall we say—common interests."

"You're putting us in the hands of pirates?" Abby whispered incredulously, as they all hurried to the long-boats.

"Smugglers," Harmless clarified.

"Smugglers!" Abby said, stopping short.

"Abigail," Harmless whispered, nodding toward Rye and Lottie. "Given the cargo, don't you want to be in the hands of someone who knows what he's doing?"

Harmless noticed Rye's nervous glance at Captain

Dent. The one-eyed smuggler barked orders as his men readied the longboats for launch.

"Not to worry, Riley," Harmless said, watching the freebooters loosen the moorings. "Daggett Dent has captained four sunken ships and three wrecks—swam away from each without a scratch. Yes, there's the matter of his eye, but that was courtesy of an unusually fearsome pelican. My point is—luck travels with him on every voyage."

Rye frowned. Apparently, luck was in the eye of the beholder.

The longboats were ready. Rye hesitated before approaching them. She smiled sadly at her friends. Folly chewed her lip. Quinn shifted awkwardly from one foot to the other.

Harmless took a knee in the sand and placed a reassuring hand on Rye's shoulder. "Something tells me you'll like the Isle of Pest. Really."

"It's not terrible—for a barren pile of sea stacks," Bramble added from over his shoulder. Harmless ignored him.

"You won't come?" Rye asked, although she already knew the answer.

"They wouldn't be so glad to see me again," he said. "I'm afraid my head would fetch a hefty price on High Isle."

"Why wouldn't they be glad to see you?"

Harmless gave her a wry smile and looked like he might answer, but a shout from the bridge drew him to his feet. A dozen men in Longchance tartan spilled over the embankment under the archway, weapons drawn.

Harmless pressed a hand to Rye's chest and steered her toward a freebooter.

"Get the children in the boats!" he called to Captain Dent, pointing at Lottie.

Harmless's eyes caught Rye's and seemed to bid her farewell, then he drew his swords from his back and charged in the direction of the advancing soldiers.

Rough hands grabbed Rye before she could protest, and she felt herself lifted off the sand and deposited into the leaky hull of a longboat. Abby and Lottie appeared next to her, and the heavy bodies of several freebooters crowded in alongside them. She struggled to spot Folly and Quinn—to be sure they were safe and at least wave good-bye—but the thick shoulders of the sailors blocked her view.

Captain Dent was soon in the boat himself, barking orders to the men who were still onshore. They pushed the longboat through the surf line, waves crashing against its bow and bathing Rye with salt spray as the freebooters heaved the oars. Looking back at the Flats, Rye lost sight of Harmless, Bramble, and her friends.

"They'll be fine," Abby said reassuringly, and handed Rye a wooden bucket.

"Is this if I get sick?" Rye asked.

"No, it's so we don't *sink*." Abby pointed to the pool of water at their feet. "Bail."

Shivering, wet, and miserable, Rye tried to empty the bottom of the longboat as quickly as possible. Lottie did the same, but only managed to deposit buckets of frigid water into Rye's boots. Squinting at the beach, Rye saw that one of the other longboats had left the shore and was close behind them, and the remaining freebooters were just pushing the last boat into the surf. The *Slumgullion* loomed closer now, rocking in the turbulent sea as they rowed toward it. Its sails sagged and its hull was pockmarked. It seemed to Rye that the ship had seen better days.

Rye looked down the coastline, where Drowning's jagged silhouette rose like thorny branches. Plumes of black smoke rose from the Shambles, growing ever more distant. What would become of it? The village was prickly—but it was still her home. She wondered when, if ever, she might see it again.

Her spirits only darkened when she realized she hadn't even gotten a chance to say a proper good-bye to Folly and Quinn. She hoped Harmless and Bramble would see them home safely. She could still hear the echoes of her best friends' voices.

"Rye! Rye!"

Rye shook her head, as if bees were buzzing in her ears.

"Rye!"

But it wasn't a memory, it was Folly's actual voice.

"Rye! Over here!"

Rye looked to the other longboat, where a soggy mop of white-blond hair dripped over Folly's smiling face. Folly waved frantically from the bow. Quinn was there too, looking more green than pleased.

"Dent!" Abby yelled. "What are you doing with them?"

"Gray said to get the children," the Captain called back, incredulously.

"Not all of them!"

"Well, next time he should be a little more specific," he huffed.

That put a smile on Rye's face for the first time all day.

14
The *Slumgullion*

"My father's going to be furious," Quinn said with a grimace, then hugged the side of the ship and deposited what was left of his breakfast into the churning sea.

"Quinn," Folly scolded, peering over the bow. "You almost got sick on that sea turtle."

"Gray will get word to Angus," Abby reassured. "Your parents too, Folly."

Folly shrugged. "It will probably be days before they even notice I'm gone."

"How long *will* we be gone?" Rye asked.

Abby glanced over at Folly and Quinn, then gave Rye a slight shake of her head. That meant she didn't know either.

Rye stared up at the patched canvas sails as the *Slumgullion* now bobbed and lurched over open water. The freebooter flag snapped in the breeze—emerald green with three soaring white gulls silhouetted in the corner. She examined the deck's worm-riddled timbers.

"Don't let her looks fool you," Captain Dent said, joining them at the rails. "The *Slumgullion* may look like a barn-dwelling nag, but she's swift as a filly when she needs to be."

The Captain fumbled through his breast pocket and retrieved several walnuts. He placed two side by side in his hand, closed it into a fist, and punched it into his other palm. When he unclenched his fist the shells were cracked, exposing the nuts inside. He handed them to Quinn.

"You look a little green around the gills, lad. These will help."

Quinn carefully nibbled them with his front teeth.

"If that doesn't work, we'll try dipping you in the drink. Cold water does wonders for greenies like you."

Quinn handed the rest of the nuts back to Dent and rushed for the ship's rails again.

Dent shrugged, took an unshelled walnut and wiggled it into the vacant hollow of his missing eye socket. He flashed a jagged smile that made him look like the carved-pumpkin head of a Wirry Scare.

Folly giggled. Rye cringed. Dent leaned forward, slapped the back of his own head, and the walnut fell out into his awaiting hand.

"You can eat that one," Rye said.

"You should wear a patch over that," Abby said dryly. "You'll scare the women and children."

"Eye patches? You've read too many fairy tales, Mrs. O'Chanter," Dent protested. "There's no place for vanity at sea."

Rye would have liked to hear more about the Captain, but he became noticeably alarmed at the sight of a large brown pelican perched on a boom overhead.

"Be gone!" he yelled and shook a fist. "I'll deliver you to the cook, you floppy-necked devil!"

Abby just shook her head. "Smugglers," she muttered.

Rye watched the Captain chase the large bird around the deck. She only hoped this voyage wouldn't fall victim to the special brand of luck Harmless had told her about.

It didn't take Rye long to discover that men at sea were an unusually supersitious lot. Women and children were considered bad luck on a ship, but fortunately the crew seemed to warm to them quickly. They told stories of mermaids and leviathans, although Rye never spotted anything more interesting than a distant dolphin. Lottie was still smarting over the loss of Newtie and, at one point, a crewman let her climb the rigging to boost her spirits. Abby put an end to that before Rye got a turn. She tried to help out on deck, but found that a sailor's work involved a remarkable amount of rope to trip over or become tangled in. Eventually, the Captain put her to work chopping potatoes in the galley.

Time spent belowdecks was dark and noisy with the groans of the sea. It stunk of the unwashed hammocks of the *Slumgullion*'s crew, but Dent had set Abby and the children up in private quarters. On their second day it rained, and Rye, Folly, and Quinn found themselves alone in the cramped space for the first time.

Rye removed one of her oversize boots to replace the damp straw with new padding. The stitching on the boots had become loose, and strips of leather flapped when she walked. She wiggled her toes, examining the black, crusty skin between them.

"I think I've got skunk foot," she said with a frown.

"What do you expect?" Folly said. "You're always running around in those big, wet boots."

"They itch," Rye said, cringing. She scratched frantically at her feet and almost tore off an iron anklet charm

Harmless had given her.

"Don't do that," Folly said. "It'll just spread. My mother makes a balm out of mushrooms whenever I get skunk foot. When we get to the island I'll see what I can find."

Folly hardly ever wore shoes around the Dead Fish Inn. Rye figured if anyone knew how to cure skunk foot, she would.

Quinn spread out on the floor a worn nautical map that he'd borrowed from the freebooters. He was always reading or studying something—his cottage on Mud Puddle Lane was full of all sorts of books, even a banned one the three friends had come across and stashed under his bed. Quinn reached into his pocket and placed a little stickman next to the map as he sprawled on his stomach and pored over the map's markings. Rye recognized it as the Strategist's Sticks, a gift from Harmless, like Rye's anklet and Folly's Alchemist's Bone.

"Helps me concentrate," he said, with a sheepish shrug. He ran a careful finger over the map's yellowed linen surface. "Here's Pest."

"I heard . . ." Folly began.

Rye and Quinn exchanged glances. Folly's most outlandish stories always seemed to start that way.

". . . that the tide washes gold grommets ashore every morning."

Rye and Quinn looked at her as if a flock of pigeons had roosted on her head.

"From the shipwrecks," she clarified.

"You heard that at the inn?" Quinn asked.

"Of course," Folly said. She was always picking up snippets of conversation at the Dead Fish Inn. And they usually seemed to involve hidden treasures or beasts that might eat you.

"I don't know anything about golden tides," a voice said with a chuckle. "Although with your ear for stories, you fit right in with my crew."

It was Captain Dent, leaning against a timber.

"These waters *were* once stalked by sea rovers," he went on. "The most notorious of them proclaimed himself the Sea Rover King and amassed a fortune raiding the real king's treasure galleons as they made their yearly runs from Drowning to O'There. The swabs prone to gossip will tell you the Sea Rover King's greatest treasure is still hidden somewhere on Pest."

"Ow!" Quinn groaned.

Folly had smacked him on the shoulder. "See?" she said. "I told you there was treasure."

"I'll just be happy if we find dry ground," Quinn said, rubbing his arm. "And a souvenir to show my father. He's never left Drowning. I'll still be in for it when we get back, but at least he'll be impressed."

"This is High Isle," the Captain said, ignoring the children's jousting and pointing to the map. "Anything worth seeing on Pest can be found there. These," he said, hovering his finger around a cluster of smaller dots, "are the Lower Isles. They are harsh and unforgiving islands. The most remote of them home to clans who dabble in dark currents. Hags whose dreams reveal the future . . . and drive them to madness."

"More fish tales from bored sailors?" Rye asked.

"Perhaps," Dent said grimly, "but I've never been inclined to sail there and find out."

Rye exchanged nervous glances with Folly and Quinn.

"In any case," the Captain said, returning to his usual good cheer, "could I please have my charts? Just to be sure we don't take a wrong turn."

"Go on, Quinn," Folly said quickly, giving him a nudge. "Give him back his maps."

Sleeping in a hammock took some getting used to, and by their third night, Rye still hadn't. She slipped out of their cabin while Folly, Quinn, and Lottie still dozed. Her mother's hammock was empty, but Rye knew where she might find her. She pulled on her coat, its elbow repaired by Abby with a green swatch made from the same heavy sailcloth as the freebooters' flag. She'd also sewn on custom loops so Rye could stow her cudgel and spyglass across her back. Abby was bundled in a heavy blanket on deck, staring out at the stars. The sea was calm, the sky crystal clear.

"Mama," Rye whispered.

Abby looked up, smiled, and lifted the folds of the blanket, making room. Rye curled up beside her and Abby wrapped her tight.

"When will we be at the Isle of Pest?" Rye asked.

"I've only made this journey once myself—going the other way," Abby said. "But I think we'll be there soon."

"How can you tell?"

"I can smell it," Abby said.

Rye crunched up her nose. "It smells bad?"

Abby stared up at the stars again. "No, not bad at all. It smells earthy, like soil and wild grass. Lavender in the springtime. Spring comes early on Pest."

Rye sniffed hard and shook her head. "I can't smell anything."

"You will," Abby said. "Soon enough."

"What's it like?"

"It's beautiful, often breathtakingly so. But it's a time-hardened place—harsh around its edges." Abby's eyes flickered at a distant memory. "It's seen its share of strife."

Pest sounded a lot like her mother, Rye thought.

"Pest has been occupied by the soldiers of many noble houses over the years—each house claiming it for the Shale. Each with varying degrees of success. Belongers—that's what islanders call themselves—are not a people to be quelled. But that hasn't stopped the Uninvited from trying."

"The Uninvited?" Rye asked.

"Anyone who's not a Belonger."

"Oh," Rye said. She picked her fingernails nervously. "Is Pest rich with treasure?"

Abby smirked. "That sounds like something Folly might have heard."

Rye shrugged. Sometimes it seemed her mother knew her friends as well as she did.

"Pest *is* rich with legends," Abby went on. "But, no, I don't believe there's buried treasure on Pest. If there was, Dent or someone like him would have found it."

Rye wondered what else might make Pest such a sought-after prize. "Is it an important port?"

Abby shook her head. "No, its reefs and shoals are far too treacherous."

"Then why have the nobles fought so hard for it? Why not leave it alone?"

Abby sighed. "Because the Belongers say they can't have it. And sometimes, unfortunately, that's all it takes."

Rye considered the enormous lengths men would go to in order to claim something out of their reach—regardless of whether they really needed it.

"I was just a girl the last time a noble house laid claim on Pest," Abby said. "They stationed a constable in Wick, along with a small army of soldiers. They tried to impose their own laws on the Belongers. They weren't the same as the Laws of Longchance, but they were hardly any better."

Rye's stomach turned at the thought of the Earl and his laws.

"One day, by chance, the wind brought a mysterious young man to Pest. A Luck Ugly. He approached my father and offered his assistance."

"Harmless?" Rye asked.

Abby nodded. "Of course, your father's assistance always comes with a price. The bargain they struck was harsh, but it was one that had been accepted by generations of Belongers before them."

"What was it?"

Abby stared out at the darkened sea. "Pest's freedom . . . in exchange for one of its sons." Abby was quiet for a moment before continuing. "With the Luck Uglies' help, Pest was soon free once again."

"But Harmless said he wouldn't be welcomed back. Why?"

Abby sighed. "It's complicated."

Rye furrowed her brow. With Harmless, it always was.

"When he left, your father took not only a son of Pest but me as well," Abby said, her eyes flickering at a memory. "I went willingly, of course." She looked to Rye and gave her a tight smile. "But there are those who would say he claimed more than he was promised."

It reminded Rye of Slinister's accusations—that Harmless had stolen away something he had cherished. She wanted to ask her mother about it but feared both the answer and her mother's reaction. She tried to push the unpleasant thought from her mind.

"Why have you never gone back home?" Rye asked.

"When I left Pest, I was just a young woman—still a girl, really. Your grandfather didn't think I was ready. He insisted your father was a terrible choice for me. I disagreed—strongly—in that special way that young women reserve for their parents. The war Waldron and I had on the day of my departure rivaled the fiercest battles Pest has ever seen. I said things—we both did—that have left scars to this day."

Rye was silent for a long while as they both watched the sea.

"I'm nervous," Rye said finally. "To meet . . . my grandfather. I know nothing of him."

"Don't be," Abby reassured.

"What's he like?"

"He's a strong man. Proud. Wise. Stubborn at times—but you'll learn that is the way of many great men. All of Pest respects him. As long as he leads them, no Uninvited will ever rule the Isle again."

Rye shivered as the wind whistled across the bow. Abby pulled her close. "When I was your age, Waldron would put a gentle hand on my head and it would warm my whole body, even in the fiercest storm."

Rye thought of Harmless. That was something he had done for her.

"I'm still nervous," she said.

"Me too, Riley," Abby whispered, with a knowing smile. "But just a little."

The moon slipped behind a cloud and the sea went dark.

"Now go belowdecks and try to get some rest," Abby said kindly. "Tomorrow's a new day. Let's welcome what it brings us."

"All right, Mama," Rye said.

Rye returned to their cabin and climbed into her hammock. Despite the rocking of the sea, she finally drifted off, dreaming of the lush island that might soon greet them on the horizon.

Unfortunately, when she woke the next day and joined her friends on deck, she found the *Slumgullion* engulfed in an ominous fog so dense she couldn't see anything at all.

15
The Salt

"It's called the Salt," Captain Dent said as they peered out over the rails blindly.

Rye felt the fog settle on her face. It left her tongue thick and heavy, like she needed a drink.

"Where did it come from?" Folly asked.

Quinn spread his fingers in front of his eyes. By the time he fully extended his arm, his hand had disappeared.

"Islanders say Pest wears the Salt like a cloak," the Captain explained. "The High Isle draws the Salt around her shoulders to protect her from unwanted strangers."

Abby raised a suspicious eyebrow at him, as if the Captain might be to blame.

"The Pests are a superstitious lot," Dent said, returning a frown. "Even worse than sailors."

"So we're at the island?" Rye asked, nerves and excitement rising in her voice. She couldn't see the far side of the ship, never mind any shore on the horizon.

"We are," Abby said. "I suspect the Captain will have us in port shortly."

The Captain waved both hands in protest. "That I will not, Mrs. O'Chanter. This is as far as I go."

"What?" Abby said, her voice even but severe.

"The *Slumgullion* is built for speed and stealth. There's not a ship in the king's fleet we can't outrun or a cove into which we can't disappear. But I can't steer where I cannot see. Pest's reefs are littered with the bones of captains who've believed otherwise."

Abby stepped close to the Captain and stared hard into his one eye. "Your bargain was to deliver us to the Isle of Pest. It was a bargain you made with the High Chieftain of the Luck Uglies."

"The ocean is measured in miles, not inches," Dent replied. "You're much closer now than when we left Drowning."

Abby's body had become stiff with menace. Rye

noticed the crossbow slung across her mother's back. Abby was known to hide even nastier bits under her dress. But Rye could also feel other eyes upon them. She sensed more bodies gathering around them in the fog on the deck. Abby must have felt it too.

"Mrs. O'Chanter," Dent said, his voice quieter. "If I ordered my crew to try to sail us into port, I'm quite certain we would all find ourselves strung from the mast."

"So we're to swim?" Abby said.

"Daggett Dent is no cutthroat!" he corrected, taking great offense. "I have a perfectly seaworthy longboat ready for you."

Rye felt her ears burning. Were they being betrayed by this man who'd pretended to be their friend?

"You're going to set us adrift?" she said, unable to contain herself.

"Of course not, lass," Dent said with a dismissive wave. "You'll have oars."

And so it was that Rye, her family, and friends found themselves back in a longboat, being lowered into the waves. At least the crew had loaded a supply of fresh water.

"Farewell, Mrs. O'Chanter! Good-bye, children! Be well, Pickle." Dent waved from the rails above them. "I'm truly sorry about all of this. But if you row east with haste, I'm sure you'll reach the shore by midday."

"I hope a pelican gets his other eye," Rye said glumly.

"Pelican? Where?" Dent said, his good eye darting anxiously at the sky.

"We'll find our way," Abby reassured Rye. "Children, take up the oars."

They did, and after just a few strokes, the *Slumgullion* disappeared behind the wall of fog.

The small boat inched along blindly at the mercy of the Salt. Quinn did an admirable job of manning the oars long after Rye and Folly had tired. Folly entertained Lottie while Rye and Abby traded Rye's spyglass back and forth. But neither of them could see anything through the thick stew that hung in the air. Fortunately, the sea and the winds remained gentle.

"How do we know we're heading the right way?" Rye asked.

"It feels right," Abby said. Rye raised a suspicious eyebrow. "And if we're not there by dark," Abby added, "we know we've veered off course."

"Did you see that?" Folly called.

"What?" Rye said.

"There," Folly pointed overhead. "I thought I saw a bird fly past."

"She's right," Quinn added. "It looks like a break in the fog."

Rye looked carefully. The Salt was turning wispier, less dense. Abby tried to peer through it.

Rye watched the sky for signs of another bird. Suddenly a large dark shape appeared overhead and fell upon them. Something damp and stringy clung to her face. She moved to pull it away with her fingers but it was now tangled around her hands too. Quinn stopped rowing and struggled to free his arms. Lottie screeched as if caught in a spider's web. The longboat rocked as they all flailed.

They had been captured in a net.

"Be calm, children. Stop struggling or it will just get worse," Abby said. She dug into the folds of her dress and retrieved a sharp blade. "Riley, use Fair Warning. Quickly."

Abby began to cut the fibers. Rye removed Fair Warning from the sheath in her boot and carefully did the same. When they had finished, Rye examined the delicate net strands in her hands. The longboat was no longer moving and she was surprised to see that the fog had suddenly lifted, the last wisps rising off the water like steam from a kettle.

"Mama," Rye said. "Who's trying to capture us?"

"He is," Abby said quietly. "Although I suspect he's rather disappointed in the day's haul."

The longboat had come to rest on the sand of a tiny

beach. Chains of jagged rocks jutted out on either side, sheltering the cove. From atop a bird-soiled boulder, a weathered old man with a head of closely cropped white hair blinked down at them in surprise.

"Good morning, fine seas," Abby called to the man, blending the words together as she spoke them so that it sounded like *Goomurnin-fi-seas.*

Rye had never heard her mother talk that way before. She'd never heard that expression either.

The old man seemed surprised but mumbled back, "Aye, fair winds to you," which sounded a lot like *I-fair-wins-t'ya.* He hopped down the rocks and made his way toward their landing spot on the beach.

Folly and Quinn climbed onto the sand while Abby helped Lottie out of the boat. Rye just sat and gaped at the landscape around them. The gray fog of the Salt still blended into the horizon in the distance, but overhead the sky was clear, bathing them in warm sunlight. The rocky crags of the island's cliffs were dotted with lush grass capped by crowns of wildflowers. Rye watched as legions of seabirds busied themselves making nests in the highest nooks and crannies. A small herd of woolly sheep as white as clouds made their way down the rolling green hill above them. They blinked at the seafarers curiously but soon lost interest, munching on the piles of kelp delivered by the tide.

"Rye, come on," Folly urged.

Rye stopped her gawking and took a deep breath. It was the most beautiful place she had ever seen. She splashed ashore.

When the old man reached them, his wide eyes darted from Abby to the children and back again. He was lean and wiry, barely taller than Quinn. His weathered face appeared as dumbstruck as Rye's. She supposed it wasn't every day that a boatful of children washed up on the beach.

"Sorry about your nets," Abby said, handing the pile of shredded ropes to him. "I'll mend them for you myself."

The man looked at the nets in his hands and frowned.

"I'm Abigail."

He shook out the nets, surveying the damage.

"Cutty," Abby added.

The man looked up from the nets with a start.

"You may not remember me, but these are my daughters, Riley and Lottie," Abby continued. "And these are our friends, Folly and Quinn."

He blinked again, his eyes changing as he seemed to recognize something in her face.

"Huh," he grunted.

Abby flashed him a smile.

"Shoo-gay-yoo a Wick, den," he mumbled finally. "S'be off."

"Did he say he's going to whip us?" Rye asked in alarm.

"No," Abby said, and put a reassuring hand on her shoulder. "He said he should get us to Wick. It's the local village."

Rye puzzled over the strange accent.

"It's called Mumbley-Speak," Abby whispered. "Some of the old Belongers still talk that way. You'll catch on soon enough."

The man turned and marched up the beach and the rolling hill, his nets dragging behind him. He gave a shrill whistle and the sheep stopped their grazing to meander after him. One of the sheep glanced back with its woolly head, as if waiting for them to follow. Rye, Folly, and Quinn looked at one another, then to Abby.

"You heard him," Abby said. "Let's not dawdle."

The old man set a quick pace, pushing himself up steep hills and worn footpaths with a walking stick that reminded Rye of a longer version of her cudgel. Rye removed her own from its sling and tried to match his stride, but still found herself trailing behind. Quinn carried Lottie on his back when her short legs tired.

Spring had indeed taken hold on the island. Cool sea breezes stirred the air, but the children found themselves loosening their collars as the sun warmed their backs. Rye was relieved when they reached the top of a tall bluff and the old man paused to take a breath. The Salt had lifted entirely and disappeared, and Rye could see the white-capped sea in all directions around them. Wind-scarred rocks and outcroppings stretched from the island, like the protective spines of the midnight sea urchins Harmless had collected at Grabstone. Nestled between them were small, sheltered coves and crescent beaches similar to the one they'd landed on. Littered among the outlying rocks, Rye saw the fractured remains of dozens of hulls and masts—the wrecks of ships that had never found those hidden harbors. She realized that luck had indeed been on their side that morning.

The island itself was mostly treeless, covered by lush but hardy turf that clung stubbornly to the ground. The hills were dotted with isolated stone cottages, gentle plumes of smoke wafting from their chimneys. White tufts flecked the rolling green meadows like dandelions. Rye squinted. They were countless flocks of sheep.

"Look over there," Folly called. "What are those?"

At a far end of the island, a half dozen twisted pillars of earth seemed to rise from an open clearing. From that distance, Rye guessed they must be at least thirty feet tall. Rye extended her spyglass and was stunned to find that they weren't natural outcroppings at all. Rather, they were boulders, each one as large as a horse, stacked and impossibly balanced into tall, narrow piles like plates in a cupboard.

Rye handed the spyglass to Folly, who took a long look and then passed it to Quinn. Lottie impatiently called for her turn, and Rye, Folly, and Quinn ignored her for as long as possible, as was their custom.

"Who built those?" Quinn wondered out loud.

"Jack-in-Irons, o'course," the old man chimed in without looking up from lacing his boot.

"What?" Quinn whispered to Rye.

"A giant," Abby translated, and flashed the children a knowing smile.

"What?" Rye echoed in alarm.

They were interrupted by Lottie's yelling. Her calls were not a product of her impatience this time. She ran around in a circle, angrily swatting at the air around her head.

"Bees! Bees!" she called.

Several large insects buzzed in and out of Lottie's hair.

Abby chuckled and tried her best to corral her.

"No, Lottie, not bees," Abby said, kneeling down and carefully plucking one of the insects from its perch on Lottie's ear.

She extended her palm to show them the emerald green dragonfly. It gently opened and closed it wings. The air was filled with a colorful swarm of the harmless creatures.

The old man decided they'd rested long enough and they soon set off again. This time the footpath meandered down more hills than up, and Rye stumbled in her boots as her body got ahead of her feet on some of the steeper slopes. Eventually, Rye caught sight of numerous buildings clustered on narrow roads overlooking a harbor. The small fishing boats moored at the harbor's wharfs and piers were sheltered by a grand rock seawall that must have taken years to build. But instead of following the footpath down toward the village, the man veered to the left, where a crushed-shell path climbed back into the hills.

"Excuse me," Abby said, stopping at the fork. "Cutty House is that way. In the village."

The old man stopped and nodded. "Aye," he mumbled. "Cutty House 'sin Wick. But Cutty's *house* 'sup dar. He ain't lived in town for years."

"Oh, I see," Abby said, sounding confused, and not just by his speech.

"Come, step lively," the man said, waving them on.

Traveling over a stone bridge and up another green slope, they came to a rather rundown-looking homestead balanced on top of a high bluff. A small collection of livestock wandered in and out of pens in various states of disrepair, coming and going as they pleased. The hull of a large fishing boat lay upside down at the cliff's edge, although the jagged coastline was so far below, this seemed to be an impossible place to launch a ship. Several small outbuildings were clustered behind a rambling stone farmhouse with a turf roof that had deteriorated into a giant bird's nest. But what really caught Rye's attention was the farmhouse's crooked wooden door. Although any paint had long since peeled away, there was, undeniably, a silhouette of a dragonfly carved into the wood. Just like the door of the O'Chanters' own cottage an ocean away on Mud Puddle Lane.

Rye was about to ask her mother about it, but Abby seemed to have fallen deep into thought at the sight of the place.

The old man gestured for them to stay where they were and approached the door. Placing his ear against it, he listened carefully. He rapped with his knuckles. There was no reply. He rapped again.

"Waldron," he called. "Yer in?"

There was still no reply. He banged louder with his fist.

"Wall!" he yelled. "There's some folk you need t'see."

Just when Rye assumed nobody was home, the door burst open and a towering man appeared in the doorway, his creased forehead flush with anger. His hair was an unkempt silver mess befitting his age, but his bristly beard was red as anchor rust and shot out in all directions.

"'T'is it, Knockmany?" he barked. "Why must you call on me every day?"

"Pardons, Waldron, but there's sum'n you need see."

"I've told you, I want nothing to do with the Crofters or the Fishers or the Fiddlers, neither."

Knockmany nodded as if he'd heard this numerous times before. He simply stepped aside and pointed.

"It's Abigail," he said quietly.

It seemed to take a moment for the words to register with Waldron. He didn't move at first, then took a step out of the door with the aid of a thick wooden staff. His chest and shoulders were massive under a tattered, unwashed shirt, his legs just twigs by comparison. The knotted blue veins in his forearms bulged, his grip tightening on his staff as he drew closer. His feet were bare and black with grime.

Rye saw his eyes squint suspiciously. They seemed to soften as he examined them, despite his efforts to keep their hard edge. Rye had seen that look before. They were her mother's eyes.

He opened his mouth, but nothing came out.

Abby took a step forward, and for the first time Rye could recall, her mother's eyes were moist.

"Hello, Papa," she said.

Waldron's face drained to a stunned pallor.

Abby took a breath and looked back at Rye and Lottie, who had frozen next to Folly and Quinn. She beckoned for them to join her. They stepped forward hesitantly.

"These are my children," she said.

Waldron blinked slowly as he regarded each of them.

"*All* of them?" he grunted.

Abby stifled a giggle. "No, Papa. Just these two." She put her hands on Rye's and Lottie's heads as they pressed close to her on either side. "Riley and Lottie."

Waldron started to smile, then his face fell, then he seemed caught in an expression between happiness and great remorse. With much effort, the towering man carefully lowered himself onto one knee to better see them. Rye wasn't sure what to do herself, so she gave him a tight lipped smile.

"I . . . ," he started, then paused. "It's . . ." His eyes jumped from the girls to Abby and back again.

"Goomurnin-fi-seas," he said, finally.

"Hello," Rye said.

"Hello," Lottie parroted, flashing a mouthful of crooked baby teeth.

They all fell into an awkward silence. Rye shifted from foot to foot. She always lost the who-could-stay-quiet-the-longest game.

"Should we call you Grandfather?" Rye asked, trying to keep the conversation going.

He pushed himself back up to his feet and scratched at his head. "You can . . . I . . ."

Waldron turned back toward the house. "I'll go . . . inside . . . wet some tea."

He stumbled back inside the house as if thunderstruck, leaving the door open behind him. Folly and Quinn exchanged curious glances. Rye looked at her mother with alarm.

"Maybe he would prefer Waldron?" she asked.

Abby patted her shoulder.

"Went well, all t'ings considered," Knockmany said, sucking a tooth. "Least he didn't chase you off with his stick."

16
The Pull

Abby thought it best that she speak with Waldron alone at first, and left the children to play outside. Folly enlisted Quinn and Lottie to help her gather some mushrooms she'd spotted growing in the fields. Rye preferred to explore the grounds around the little homestead. Although rundown and in need of serious repair, it seemed to Rye that it must have been a marvelous farm at one time. Even now, standing on the gently sloping hills of the grazing field, she was spellbound by its sweeping view of the vast, rolling sea. A blue dragonfly paused to examine her before fluttering away.

A rustle of grass at her feet startled her. She looked down and found two angular yellow eyes returning her gaze from some overgrown bracken. They belonged to a large smoke-gray cat with long, unkempt fur matted into clumps. It reminded her of Shady, even though, despite his appearance, Shady was no cat at all. She bent over to call for it, but the cat turned its back to her and skulked away. Only its bushy tail was visible as it made its way toward Knockmany's quarters—a glorified potting shed set back among the sheep pens.

"Riley," a voice called.

It was her mother in the doorway of the stone farmhouse. Abby beckoned to her.

"Waldron's resting," she said quietly when Rye arrived. Rye could hear his snores echoing down the snug hallways. Abby appeared weary herself.

Rye stepped inside and cast her eyes around the rustic farmhouse. At first glance, it seemed to have the ordinary trappings of a normal home—albeit one suffering from years of neglect. However, upon closer inspection, she found a number of unexpected oddities. A window opened into an empty closet. A set of wooden stairs simply ended at the timbers of the ceiling—there was no second floor.

"Mama, did Waldron build this place?" she asked.

If so, Rye thought, he must have been drinking homebrewed bilge wash at the time. She eyed the pile of empty, earthen jugs stacked by the hearth.

"No, my love," Abby said, taking a broom. "This was my mother's childhood home—your great-grandparents' farm. They're all long gone now."

In a corner, Rye found a small purple door, too small for even Lottie to fit through. She pulled its tiny handle but found nothing except solid wall on the other side.

"They weren't the finest architects," Rye said, closing the little door and noticing a sideways cupboard tilted like a seedling bent in the wind.

Abby smiled. "This was all by design."

"They wanted a crooked farmhouse?"

"Yes," Abby said, "as peculiar as that may seem. Belongers are superstitious folk, the older generations particularly so. The house is built like this for the Shellycoats."

"Shellycoats?"

"You may hear them called the Trow . . . or imps. Spirits."

Back in Drowning, they called such things wirries. Those who still believed in them erected scarecrow-like stickmen to ward them off. *Shellycoats* had a nicer ring to it.

"Belongers say Shellycoats dot the island like sheep,"

Abby continued. "They live in walls and under bridges. They're harmless enough—most of them, that is. But when they grow bored, even the most benign of Shellycoats can be mischievous—stir up trouble. The endless staircase, the doors to nowhere . . . they're designed to keep the Shellies busy. You'll find that all houses on Pest have one or more of these quirks."

Rye mulled over the strange custom. She doubted that her mother believed in wirries, or Shellycoats for that matter.

"Did you grow up in this house?" she asked.

Abby shook her head. "I was raised in Cutty House. Down in Wick. That's where my family lived. Where Waldron lived when I left this island. I'm not sure what brought him here to the farm." Abby looked over the unkempt house. "Whatever it was, he hasn't been the finest housekeeper."

Rye couldn't disagree. Even the Quartermasts were clean-sweeps by comparison.

"I'll give you a choice," Abby said, extending the broom. "You can help me tidy . . ."

Rye's shoulders slumped.

". . . or go explore with Folly and Quinn for a bit while Waldron finishes his nap. I'll mind Lottie."

Her eyes lit up.

"Don't stray far," Abby added hastily. "And please try

to stay out of the village for now. There'll be time for that later."

But Rye was already out the door.

Village Wick came into view as Rye, Folly, and Quinn crossed the small stone bridge and traipsed down the footpath.

"Look at that," Folly said in surprise.

"We must have taken a wrong turn," Rye said, and pursed her lips.

"Will your mother be terribly upset?" Quinn asked, slowing.

"She said *try* to stay out of the village," Rye recalled with a sly smile. "That's not the same as *don't* go in the village."

Wick occupied the crescent-shaped harbor at the seat of the hills. Its stone buildings jutted out in irregular shapes and sizes like headstones in an ancient boneyard, their roofs topped with grassy turf. A tall waterwheel churned at the mouth of a narrow river that divided the small hamlet. The whole place could have fit into a corner of Village Drowning.

The village streets were lined with crushed shells that chattered under their heels as they approached. Rye wondered if the shells' gravelly voices were meant to serve as a warning of outsiders' arrival. But, as they wandered through town, they found the streets remarkably deserted.

A fleet of fishing boats sat at the docks, even though the water was calm and Rye would have expected the fishermen to be at sea. The shops were empty. A shaggy pony tethered to a post eyed them expectantly as they passed. Quinn tugged some grass from the ground and held it out for him to chew.

"It's as if the town's been abandoned," Folly muttered out loud.

Mixed in among the shops were other buildings Rye took to be private homes. The doors were painted in colorful hues that mirrored the moods of the sea—aqua, deep blue, seafoam green. Over each door was a carved wooden placard: GILLY'S ROCKS. TARVISH DWELLS. DUNNER PLACE. In each case, nobody was home.

Rye stopped at a house in the center of town whose paint was more faded than the others. It sat in shadows, as if the building itself was deep in sorrow. She looked up. The placard read CUTTY HOUSE.

Rye hesitated, then gently placed her fingers on the door to see if it was unlocked.

"Y'er late too?" a friendly voice called out.

Rye pulled her hand away and turned at the sound.

"I was stuck in the field," the tall boy said as he hurried down the street. His hair was tawny and long enough to push behind his ears. He looked to be a year or two older than Rye and her friends.

"Oh," he said, stopping abruptly and looking them over with a suspicious eye. "Y'er not from here."

"I'm Rye O'Chanter," she said cheerfully. "These are my friends—Folly and Quinn."

The boy crossed his arms.

"We're from Village Drowning," Rye offered. "In the Shale."

"Aye," he said coldly. "Uninvited."

"Well, technically, yes," Rye said, furrowing her brow. "Although we weren't entirely *unexpected.* My mother is from Pest. Abigail O'Chant—I mean, Cutty."

"Cutty, you say?"

Rye nodded. "My grandfather lives here. On a farm up on that bluff."

The boy raised his eyebrows. "*Waldron* Cutty is your grandfather?"

Rye looked at Folly and Quinn, unsure of how she should answer. She opted for truthfully. "Yes."

The boy had an astonished look on his face, as if he wanted to believe her but was unsure that he could. "In that case," he said finally, "y'er a Belonger after all. How about you two? You have kin on the Isle?"

Folly and Quinn shook their heads with some reservation.

"Hmm," the boy said, considering it. "Well, stick with Rye and me and you should be all right. I'm Hendry, by the way."

"Nice to meet you, Hendry," Rye said. Folly and Quinn echoed the sentiment.

A thundering sound rumbled from the far side of town. It was the roar of a crowd.

"Come on, then," Hendry said, waving them ahead. "Let's get to the wall. The Pull's already started."

He broke into a jog. Not knowing what else to do, Rye, Folly, and Quinn hurried after him.

"The Pull?" Rye asked as they ran.

"O'course," Hendry said. "Where else do you think everyone is?"

They arrived at the far end of the village, where it seemed the entire town had gathered at the edge of the harbor. The Belongers cupped their hands and cheered loudly. Billowing, multicolored flags and banners waved over their heads. Savory smoke from large cook fires filled the air and made Rye's stomach grumble. From the back of the crowd, she stood on her toes to get a better view.

"Up here," Hendry said. He had climbed atop a farmer's cart. Rye, Folly, and Quinn joined him.

From their perch, Rye could now see three separate segments of massive stone seawall. Two lengths extended inward from either end of the harbor's crescent tips, while a third stretched from the center. Spanning the distance between them was a long, triple-ended rope thick enough to tether the largest of ships. The rope ran through an iron-and-stone pulley system housed on a solitary rock that formed a tiny, uninhabited island in the center of the harbor. Some sort of weathered wooden circlet was strung at the top of the pulleys, rotating clockwise and back as their wheels creaked. Each of the rope's three ends was held by a team of a dozen burly men—and more than a few stout women—on each seawall. *Held* was probably not the most accurate word, as they all gripped the rope for dear life while pulling their end toward the shore. All of the pullers wore tartan kilts.

It was a giant tug-of-war, like the ones children sometimes had in Drowning, except this one included three teams made up entirely of adults. Nobody seemed to be at play.

"This is the Pull," Hendry explained. "It's held every spring here at the harbor, and everyone on High Isle attends. Surely you've heard of it where you come from?"

Rye gave Folly and Quinn a quick glance. They shrugged.

"Even some folks from the Lower Isles sail in," Hendry went on. "You can always spot the Low Islanders right off. They're usually a bit wild-looking."

He nodded to a large family with numerous children,

all of them with long, matted hair and nervous eyes that twitched like foxes'.

"Probably haven't left the Lower Isles since last year," Hendry whispered.

All of the Belongers struck Rye as a little rough around the edges. They were generally large people, robust through the shoulders and hips but not soft, with weathered faces and eyes that brimmed with life. Many had painted their faces in colors that matched the kilts of the men and women on the seawalls. She saw quite a bit of red hair, which was uncommon back in Drowning. She finally understood where Lottie's raggedy mop came from.

"Is it some sort of competition?" Quinn asked.

"It's *the* competition," Hendry clarified. "To determine which of the three clans will govern Pest for the next year. The Tarvishes, Dunners, or Gillys, although the families are all jumbled now anyway so the names really aren't important. What matters is whether it's the Crofters, Fiddlers, or Fishers."

Folly squinted toward the three teams on the rock walls. "How do we tell them apart?"

"Well, Miss Uninvited," Hendry said, in a way that was more of a gentle tease than a mean-spirited slur, "if you lived here you'd know. But since y'er new, the Tarvishes are the Crofters. That's them in the green-and-white tartan. Most live in the hills, tending sheep and farming the crofts. The Gillys represent the Fishers. They're in gray-blue tartan and, as you might expect, are fisher folk."

Rye watched as the teams of Fishers and Crofters strained at the rope.

"The Dunners—they're the Fiddlers, and you'll spot them soon enough. They're always the first ones pulled into the drink."

"They're musicians?" Quinn asked.

"No, no," Hendry chuckled. He waggled his fingers. "They tinker and fiddle with things. Great with their brains and thumbs, the Fiddlers—they devise ingenious crab traps and keep the waterwheel churning. But their brawn . . . not as much."

There was a scream and a splash and most of the crowd erupted in cheers. Hendry threw up his arms, cupped his hands to his mouth and whooped and hollered. The first few members of the team in rust-colored tartan had tumbled off the rocks and into the water. Several dinghies rowed quickly from the docks to collect them before they drowned. A third of the crowd groaned and cursed, shaking their heads in resignation.

"Told you," Hendry said with a smile. "The Fiddlers keep claiming the pulley system is rigged. We just ignore them—after all, they're the ones who built it!" Hendry let out a hearty laugh. "The Fishers and Crofters on the other hand, they're a bit more evenly matched."

"Which team is yours?" Folly asked.

"Hendry Tarvish, First Apprentice Sheepherder," he said with a little bow. "And eighth-generation Crofter."

On the seawalls, the Crofters and Fishers took little time to relish in their first victory. The teams quickly turned their attention to each other. The prize at the center of the rope wobbled but did not rotate far either way.

"What's that in the middle?" Quinn asked.

"The Driftwood Crown," Hendry explained. "It's just an ornament. No one actually wears it—that would just be foolish."

It all struck Rye as a bit foolish.

"The Fishers have won the past two Pulls," Hendry said. "But I think this may be our year."

"How long will they go at it?" Quinn asked.

"As long as it takes," Hendry said. "Last year it lasted nearly a week."

"A week!" Quinn exclaimed.

"You can swap pullers out for a rest, as long as there are never more than twelve mates touching the rope at any one time. Substitutions are tricky."

"Will you be one of the substitutes?" Folly asked.

"No, still too scrawny," he said with a smile. Hendry flexed a bicep that produced an impressive bulge for a boy his age. Folly blushed. Quinn glanced down at his own arm and frowned. "Maybe someday," Hendry added.

Rye continued to study the teams battling each other on the seawalls.

"Isn't there a better way to decide who's in charge?" she asked.

"Of course," he said. "It should be the Crofters every year. But ask three Belongers and you'll get three different answers."

"Still, it doesn't seem like the best way," she replied.

"No?" Hendry asked. "It's certainly better than the old way. That involved much blood and broken bones."

Rye turned to him. "How long has Pest chosen its leaders like this?"

"Most of my life," he said, then hesitated. "Although there was a time when the clans weren't so quarrelsome."

Rye raised an eyebrow.

"There was once one leader who everyone agreed on," Hendry said. "But he abandoned us long ago. It's been like this ever since."

"Can't he be replaced?" Rye asked.

Hendry gave her a tight smile.

"Maybe," he said. "But as far as I know, there's only one Waldron Cutty."

17

Belongers

Hendry took Rye, Folly, and Quinn on a tour of the vendors' tents and stalls. Drowning's silver shims and bronze bits were of no value on Pest, but after Hendry introduced Rye as a Belonger the peddlers were willing to let them sample the local fare. The face painters even added a touch of decorative color to their cheeks. Quinn filled up on something called offal pie, and when he asked Hendry what was in it, Hendry just slapped him on the back and said, "You've got so many goat bits in your belly you'll probably be bleating in your sleep."

They all made their way back up the crushed-shell path as the sun hung low in the sky. Other groups of children followed the occasional adult out of the village, but most of the Belongers still crowded the harbor where the Crofters and Fishers continued to labor at the ropes. Hendry explained that many of the Isle's daily chores would be left to the children until the Pull was complete.

Rye heard the crush of shells behind them as two other children hurried to catch up. The boy was about Hendry's age but short and squat. His hair was shaved down to his scalp over each ear and around the back of his head, with a thick thatch of auburn hair sticking up on the crown like a plume. The girl was younger, perhaps seven or eight, and thin as a spring wildflower. She had perfectly round, green-flecked eyes that seemed to reflect the dull innocence of a halibut, and wore a crooked smile that reminded Rye of the bent cupboard back at the farmhouse. And yet her most striking feature was her hair. Her brown locks fell as straight and fine as thread past the hem of her frock, just short of the heels of her bare feet. Rye had never met anyone with hair so long.

"Is this them?" the boy asked, his cheeks ruddy with excitement.

Hendry nodded. "Rye, Folly, and Quinn, this is my second cousin twice removed, Rooster Dunner."

Rooster gave them a cheerful wave.

"Do they call you Rooster because of your hair?" Folly asked with a smile.

Rooster's cheeks flushed even more. "Um, no," he stammered, and he tried to flatten his auburn tuft over the bare skin of his scalp. "It's because I wake up so early."

"Oh," Folly said as Rye flashed her a reproachful look. "That makes more sense," she added quickly.

"And this is our friend, Padgett Gilly," Hendry continued. "We call her Padge."

Padge kept smiling without blinking.

"Is it true?" Rooster asked, looking toward Rye as he grappled with his uncooperative cowlicks. "Are you really a Cutty?"

Rye had to think before answering but said, "Well, yes. I suppose I am."

"Have you met him?" Rooster asked.

"Who?"

"Waldron, of course," Rooster clarified.

"Yes. Well, barely. Folly and Quinn have too."

"Told you," Hendry said.

The three Belonger children exchanged wide-eyed glances, although Rye was beginning to get the sense that Padge's eyes always looked that way.

"Your grandmother's mother was my grandmother's

aunt," the younger girl chimed in unexpectedly.

Rye returned a blank look.

"My great-grandmother was your mother's great aunt," Padge clarified, in a way that was entirely unhelpful.

"Oh," Rye said, "That makes us . . ." She wasn't exactly sure.

"*Related*, silly," Padge said with a roll of her eyes, as if the answer should be obvious to anyone.

Quinn furrowed his brow. "I think she means your great-grandmothers were sisters."

"Exactly," Padge said, and blinked her eyes for the first time, batting them at Quinn. "You must be the smartie of the bunch."

"Padge comes from a family of whalers," Hendry explained. "Her father was a legendary seaman, but he was swallowed by a humpback when she was just a baby. We keep an eye out for her now." Hendry flashed her a warm, brotherly smile, then leaned in and whispered to Rye. "He actually tangled his foot in a net and fell off the dock, but we tell her the whale story to make her feel better."

Hendry leaned back out. "Padge also happens to have an uncanny ability to guess things before they happen."

"It's true," Rooster confirmed.

"We keep that to ourselves, though," Hendry added warily. "We wouldn't want the adults to get the wrong idea and ship her off to the Lower Isles."

"Why would they ship her off?" Rye began to ask, but Rooster had already jumped in.

"Who's going to win the Pull this year, Padge?" he asked.

"I already told you. Nobody."

"Come on," Rooster coaxed.

"You don't have to believe me, Rooster. But you can be sure who's *not* going to win—the Fiddlers." She stuck her tongue out at him.

Rooster scowled. Folly giggled. Hendry suggested that they all move along, offering to see Rye, Folly, and Quinn back to Waldron's farm before dark.

Rye started after Hendry but stopped when she felt a small tug on her sleeve.

"My father wasn't swallowed by any whale," Padge whispered, and winked a big round eye. "I just pretend to believe that to make Hendry and Rooster feel better."

The children made their way along the footpath. Quinn chatted with Hendry while Rooster eagerly quizzed Folly about what is was like to live in a tavern. Padge followed closely at Rye's heels, so close she accidentally stepped on Rye's boot and sent her reeling. The little girl didn't say much but just kept smiling her crooked grin.

Rye saw Quinn pause as they reached the small stone bridge.

"What's that?" he said, pointing to something nestled underneath. It looked like a leather pouch. "Someone's dropped their coin purse." Quinn started down the embankment.

"Don't touch it!" Hendry cried. "We leave coins under bridges for the Shellycoats—to keep them happy and out of mischief," he explained. "Disturbing their coins . . . that could be trouble."

"What's a Shellycoat?" Folly asked.

"Like a wirry," Rye said.

Padge leaned in close to Rye. "Silly boys," she whispered. "The Shellycoats don't want coins."

"No?" Rye asked.

Padge shook her head adamantly.

"What then?" Rye asked.

"Blood," Padge mouthed.

Rye pinched her face tight at the thought. Padge just looked at her without blinking, then her shoulders began to shudder and a little wheezing sound came from her throat, like Shady coughing up a hairball. It took Rye a moment to realize it was laughter.

"I'm just tickling you," Padge said, and jabbed a

small, bony elbow into Rye's ribs.

Hendry glanced at the sky. "Smells like we've got weather coming in. We should all get home ahead of it." He turned and pointed up the path that Rye, Folly, and Quinn had descended earlier. "Keep to the footpath and you'll be fine. Don't stray north of your grandfather's farm, though. Beyond that is the old Varlet homestead—and you don't want any business there."

"What's wrong with the Varlet homestead?" Folly asked.

"It's haunted," Rooster jumped in. "And cursed on top of that."

Rye, Folly, and Quinn had heard their share of ghost stories around Drowning. Rye had come to discover that the stories were mostly bogwash. She heard Hendry call out as the new friends parted company at the edge of Waldron's farm.

"Meet us in Wick tomorrow! Don't stray from the farm after dark—you don't want the Shellycoats to get you!"

Rye smelled the familiar scent of her mother's cooking wafting from the farmhouse. Overhead, the glowing clouds that had reflected a golden sunset over the hills now turned to dark bruises. The children hurried through the field, ducking under an enormous pair of billowing men's trousers Abby had hung on a line to dry.

Behind them, the seas churned the color of metal. On the horizon, a large ship bobbed on restless waves. Then the Salt materialized like a massive ghost from the depths of the ocean, obscuring it behind its murky wall.

Abby had done her best to arrange a proper setting around the farm table for supper. She'd cut wildflowers and placed them in an empty bottle as a centerpiece, and everyone blinked at one another from their seats without saying anything at all. Rye and her friends sat up straight and smiled politely in their chairs for the benefit of Waldron and Knockmany.

Their good manners lasted all of a minute, the children resuming their usual suppertime antics by the time Abby had filled their goblets. Rye was starving and the floor around her was soon covered with crumbs and soup stains. Folly and Quinn loudly debated the veracity of one of Folly's stories. Lottie, whose own story was getting lost in the argument, banged her spoon on her plate.

Abby was well accustomed to such commotion, if not altogether enamored with it. But Waldron and Knockmany seemed as baffled as if a flock of geese had joined them at the table. Waldron slurped at his stew, his large frame spilling out of his chair. He didn't have much to say, although the wildflowers made him sneeze now and again. Knockmany sat next to Lottie and flinched at some of the louder shrieks and more boisterous laughter. He hunkered down behind his bowl and mug.

"So how was Wick?" Abby asked matter-of-factly, cocking a knowing eye at the children. They fell silent.

Rye exchanged glances with Quinn. His face was still smudged with the festive green and white paint of the Tarvish clan. She looked to Folly. A craftswoman had plaited strands of Folly's white-blond hair into a traditional Pest braid. It didn't take a sage to figure out where they'd been.

"We tried to stay out," Rye explained, "like you asked. It just didn't work."

"My father says a strong effort is sometimes worth more than a good result," Quinn added helpfully.

Abby just shook her head.

"So who do you think will win the Pull?" Folly asked Rye and Quinn.

Waldron's eyes narrowed from across the table.

"The Pull?" Abby asked.

Folly jumped in before Rye thought to stop her, telling Abby everything they'd seen and learned from Hendry. Abby's face frowned as Folly rambled, although Rye sensed that her mother's annoyance was not with her friend but at the state of affairs in Wick. Rye watched Waldron's reaction even more carefully. He didn't speak, but his eyes darkened with every word. It was the same sort of quiet anger she'd seen in her mother more than once.

Rye nudged Folly under the table in hopes it might quiet her, but Folly didn't take her cue. Rye felt the pit in her stomach move to her throat. Surely Folly knew better than to mention Hendry's words about the leader who'd abandoned them.

"They said it wasn't always this way," Folly continued between bites. "Once, there—"

Rye forced out an enormous belch—one loud enough to abruptly halt Folly's chatter. Abby gave her a reproachful look and Rye's eyes darted to Waldron. His forehead had gone scarlet. The muscles in his neck tightened as if he were trying to contain himself.

Uh-oh, Rye thought. Apparently that wasn't the custom on Pest either.

"Thank you for the dinner?" she said meekly.

Waldron's chin wrinkled, his brow furrowed, and he could control himself no longer. A sound escaped his throat. To Rye's surprise, it was a deep chuckle.

Rye looked at her mother. There was another burp.

Lottie smiled. "Tu, tu," she said, which meant "thank you" in Lottie-speak.

Waldron's chuckle turned to a belly laugh. The children laughed too.

Folly let out a burp. Then Quinn.

"Thank you for the dinner!" they called in unison.

Waldron's great barrel chest heaved. Abby crossed her arms and stiffened in her seat, but Rye could see the hint of a smirk on her face. Finally, after the children had forced out as many belches as they could, Waldron's laughter drifted off and he paused in his chair as if catching his breath. He refilled his goblet, drained it with a vigorous gulp, and buried his chin in his chest. Within seconds his eyelids drifted shut and his red beard was rising and falling in deep breaths.

Rye and her friends exchanged curious glances.

Rye leaned across the table toward Abby. "Is he asleep?" she whispered.

Waldron's eyes snapped open and he abruptly pushed himself up from the table with great effort.

"Yes, to bed, then," he said, and lumbered off to his bedroom, closing the door behind him.

That night the island was lashed by a storm the likes of which Rye had never before seen. She huddled with Folly and Quinn in a spare room of the farmhouse as the wind howled and shook the roof. Lottie had taken refuge with Abby in a second bedroom. Waldron seemed to sleep right through it, but Rye feared Knockmany would be blown out of his rickety shed.

Despite her exhaustion, Rye barely slept. Her first night back on dry ground, the floors of the cottage seemed to shift under her back like the decks of a ship. She had finally drifted off when the sound of moaning flooded her ears.

Rye awoke breathing heavily, her forehead damp with sweat. She leaped up, afraid it was Folly or Quinn, but both friends were still dozing on their straw pallets. She turned to the windows. The shutters were thrust open and she could hear the rage of the gale outside. A shadowy, four-legged mass sat on the sill with its back to her, watching the storm. It seemed to sense Rye's surprised gaze, and two yellow eyes looked back over its shoulder.

It was the gray cat she'd seen earlier that day. It must be seeking shelter.

Rye called to it softly and moved to coax it inside, but the cat leaped out into the darkness just before she could reach it. Rain splattered Rye's face as she peered outside.

The cat might have disappeared, but the low, guttural moaning hadn't. It came as if carried by the wind, and was full of a sadness more chilling than the damp coastal air. Rye quickly closed the shutters and returned to bed, her eyes pinched tight, wishing for the sound to go away. It seemed to ebb as the night wore on and, finally, as the tiniest sliver of pre-morning light peeked through the cracks in the window, she climbed from her covers.

She saw that one shutter was slightly ajar, as if forced open again by the storm. But there, on the sill, was an object that had become all too familiar.

A cold, black rock, polished smooth by the tides.

18 The Curse of Black Annis

Rye snatched up the stone and held it tight in her hand. It couldn't possibly be the same one she'd dropped in the Shambles, nor the one she'd discovered in her boot. What were the chances that the storm could have blown an identical stone up onto the sill? And if not, who would have put it there? Quinn and Folly would know better than to play such a prank. This time she tucked it into the pocket of her coat. She slipped outside without waking anyone.

From the cliff at the edge of the pasture, she found

the seas calm and glassy. The coves below were covered in piles of driftwood and kelp. Although there was some new damage to the fences and animal pens, hardly a breeze rustled her hair. She climbed onto the hull of the old, overturned fishing boat and took a seat.

"*Goomurnin-fi-seas*," Knockmany's voice grumbled. Rye looked over her shoulder and watched him shuffle from his potting shed.

"*I-fairwins-t'ya*," Rye called back, in the best accent she could muster.

Knockmany set a small tin plate on the ground. The gray cat appeared from the bracken and hurried to the plate, its yellow eyes flicking warily as it lapped a shallow layer of milk. Rye was glad to see it had made it through the storm.

"Is that your pet?" Rye asked.

"Gristle wouldn't like to be called that," Knockmany said. "She comes and goes as she pleases, though she sometimes keeps me feet warm on a cold night." He shambled back inside the shed and returned with some tools.

Endless flocks of white sheep were already grazing on the hills. Rye wondered which ones were Hendry's. She extended her spyglass and turned the lens toward the sea, where two large ships bobbed on the horizon, too far away for her to make out any colors. Merchant galleons, she guessed, probably sailing east to O'There.

"Y'er awake early," a different voice said behind her. It was Waldron.

"So are you," Rye said, lowering her spyglass and offering a smile. It was the first time he'd truly greeted her.

"Looks like I've got a busy day mending fences," he said, although his eyes were on the farmhouse, not the broken pens. "But y'er too young to have those dark bags under y'er eyes. I've already got plenty."

"The storm kept me up most of the night. It was the worst I've ever heard."

"It was a bit of a blow," he said. Gripping his staff, Waldron propped himself against the hull and returned her smile.

Rye ran her fingers over the weather-beaten wood. "Do you ever take this out for a sail?"

"Oh, this isn't my boat," Waldron said with a chuckle. "Knockmany found it out here one morning after a *real* storm."

Rye glanced at the surf lapping the base of the cliff far below. She'd hate to see a storm like that.

"There was a noise last night," she said. "A moaning . . . like something was in pain. Did you hear it?"

Waldron crinkled his thick brow, but his face seemed blank.

"I've heard noises like that before, back in Drowning—well, not exactly the same," she explained. "That time, it was a Bog Noblin."

Waldron grunted and shrugged. "Closest thing we've got to one of them is bony old Knockmany. Knockmany!" he called. "You ever seen any Bog Noblins on Pest?"

Knockmany had set down his tools and now studied a broken fence with crossed arms.

"I walked ever' inch o' this isle and I can tell ya we got none of those," he called back. "Them knobblies ain't good swimmers. They like the muck and mire . . . shallow canals . . . but anyt'ing over they heads and they sink like stones."

Rye had never heard that about Bog Noblins before. Knockmany started work on the fallen post and didn't offer more.

A thought seemed to dawn on Waldron. "You might have heard the Wailing Cave," he said, raising an eyebrow at Rye. "I forget it takes some getting used to."

"The Wailing Cave?"

"Have a look."

Waldron nodded to her spyglass. When she lifted it to her eye, he guided it so that it pointed to the shoreline some distance to the north. The mouth of a towering black cave rose from the side of the cliffs, its arched peak as tall as a cathedral's. The entrance to the cave was lined with natural basalt pillars. The waves swelled into its maw and disappeared, as if the cavern was swallowing the ocean itself.

"A bit closer and you can hear the current echo inside her," Waldron said. "It's a beautiful sound, but haunting. When the winds pick up, it carries her song across High Isle."

Rye lowered the spyglass. "What's in there?"

"Nothing," Waldron said quickly. "At least nothing anyone should go looking for." He seemed to hesitate. "Many a young man has entered the mouth of that cave. But none have ever returned." His face grew heavy. "The last one was your uncle Bramble."

Rye looked to Waldron in surprise. "But Bramble is fine," she said. "Well, he does keep strange company—his best friend is a monkey. But he's back in Drowning right now."

"You don't understand what I mean." Waldron measured his words for a long while before speaking again. "There have been dark times when the Uninvited would come to Pest in such numbers that we couldn't withstand them on our own. The Belongers are resilient people, but sometimes we've been forced to turn elsewhere for help." His eyes hardened. "There are men of shadows willing to render their services to the highest bidder. They named their price to join our fight against the Uninvited. And it was a steep one."

Rye knew he was talking about the Luck Uglies.

"A son of Pest," she said, remembering the words Abby had shared with her.

"Your mother's told you," Waldron said, nodding gravely. "Once these shadow brokers fulfilled their bargain, they would choose a Belonger and summon him to the Wailing Cave. There the young man would bid farewell to his family and enter the cave alone. And no one on High Isle would ever see him again.

"It was a cruel bargain," Waldron continued, "but one the Belongers grew to accept over time. Bramble was the last one—he was the toll paid when Pest last suffered under the rule of the Uninvited. I offered my own son so that no other family would have to." Waldron stared at the sea. "Bramble would have left High Isle on his own sooner or later, but not a day goes by that I don't regret my decision."

"But the Luck Uglies are not so awful," Rye said.

"Riley," Waldron said, his cheeks turning as red as his beard. "I know it is difficult for you to hear such things about your father's kind. But the Luck Uglies blacken all they touch. There's no honor among them."

"Harmless always keeps his bargains!" Rye said, her ears growing hot.

"We have an expression here," Waldron said. "*What the wind brings, the tide takes away.* It is the same with the Luck Uglies. What your father promises with one hand, he takes twofold with the other."

"That's not true!"

Waldron pushed himself up to his full height, so tall that he could look Rye in the eye even as she sat on top of the boat's hull.

"Pest will never lose another child to the Luck Uglies," he said, his voice rising. "I told your father long ago that any Luck Ugly foolish enough to return to this Isle will be greeted by my staff and my hammer." He shook his staff, then his fist. "Look around. There are no forests to cast shadows on Pest. No sewers to lurk in. Do you know what happens to a serpent when you pull it from its hole and clutch it by the throat? It squirms, and snaps its jaws, and wraps its tail around your wrist." He clenched his fist around the staff so hard his knuckles turned white. "Then it stops breathing."

Despite his age, Rye didn't doubt for a moment that he could wring the neck of a serpent, or a man, with his huge, basketlike hands.

They locked eyes, both of their tempers flaring. Rye struggled to not be the first to break their gaze. To her surprise, it was Waldron's eyes that softened, and welled with great sadness.

"I'm sorry, Riley," he said, shaking his head. "I am a combustible old man. Those words weren't meant for you."

"I understand," Rye said, although she really didn't.

"I was more patient once," he said. "But after your mother and uncle left I had little tolerance for the petty squabbles that arise in a place as small as this. My own family was gone—what did I have left to quarrel over? So I moved out of Wick, leaving the clans of High Isle to resolve their own differences."

"You came here because you're lonely," Rye thought, but actually found herself whispering the words out loud. She stiffened, hoping Waldron wouldn't be angry with her observation.

But her grandfather just extended a hand to help her down from the boat.

"Join me on a little walk," he said. "I want to show you something. And tell you a story."

Rye hopped down from the hull. She was relieved to see Waldron was wearing shoes today.

"Take it easy on me," he added. "My legs are long but old. They can't possibly match your young, spry ones."

Rye followed Waldron up the crushed-shell path where it wended north of his homestead. A thick, gray-maned bundle of fur skulked through the heather as they went. Gristle kept her distance, but seemed content to shadow them on their walk. Waldron pushed himself along with his staff.

"When I was much younger, a woman named Annis lived in Wick," he began. "It was said her soul was as dark as her face was beautiful. She was suspected of witchcraft and sentenced to banishment on the most remote of the Lower Isles."

"So it's true the Lower Isles are home to witches and hags?" Rye asked, remembering Captain Dent's far-fetched story on the *Slumgullion*.

"*Intuitives*, they call themselves," Waldron said, returning a tight smile. "And the wisest woman I've ever met was a Low Islander," he added, as if that explained it all. He pushed along in his own thoughts for several strides before resuming the story.

"But Annis was with child, and it was agreed that she would be allowed to give birth before she was sent to her fate. She bore a son, and with no father to be found, the new baby became the source of much debate. Most thought the infant should be shipped off with its treacherous mother, for what good could come of a child bred from such terrible stock? But gentler tempers prevailed, and it was agreed that the baby could stay. Of course, Annis disagreed. She cursed and railed against the villagers so furiously that her eyes rolled back in her head, and she had to be dragged aboard the waiting boat."

"They thought that was better?" Rye asked in disbelief.

"I wasn't an elder at the time," Waldron said with a shrug, "but so it was decided." He labored up a steep stretch of path.

"Everyone felt it was best that the child never know his real origins," Waldron continued. "So a kind family—the Varlets—agreed to take the boy in. They named him Slynn, after an honored ancestor, and raised the boy alongside their only son."

Rye took pause at the unusual, yet strangely familiar name.

"Riley," Waldron said, stopping several steps ahead of her. "Are you coming?"

Rye realized that she'd stopped walking. She hurried to catch up and Waldron went on.

"The other parents on High Isle kept their own children away from Slynn, certain that the rotten apple would someday reveal its core. As he grew older, he spent most of his time with his older brother, who was known to be the best climbing boy in all the Isles."

Rye had heard of climbing boys. They scaled the cliffs to harvest eggs from the seabirds' nests.

"One day the Varlet boys were alone collecting eggs when Slynn's brother slipped and . . . well . . . if you've ever seen an egg fall from a nest, you can imagine the result. Slynn hurried home, hysterical, crying for help along the way to anyone who would listen. But rather than comfort him, the villagers lashed out in anger. Surely, Slynn's brother didn't slip—after all, wasn't he the finest climbing boy in all the Isles? No, the young monster must have shoved him off the cliff out of jealousy." Waldron's face grew tight. "Harsh and hasty words were cast, and the truth of Slynn's parentage was revealed."

"What a terrible way to find out such a secret," Rye said. She knew what it was like to discover unexpected surprises about your parents. "And what an awful thing to accuse someone of," she added.

Waldron nodded in agreement. "The Varlets *did* believe him, and refused their neighbors' pleas that he be cast off to sea. To keep him safe, they confined him to their stables, where he tended the sheepdogs and livestock from dawn until dusk. But that didn't protect him from the taunts and jabs. From that day forward, the children of Wick called him 'Slinister.' Their parents whispered warnings about Black Annis's malevolent son hidden away on the Varlet homestead."

Rye felt the blood drain from her face. Her heart raced with the realization that Slinister was from the Isle of Pest.

"An outcast on his own island, a change came over Slynn," Waldron continued. "He began sneaking out after dark, sometimes disappearing for days. Once, when he'd been gone for over a week, the Varlets set out in search of him. They finally found him soaked and half-starved at the mouth of the Wailing Cave." Waldron's jaw tightened. "Slynn wasn't chosen by the Luck Uglies—he'd gone there on his own."

Waldron came to a stop when they'd reached the top of a ridge. He leaned on his staff.

"They brought him home, and the very next day, we discovered this."

He pointed down the slope, where the blackened skeleton of a stone house sat in overgrown grass. There was no roof, and its floors and foundation had long since been reclaimed by the isle. Rye shivered. The wind was brisk here as clouds hurried across the sky.

"The Varlets' cottage was left smoldering," Waldron said. "Burned to the ground . . . with the Varlets still inside."

Rye's was stunned. "Where was Slinister—I mean, Slynn?"

Waldron shook his head. "The boy was never seen again."

She stared at the grim remains.

"There was one more thing," Waldron said. "When

a Belonger hurried through the ashes to search for him, he found something on the wall. A symbol scrawled in ash. I remember it clearly—because I was that Belonger."

"What was it?" Rye asked breathlessly.

"A black four-leaf clover. The mark of the Luck Uglies."

The Ragged Clover, Rye thought.

The story chilled her into silence. Although she knew the Luck Uglies came from dark pasts, she'd never heard such details.

"It was only then that we recalled the curse that Annis had hurled on them the day they banished her," Waldron continued. "She'd promised that one day her son would grow up and find her. And together they would make all the Belongers pay for their wrongs."

Rye wanted to mention her encounters with Slinister. She wanted to confide in her grandfather about the troubles in Drowning and the growing rift between the Luck Uglies and Fork-Tongue Charmers. But that would mean talking about Harmless, and she pictured Waldron's clenched fist as he spoke of wringing the necks of serpents—and Luck Uglies.

"Did . . . *Slynn* ever come back to Pest?" she asked instead. In her pocket, her fingers grazed the cold stone she'd collected from the sill.

Waldron shook his head. "No, and none of his kind have ever returned since Bramble left High Isle." He placed a heavy hand on her shoulder. "You are old enough to make your own decisions about the Luck Uglies, Riley. But before you do, you need to hear the real stories. Not just the myths and legends."

Rye averted her eyes from the scorched cottage.

"And what became of Black Annis?" she asked.

"It's said she's still out there on the most remote of the Lower Isles." Waldron cast his own eyes toward the sea. "Woe betide the unlucky man who finds himself marooned on the Isle of Black Annis."

The stone was icy in her palm. She thought of Slinister and Bramble, of other boys of Pest who'd joined the ranks of the Luck Uglies. Were they once so different from Hendry and Rooster?

"Waldron," Rye asked in a near whisper, "you said Slynn Varlet wasn't chosen by the Luck Uglies. How were the sons of Pest selected?"

Waldron shook his head. "Nobody knows why some were picked over others. But late at night, when all was quiet, a black stone would be left where only the Luck Uglies' chosen boy could find it. On a doorstep, or in a shoe."

Rye stiffened. *Or perhaps outside a window?*

"That's how he knew it was time to say his

good-byes," Waldron added.

Her hand clenched around the stone. This time, her heart pounded so hard she couldn't even hear the rest of Waldron's words.

19 The Stone on the Sill

"You really think Slinister could have followed you here?" Quinn asked Rye skeptically.

He hurried along with Rye and Folly toward a low-lying meadow not far from Wick Harbor.

"I don't know, Quinn. Did you and Folly put this on the sill?"

Rye held up the black stone for him to see again. She had already explained how she'd found identical stones on Silvermas and again in the Shambles, and told them everything Waldron had said about the Wailing Cave and Black Annis.

"Of course not," Quinn replied.

"Does it seem like the type of trick my mother would play?"

Quinn pursed his lips. "She did throw my shoes in the bog after I tracked in the cowplop, but I don't think she was trying to be funny."

"And yet it seems like *someone* on Pest wants me to go to the Wailing Cave."

"Slinister could have come back here any time. Why follow *you*?" Quinn asked.

"He thinks Harmless took something from him . . . and that I know where it is."

"Well . . . ," Quinn said. He and Folly flashed Rye dubious glances. They had both grown fond of Harmless, but they'd heard enough about him to know that Slinister's accusation wasn't out of the question.

"No," Rye said, guessing their thoughts. "If he stole something, I know nothing about it."

The meadow came into view around a bend.

"I still think the wind could have blown that stone onto the sill," Folly suggested.

"It's just like the ones I found in Drowning," Rye countered. "Did the wind blow them across the ocean?"

"Stones are stones," Quinn said, still unconvinced. "If you've seen one, you've seen them all."

He had a point. Rye had skipped her share of rocks across puddles, even off the helmets of some particularly rude soldiers one or twice. She hardly ever took much notice of them, but that was exactly what made these stones so unusual.

"If you're so concerned," Quinn said, "shouldn't we tell your mother?"

Rye had already thought about that. "Not just yet," she replied. "She needs to spend her time with Waldron now. You might be right, this could all be nonsense. But you know her—if she catches even a whiff of trouble we'll spend the rest of our time here locked up at the farm."

They had already spent most of the day helping Abby and Knockmany patch the farmhouse's tattered roof and chase mice from its walls. It was late afternoon and only now were they able to go find their new friends in Wick.

Rye repocketed the stone. "There's only one way to find out for sure."

"Uh-oh," Quinn said. "And what is that?"

"We go find out what—or who—is in the cave."

"We don't even know how to get there," he pointed out.

"No, but I bet some Belongers do . . ."

They arrived at the edge of the grassy field, where they were greeted by a raucous chorus of squawks and grunts. Rye blinked her eyes in disbelief. The grassland

was filled with hundreds of the strangest birds she had ever seen. The black-and-white feathered creatures were smaller than chickens, and waddled about calling madly with their oversize orange-and-blue beaks. A large group of talkative Belonger children marched away from the flock, making their way back to Wick. Rye spotted Hendry, Rooster, and Padge among them.

"I almost had it," Rooster was saying, with a shake of his head.

Hendry consoled him. "There's always next year."

"More practice," Rooster sighed.

"Rye!" Hendry called, catching sight of them. "You missed the Puffin Hunt!"

A bird scurried between Rye's legs and looked up at her expectantly.

"They're so cute," Folly said, reaching down to pet it before it bobbled away on its bright, webbed feet.

Rye looked at the innocent-looking creatures, none of whom appeared the slightest bit fearsome. "You hunt these little things?" Rye asked. "I don't think I'd want any part of that."

"Not exactly," Hendry said.

Rye noticed a fishing line strung with the well-picked bones of several large fish. Inexplicably, it was tucked down the back of Rooster's trousers.

"Every spring, while the adults are at the Pull, we

have a Puffin Hunt," Hendry explained. "Contestants stuff fish in their britches . . . then run. The last one to keep his fish wins." Hendry gave Rooster a slap on the back. "Don't worry about it, Rooster. That little Fisher girl came out of nowhere. Who'd have guessed she was so fast?"

"*I* did, you just didn't listen to me," Padge said.

Rye and her friends joined the Belonger children on their way back to Wick. Her hand dipped into her pocket again, fumbling with the stone.

"Hendry," Rye called ahead. "Do you think you could show us around the island?"

"Sure," he replied over his shoulder. "It's getting late, but tomorrow we could hike up to the north shore—it's got a great view of the Lower Isles. Or maybe the cliffs where the seabirds nest . . ."

"I could show you how we clean the gears of the waterwheel," Rooster chimed in enthusiastically.

"Nobody's interested in that, Rooster," Hendry said.

"That would be great," Rye said, "but I thought, first, maybe we could go see . . . the Wailing Cave?"

Hendry and Rooster both stopped abruptly.

"I don't know about that," Hendry said. Rye thought she heard a touch of nerves in his normally confident voice.

"It could be fun," she added, trying to sound convincing.

Quinn and Folly glanced at Rye, then each other. They knew she was interested in more than just sightseeing.

Hendry furrowed his brow. "It's a bit far. And with the Pull, I've got a busy day ahead of me tomorrow," he said unconvincingly.

Rye frowned. "I understand. Maybe we'll try to find it ourselves."

"No, don't go alone," Hendry said quickly. "I mean, it's too easy to get lost." He seemed to weigh a decision, then sighed. "We'll take you. Come find us in the morning. But please don't be too late. We'll want to be back well before dark."

Rooster gave him a wary look, and the two boys resumed walking. They all followed.

Rye smiled to herself. After a few paces, she was stopped by a tug on her sleeve.

"What are you looking for in the Wailing Cave?" Padge whispered.

Rye hesitated. "I'm not sure," she answered honestly.

"Come on, Rye," Padge said. "You can tell me. After all, my grandmother was your mother's mother's cousin."

Rye just shook her head, stumped again by the muddled reference. "I really don't know. It's just—"

"I had a dream," Padge interrupted excitedly. Rye paused to indulge her. Having a discussion with the little girl was like trying to paint a live dragonfly.

"About you," Padge added.

Rye raised an eyebrow. "Really?"

She nodded. "You were alone. On a rock in the middle of the sea. The tide was rising . . ."

That doesn't sound promising, Rye thought. "What happened?"

Padge pinched her lips and studied Rye closely with her round eyes.

"I like you, Rye, even if you're not the sharpest hook in the tackle box," she said finally. "So try to stay away from rocks in the middle of the sea."

The little girl gave Rye a smile before heading after the others, her long hair flowing behind her bare feet like a cape.

Rye looked out at the endless waves stretching off into the distance. It seemed that just one arbitrary roar of the ocean could make them all disappear in an instant. Padge might as well have told her to eat with her mouth shut, or paint with her toes.

Rye collapsed on her straw pallet after their busy day. Tomorrow's trek would be a long one. Quinn moved to the window.

"Just in case," he said, latching it firmly shut. "So we don't end up with another stone."

"Not a bad idea," Rye agreed.

Folly hurried into their shared room.

"Take off your boots," she said eagerly.

"What?" Rye asked.

"Your boots," Folly repeated. "Take them off. I have something for your feet."

Rye pulled off a boot and shook out the straw. The leather soles had grown even more ragged. Folly held out a bowl filled with a grayish-white paste.

"What is that?" Rye said.

Folly's blue eyes shone. "Fungus for your fungus."

Rye crinkled her nose as Folly slathered it between her toes. "It stinks."

"No worse than your skunk foot," Folly said, working some into Rye's heels. "I made it from the mushrooms we found in the fields. They're popping up everywhere—the island's littered with them. Of course, I didn't have all of my potion-making supplies. I wish I had my Alchemist's Bone . . ."

Folly paused to examine her work.

"There," she said. "How do they feel?"

"Like I stepped in sap."

"Do they still itch?" Folly asked.

Rye paused. "No . . ." She grimaced. "Now they burn. Ow! Folly, get it off!"

"That means it's working."

"No it doesn't . . . Quinn, get some water, quick!"

Rye waved her feet in the air trying to cool them.

Quinn hurried off and returned with a ceramic jug.

"Rye, you're being a bit dramatic," Folly said.

Quinn splashed the water on her feet.

"Did that help?" he asked.

"Not really."

"Give it a chance," Folly said, frowning. "Sleep on it. Maybe they'll feel better in the morning."

They all settled into their bedding, Rye leaving her feet dangling out of the blankets to cool them in the air. Quinn extinguished the lantern.

"Rye," he called from the dark. "You're glowing!"

"What?"

She opened her eyes and her hands immediately went to her choker. But it wasn't her runestones. A greenish glow came from her feet, lighting the room.

"Folly," she fumed. "What did you do to me?"

Quinn laughed.

"It must be the mushrooms," Folly said, laughing too. "I'll have to remember that for my potions."

"Not funny."

Folly and Quinn stifled their giggles. Rye turned over and shut her eyes, trying to fall asleep.

"Rye," Quinn whispered.

"Yes?"

"I can't sleep with the lights on. Can you please put out your feet?"

Folly and Quinn both giggled. Rye grumbled and put her pillow over her head. But she found herself smiling too, and, for the moment, pushed her concerns about the black stone out of her mind.

20
The Wailing Cave

"*Come all would-be heroes and join me in song,*" Hendry bellowed.

"And curse the dread outlaws plagued this Isle for so long," Rooster sang even louder.

"So take heed me warning, of no favors ask, beware the dread outlaws in shadows and masks!" they called out together.

The boys continued singing off-key, trying to outdo each other in volume if not tone. They led Rye, Folly, and Quinn along the winding foot trail to the northeast of Waldron's farm.

"What are they singing?" Rye asked Padge, who, as usual, trailed close enough to scrape the heels of Rye's boots.

"It's an old tavern song," she said, twirling a wildflower between her fingers. "About the Luck Uglies."

"Your sons and your daughters, in bed safely tuck, hold tight what you cherish for that they shall pluck! In shadows and masks, in shadows and masks . . ."

"They're just trying to hide that they're nervous," Padge explained. "Old superstitions," she whispered.

Hendry and Rooster certainly seemed more enthusiastic than when Rye, Folly, and Quinn had met them that morning. Despite his normal good-natured swagger, Hendry had tried once again to talk them out of going to the Wailing Cave. He'd kept his word when they didn't waiver, but warned that he wouldn't take them any farther than the top of the nearest cliff.

"So take heed my warning, of no favors ask, and curse the Luck Uglies in shadows and masks!"

Another boy's voice hummed along quietly.

"Quinn," Rye said harshly, and elbowed him in the ribs.

"Sorry," he said sheepishly. "It's a catchy tune."

Their walk took them to the top of a ridge with sweeping views of High Isle and the numerous Lower Isles stretched out across the sea. Rye noticed that the merchant fleet had grown on the horizon. A third ship had joined the two she'd seen before, bobbing like enormous black gulls.

"I think you can see all the way to Wick," Quinn said.

"And Jack-in-Irons' rocks," Folly added, pointing to the tall rock formations they'd spotted on their first day.

"Those are called the Piles," Hendry clarified. "Been there as long as anyone can remember."

"It's funny they say they were built by a giant," Rye said offhandedly.

"Well, they were," Hendry replied with a chuckle. "What else would you expect them to say?"

Rye raised an eyebrow. "Have you ever seen a giant?"

"No, of course not. They're extinct."

"How do you know it was built by a giant, then?" Rye asked.

"That's what my parents told me."

"Have they ever seen a giant?"

"No."

"So how do they know?

"Who else could have built them?" Hendry asked.

Rye gave the question some serious thought. "Well, I don't know."

"So there you have it," Hendry said, tapping his forefinger to his head with a satisfied smile.

But Hendry's grin soon fell away as they reached the

edge of a bluff overlooking the ocean. Strings of sun-bleached shells hung from two wooden posts erected on either side of a steep, rocky trail that wound down the cliff. The trail ended at the mouth of the Wailing Cave far below.

"Are you sure about this?" Hendry asked her for the third time since they'd started their walk. "That cave is like a bottomless well there's no climbing out of."

Rye adjusted the coil of rope on her shoulder. "We're just going to take a little peek. We won't go in if it looks dangerous."

"I can go down with them," Rooster volunteered. He seemed nervous but excited by the prospect.

"You're staying here," Hendry said. "You too, Padge. I'm not going to be the one to tell your parents we lost you in that pit." He turned to Rye, Folly, and Quinn. "We'll wait up here for you. If you're not back by mid-day, we're going for help."

Hendry and Rooster each reached out and gave the strands of shells a good shaking. The shells tinkled like delicate glass.

"What's that for?" Folly asked.

"We're asking the Shellycoats to be kind to you on your journey," Hendry explained.

Padge rolled her eyes at Rye and shook her head in exasperation.

The three friends moved carefully but quickly down the cliff's narrow path. The tides seemed angry as they stared into the mouth of the enormous cavern. They stood in a small tract of crushed shells above the reach of the tide, but the spray of crashing waves on the nearby rocks still managed to splatter their faces. The Wailing Cave groaned and called to them from deep inside its gullet.

Rye looked up to where Hendry watched them from the cliff high above and signaled that they'd reached the bottom of the trail.

Rye, Folly, and Quinn had agreed that they would only take a look from the entrance—just a peek to see if they could find a clue as to who, if anyone, had been leaving stones for Rye. They wouldn't go inside unless it seemed absolutely safe. That's why they'd brought the long lengths of ship rope—in the unlikely chance the cave looked benign.

"So you really think *this* looks safe?" Quinn was saying, as he tied one end around his wrist.

"It can't be any worse than the Spoke," Rye said.

"Folly and I have never been in the Spoke," Quinn pointed out.

"Right. Well, it's cozy actually. Much like a rabbit's warren," she fibbed. "Now, we each have a lantern, and we're tied together so no one gets lost."

Rye tied an end of the rope around her own wrist and threw the rest of the coil over her shoulder. She had gotten the idea from the Pull. Each of them had their own length of rope so that they could move in different directions, but they'd always remain joined at the center so they couldn't be separated.

"Great," Quinn said. "And what if someone falls into a bottomless pit?"

Both Quinn and Folly were looking at Rye. She scowled at them.

"Then you pull her up," she said.

They entered the mouth of the cavern once their ropes were safely knotted. Inside, the cave's height expanded ever higher upward, the basalt pillars stacked atop each other and forming an intricate maze of patterns. Rye had never been inside a beehive, but she imagined this is what one's honeycomb passageways might look like. The waves rolled in from the sea, creating a frothy cauldron before flowing down a narrowing channel and disappearing deeper into the belly of the cave.

They stood in awed silence. Rye stared up at the twisted ceiling high above them until her neck ached. The cave was both beautiful and haunting. She could feel the echoes of its sad melody deep in her bones.

"Come on," Rye whispered finally, and they made

their way along the cave wall over a path of stubby but dry pillars.

As they wound their way deeper, the ceiling sloped lower and the waters calmed. The current now branched into several azure-colored channels, each flowing into a narrower tunnel.

"Which should we try first?" Folly asked.

"How about you take the one with the sharks, Rye can take the one with the sea hag, and I'll stay right here," Quinn said.

"Quinn's right," Rye said. "It would be best if we all take a different tunnel. Just for a short distance, to see what we find and then report back. That way, if anyone runs into trouble, the others will be able to help."

"That's not *exactly* what I had in mind," Quinn muttered.

"All right," Folly said, "this will be our signal if there's trouble, if anyone falls down, or gets their foot stuck in a crack, or . . . whatever. Three quick but firm tugs." She demonstrated. "Does everyone understand the signal?"

Folly and Quinn were staring at Rye again. She rolled her eyes.

"Yes, three pulls. I understand."

"Good," Folly said. "So which do we start with?"

"I'll go down that one," Rye said, pointing to a tunnel where the water reflected off the cave walls.

She didn't know why, but that one seemed to draw her in with an unspoken pull.

Rye was careful to keep her rope taut as she worked her way through the snaking tunnel, a task easier said than done. The coil twisted around her and chafed her side. She tried to readjust it but almost set it ablaze with her lantern. As she followed the flowing channel, she was mindful that the echo of the waves grew fainter the deeper she traveled. She could now hear each splash of her boots in the briny puddles. Ahead, she spotted the tunnel's end. It shimmered from another light source. There was something down there.

Rye took a deep breath, hurried forward, and snagged the rope under her heels. It sent her sprawling on the rocks.

"Pigshanks," she cursed under her breath.

She limped to her feet and pulled the coil of rope off her shoulder, dropping it into a pile in frustration. Rye set her lantern down and rubbed her scraped shins through the new holes in her leggings.

Something on the ground caught her eye—a damp rock at her foot. She reached down and picked it up, feeling its glasslike texture between her fingers. In the light of her lantern it was as dark as midnight under a Black Moon.

She stooped and pressed her lantern closer to the ground. She dug into her pocket and retrieved the stone from the sill. There were other similar ones, a scattering at first, but increasing in number as she followed them closer to the light source at the far end of the tunnel. Rye was so intent on examining the stones she didn't notice the first tug on her wrist.

Creeping along, she picked up more of the strange stones as she went. They were all smooth and dense, just like the ones that had been left for her in her shoe, her coat, and on the windowsill.

Finally, she found herself at the mouth of a hollowed-out grotto. Sunlight beamed down from the crevice in the ceiling high above. The light reflected off a mirror-like pool of turquoise water and cast the whole space in an otherworldly glow. No person was there to meet her, but the grotto's walls were covered in rambling, black markings of those who'd been there before.

Two more tugs caught Rye's attention, but she ignored them. She looked more closely. The marks were simple drawings and hand-scratched words—some more legible than others.

A LIFE OF MISCHIEF, AND A SHORT ONE, THAT WILL BE MY MOTTO.

And, in a different hand:

FOND TIDINGS UNTIL WE MEET AGAIN, ON THAT MOST DISTANT SHORE.

They were messages. Perhaps the last messages of the sons of Pest who'd come here?

Another three tugs pulled at her wrist. Urgent, desperate.

You taught me manners, proper and prim, but now I wish I'd learned to swim.

She squinted at one more, and could feel the writer's fear in his desperate scrawl.

HELP, MUM! PLEASE! THERE'S BEEN A TERRIBLE MISTAKE!

Rye's arm jolted with such force that it nearly dragged her to the ground. She looked down. The rope was now taut, pulling her like a fish being reeled in on a line.

Realizing that Folly or Quinn must be in trouble, she ran back through the tunnel as fast as she could. She found her friends at the main chamber of Wailing Cave, both of them flush with excitement.

"Why didn't you come?" Quinn said. "We thought something had happened to you."

"I found more stones," Rye started to explain.

Quinn glanced around at the rock walls and looked at her like she was wearing pants on her head. "I can't say I'm entirely surprised by your discovery . . ."

"They led to a grotto—"

"I heard something," Folly interrupted.

"She really did," Quinn confirmed. "I checked. There's something at the end of that tunnel." He pointed to one Folly had explored.

"What is it?" Rye asked.

"Don't know, but it's making quite a racket," Folly said.

"Could be a person," Quinn added.

"Or maybe it's a Shellycoat," Folly suggested.

Together, they cautiously worked their way down the tunnel Folly had taken earlier. As they approached a curve in the wall, Rye heard the noise Folly and Quinn had mentioned. A groaning—but not the echo of the waves. It wasn't a happy sound. Rye sniffed the air. Smoke.

Then came another noise from the other side of bend.

A sneeze.

Rye raised an eyebrow at Folly and Quinn. Carefully,

they peeked their heads around the corner.

They found no sea monster, Shellycoat, or hag.

Instead, huddled over a sorry excuse for a fire on the cave floor, was a bedraggled, one-eyed smuggler, rubbing his aching knee.

"Dent!" Rye yelled, and rushed out to meet him.

The startled Captain caught his breath in fright before brightening in relief.

"Children! What luck you've found me. It seems fate still smiles brightly on the old Captain."

"What are you doing here, you cockle-knocker?" Rye said, her ears burning.

"Such language from a young girl," Dent said. "You'll make an old sailor blush."

"The way you set us adrift, you'll be lucky if the only thing we do is make you blush. Wait until my mother gets hold of you."

"Now, now, let's not be rash. I've already got myself in quite a twist—literally, you see." He grimaced and touched a knee that appeared to be swollen to twice its normal size.

"Where's the *Slumgullion*?" Rye demanded.

"At the bottom of the sea, sorry to say."

Folly's eyes were wide. "What about your crew?"

He looked up from his twisted joint. "Scattered like the wind. Some have surely washed ashore in the Lower

Isles. Others are likely paddling for the Shale. The lesser swimmers, well, they may be dancing with the crabs."

"Was it a storm?" Quinn asked.

"Of course not," Dent said, taking great offense. "It takes more than a spring blow to set me off course." His one eye looked up at them without its usual mischievous glint. "We were attacked," he said sharply. "By a full-blown warship. Three decks. Two hundred men."

"A warship?" Rye said. "Whose?"

Dent clucked his tongue. "Longchance's, of course. A small sloop had been following us since the day after we left Drowning. Surely you saw it in our wake at one point or another?"

Rye, Folly, and Quinn looked at one another blankly.

"Well, imagine that. There are still a few things a ship's captain knows that three rapscallions don't," he said, although his tone was not unkind. "I assumed the sloop was tasked with tracking our whereabouts . . . and reporting back to our friends who gave us such a warm send-off in Drowning."

"That's why you set us adrift in the fog?" Rye thought out loud.

"Aye, lass," the Captain said, narrowing his eye. "It was my only chance of getting you to Pest safely. I hoped we would sail off and lead the sloop away none the wiser. I couldn't take the chance of mooring in the cave—they'd discover our port."

"This cave is a port?" Quinn asked, looking around with new eyes.

"Aside from Wick Harbor, it's the only navigable port for heavy ships on High Isle. Few know its secrets. I wasn't keen on sharing them with Longchance or his Constable."

Dent crossed his arms and furrowed his brow.

"But what I didn't expect were the warships trailing in the sloop's wake. It took but one to sink us. The three out at sea now could sack the entire island."

Rye's skin went cold. The ships on the horizon were no merchant caravan.

"We need to warn the Belongers," she said to Folly and Quinn. She turned and rushed for the mouth of the cave, her friends hurrying after her before she dragged them off by the ropes on their wrists.

"A grand idea!" Dent called after them. "But could you help an old salt to his feet first? Hello?"

21
Ties That Bind

Abby met the children at the door with a broom in her hands. Her welcoming look turned sour when she recognized the man propped up between them. She flipped the broom upside down, gripping it like a club as she marched toward them.

"Mama, no!" Rye said, stepping in front of Dent to protect him from what was sure to be a wicked braining. "Wait until you hear what he has to say."

The Captain nodded enthusiastically and flashed a crooked smile.

"Then, if he still deserves it," Rye added, "give him a good knock upside the head."

The Captain frowned.

Abby set her distrust aside long enough to hear him out, but not so much that she was willing to let him inside. She dragged two chairs outside the farmhouse door and propped his knee up with a compress of warm herbs. That was a good sign, Rye thought, although given the look on Abby's face, a braining still wasn't entirely out of the question.

Waldron leaned on his staff and listened from the doorway of the cottage. Rye noticed Hendry, Rooster, and Padge hovering anxiously a healthy distance away. They craned their necks trying to get a better look at him. Waldron furrowed his bushy eyebrows, and Rye suspected that he hoped his ugly glance would convince them to leave. He had no such luck.

Abby approached Waldron after she finished speaking with Dent.

"We need to go to Wick," she said.

Waldron pinched his beard and shook his head. "They won't listen."

"Of course they will."

"I know them," he grumbled.

Abby stared at him hard, waiting. Rye was surprised to see that, for once, Abby's glare wasn't enough.

Waldron just shook his head again.

"I'll go myself, then," she said flatly.

"Save your breath, Abigail," Waldron huffed. "You'll only be disappointed."

She narrowed her eyes at him. "No more disappointed than I am right now." She turned to Rye. "Riley, introduce me to your new friends."

Rye introduced each of them.

"Tarvish—your aunts and I were childhood friends," Abby said cheerfully to Hendry. "We used to chase otters together in the river. And Rooster—I knew your father. He used to steal my pies from the windowsill," she said good-naturedly. "I'd recognize that Dunner haircut anywhere." Rooster blushed.

She smiled at the long-haired little girl. "Padge, are you—"

"Your grandmother was my grandmother's aunt," Padge chimed in.

"Of course," Abby said, taking Padge's hands warmly. "We're cousins. Distant—but cousins nonetheless."

Rye shook her head. She wouldn't want to climb her family tree; she might never find her way back down.

"Come, children," Abby said to Hendry, Rooster, and Padge, "let's hurry to Wick to speak with your parents and the others. I'm afraid there's no time to waste. Folly, Quinn, Rye—you too. We'll need as many voices as we can spare to spread the word."

Rye paused as Abby and the others headed down the path. She glanced back at Waldron in the doorway.

"Will you come?" she asked.

Waldron shook his head slowly and cast his gaze to the sea. "The Belongers hear nothing but their own bickering. They won't listen to Abigail. They won't listen to me."

"We have to try," she implored, but Waldron's bristled jaw remained set. He didn't move.

Rye bit her lip, turned, and ran after her mother.

Abby hurried through Wick, speaking urgently with every Belonger who remembered her. Before long, the word had spread quickly among the villagers themselves, and Rye saw animated conversations spring up in clusters up and down the winding streets. Soon the village was consumed by the angry shouts of the Belongers, and Rye eagerly waited for them to call in the teams from the seawalls and take up their arms. And yet, unbelievably, the men and women didn't lay down their ropes. Rye was dumbfounded when she realized what was happening.

The Belongers yelled not in response to Longchance's ships, but to each other.

"We'll take the children to Westwatch," a gray-bearded Fisher barked. "It's long since abandoned, but there are still walls and gates."

"We're outmanned. We should all go with them!" called a Fiddler with a white plume of hair cut identically to Rooster's.

"Who are you to say?" a different fisherman yelled back.

"That's right, Fiddler," a thick-armed Crofter chimed in. "You haven't won a Pull in ten years."

"The Fishers are still in charge until the Pull is complete," the fisherman said, crossing his arms with finality.

"Hold on now, that's not so," the Crofter said, waving both hands in protest. "Once the Pull begins, no one is in charge until we have a winner."

"Ha! Then we have as much say as any of you," the Fiddler yelled.

After much loud debate, nobody could recall whether there was any such rule, so they all turned back to the ongoing battle on the seawalls with even greater intensity than before. Cupping their hands to their mouths, the Crofters and Fishers urgently cheered for their teams to hurry up and finish off the other side.

Fingers were pointed and bodies were shoved. A few levelheaded Belongers tried to maintain the peace, but as tempers flared the crowd seemed less inclined than ever to pay attention to pleas for common sense. Abby's voice was now drowned out entirely.

The Pull itself continued, the Crofters and Fishers heaving at the rope with what little energy they had left.

Rye's ears burned in anger. How stubborn could they be?

Then it occurred to Rye. Maybe the best solution was the simplest one. And maybe it could be found right under her nose.

Or in this case, in her boot.

Rye ran to the water's edge and plunged in. The swim into the harbor was a short one, but the cold water and her nervous energy left her spent by the time she pulled herself onto the manmade rock island at the center of the seawalls. With her awkward swimming style, any onlooker could have mistaken her for a dog paddling out to chase a gull.

The thick rope slunk back and forth in the squeaking pulleys just above her head. The Driftwood Crown tottered over the intricate system of wheels and gears. Rye swallowed hard and resolved herself to her task.

She reached down and drew Fair Warning from her sopping boot.

The rope proved to be tougher than Rye had expected. She had to saw at it, strand by strand, pushing Fair Warning through each fiber with all of her strength. If anyone spotted her or called out she was too preoccupied to notice, until, finally, the remains of the rope snapped with a loud twang. She barely threw herself down in time to avoid the flail of one end as it whipsawed past her face.

The pulley system jammed and groaned before collapsing into a bent iron knot. Something clunked her hard on the skull and settled askew atop her head. On the seawalls, the teams of pullers lurched and tumbled backward, falling onto their backsides or into the harbor itself.

Rye cringed. She hadn't thought about that part.

But what struck her most was the absolute quiet. All she could hear was the lap of waves against the walls. The boisterous Belongers had plunged into silence as they stared, dumbfounded, trying to determine what exactly had happened. Had the Fishers won again? No, both teams were dazed and climbing to their feet. Had the rope broken?

Then someone called out. Fingers pointed, this time at Rye—alone on her tiny island at the center of the harbor.

Suddenly it was quiet no longer. Hordes of villagers rushed down each of the seawalls, the colored tartan of the competing factions blending together as they charged toward their common enemy. They pressed close to one another on the rocks, their ruddy, bearded faces glaring down at her in rage.

Rye looked at Fair Warning in her hand. The

Belongers had seen it too. Their eyes drilled into her, demanding an explanation. With her other hand, she carefully patted her skull. She felt a wooden circlet between her fingers, sitting low on her brow and too big for her head.

Pigshanks, she thought.

"I'm sorry," Rye called, as she carefully removed the Driftwood Crown and set it on the rock beside her. Up close, she could see that its three jagged spikes were carved into the shapes of a fish, a ram, and clockwork gears. "But you must listen. The Isle is in danger. Look! The ships are coming, and they won't wait for you to decide who's in charge."

But the Belongers did not turn their attention away from her.

"It's a child!" someone called.

"Whose is it?" another onlooker demanded.

"None of ours!"

"An Uninvited!" a different Belonger spat, as if the words themselves were distasteful.

"STOP!" commanded a voice so deep and powerful that it seemed to echo from the hills. The crowd hushed into quiet whispers.

"The girl is no Uninvited!" the voice called as it moved through the crowd. "She's as much a Belonger as any of you."

Rye's heart jumped as the man pushed his way to

the edge of a seawall. It was Waldron. When he used his staff to push himself up to his full height, he stood taller than nearly all of the other men. A stunned buzz seemed to fall over the Belongers. The faces Rye could see looked to one another in disbelief.

"And she has more sense than all of you combined," Waldron continued, voice booming. The crowd rustled. "Does your stubbornness clog your ears? Look to the sea! The true Uninvited have come for Pest once again."

Waldron thrust his staff toward the water. Following its path, Rye saw the enormous warships. Closer now, they towered like castles rising from the water.

"There will be time for petty squabbles tomorrow! For now we must stand together. The men on those ships outnumber us three to one! But they have yet to taste the wrath of Pest. Secure your children, take up your arms, and defend this High Isle, as we have always done before!"

If the Belongers were inclined to protest, the return of Waldron Cutty seemed to shock them into action.

"You, Master Dunner," Waldron called, pointing his staff to the Fiddler with the white plume of hair. "Dust off your toys of mayhem and get them into place." He turned to a group of fisherman. "Fishers, barricade the harbor. And Crofters, use those farm muscles to retrieve the weapons. Tell me you haven't forgotten where you put them!"

The Belongers tore from the seawalls and made for Wick. From the wall above her, Waldron caught Rye's eye and gave her a nod.

Rye smiled back, and for the first time recognized the man her mother had described. She knew that somewhere in the crowd, Abby would be smiling too.

22 The Shoemaker

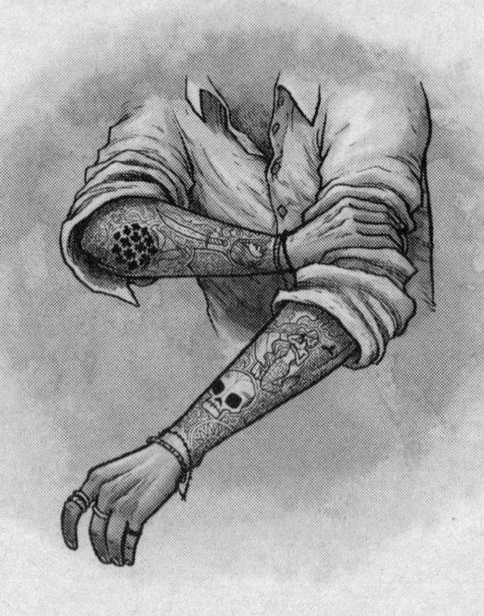

From atop the westernmost seawall, Rye watched as Wick became a hive of frenzied activity. Fishers repositioned the fleet so that their boats formed a barricade across the mouth of the inner harbor. All around the village, Belongers retrieved hidden arsenals from storehouses and long-forgotten armories. Their weapons were heavy and imposing: great two-handed broad swords, poleaxes, and maces. Rye doubted she could even lift one of them.

Rooster joined Rye at the edge of the wall. His

father, with the help of several other Fiddlers, rolled a heavy cask into the basket of a massive, wheeled catapult situated next to them. Rooster's father blew dust off the imposing war machine, polishing it proudly with the sleeve of his shirt. Obviously it had not seen any use in quite some time.

"Pride o' the Isle," Rooster's father said to Rye, with a nod at the cask. "Strongest mash this side o' the sea or any other."

"Whiskey," Rooster translated for her. "We'll hurl them right onto the ships." The Fiddlers rolled several more casks into a neat line, ready for quick reloading.

"Are you hoping the soldiers will drink it all and fall asleep?" Rye asked dubiously.

"No," Rooster replied, shaking his auburn plume. "The casks are as heavy as boulders . . . but their contents light like tinder."

A Belonger arrived with a horsecart laden with beach sand.

"And that?" Rye asked.

"Have you ever had sand in your boots?" Rooster asked.

"My boots, my leggings, my hair. I haven't been able to get it out since I arrived."

"Exactly. The barrels are for the ship, but the sand's for the soldiers." He raised a mischievous eyebrow.

"Imagine what it's like stuck in armor—and heated as hot as boiling tar."

"Stand back," Rooster's father called as he adjusted counterweights and gears. The catapult's enormous arm flung up and forward, hurling the cask through the air. Rye marveled as it sailed past the length of their seawall, over the crescent harbor, and kept on going.

"Uh-oh," Rooster said.

The cask cleared the far side of the harbor and crashed through the grass-crowned roof of a Wick home. The Fiddlers on the opposite seawall ducked and shook their fists, then returned to preparing a similar catapult.

"Looks like we may need to make a few adjustments," Rooster added with a shrug.

Rye, her family, and friends returned to the farmhouse in the early evening. Captain Dent, who had been tasked with watching Lottie and subjected to her endless dress-up games, seemed hugely relieved to see them as he quickly removed a ladies' straw hat. Dark clouds now brewed offshore and Dent said rough seas would likely keep the ships away from the dangerous coast for at least another night. While Abby and Knockmany continued preparations, an exhausted Folly and Quinn collapsed into their beds before twilight.

Rye remained anxious, wondering whether Constable Valant would risk braving the turbulent waters before morning. She wandered outside, staring at the warships from atop the fishing boat.

She tightened her fists around her cudgel.

Why did Longchance ruin everything? Why must he chase her family across the sea?

Rye swung her cudgel hard against the hull.

He'd run them out of their home.

She slammed it hard again.

He'd sent the Constable to the Dead Fish Inn. Even the Shambles weren't safe anymore.

Rye lifted the cudgel over her head and brought it down a third time.

Now his soldiers were on their way here. To her mother's island. To go to war with these people who wanted nothing more than to be left alone.

"If you put any more dents in that boat she'll never fish again," a gruff voice called.

Rye froze and turned on her heel. It was Waldron. He leaned on his staff with a bemused look on his face.

"I'm sorry," she said. "I didn't mean to cause any damage."

Waldron waved her off. "I've been telling Knockmany to get rid of that wreck for years."

Rye was relieved to see him smile.

"However, what I will not tolerate is a Cutty who swings her cudgel poorly." He set his staff on the ground and walked toward her. "Here, let me show you."

With thick but gentle hands, Waldron took the cudgel and demonstrated how to grip it.

"You swing not with your wrist or arm, but your whole body. Like this."

Waldron swung in a quick fluid motion. With a splintering crack, the cudgel didn't just strike the hull of the boat, it tore through it.

"See," he said. "You can wield it this way as well."

He pulled the cudgel free and held it across his body, over the opposite shoulder. When he swung downward, the cudgel's whipping motion doubled its force and sheared away several planks.

"A blow like that will hobble a man for life," he said.

He handed it back to her. She replicated what Waldron had shown her. It didn't break the wood, but left a substantial dent.

"Good," Waldron said. "Now try this one."

They passed the cudgel back and forth, taking turns on the unlucky boat. After she mastered one motion, he showed her another. Before long they were circling each other in the grass, where he demonstrated how to use the cudgel to disarm a man, and how to take one off his feet. Waldron was a willing subject, and despite his age he remained strong and fast. When she finally knocked him to the ground they both laughed and clapped, although it took him a long time to climb back to his feet.

"I think that's enough for one day," he said, breathing hard.

"Agreed," Rye said, brushing her hair from her eyes.

They both examined the boat's hull, which was now dotted with fresh holes.

He cocked a silver eyebrow at Rye. "Do you feel better?"

"A little," she said. The exercise had provided her with an outlet for her frustration, but now, as she eyed the sea, her worries returned. "But not really."

Waldron nodded knowingly. "Such is the way of the cudgel . . . and the sword. They may help for a moment, but seldom cure our troubles in the end. It's a good lesson to learn young—most never learn it at all."

He took notice of something by Rye's ear. The dragonfly hair clip dangled from a loose strand of hair. He carefully removed it and regarded it between his thick fingers. A look of recognition passed over his face.

"I gave this to your mother when she was your age," he said quietly. "It was your grandmother's before that." He gently clipped it back in place and curled his bushy lip in a smile. "Perfect."

The thought made Rye smile too.

Waldron turned toward the farmhouse. "Come inside and have a rest. The coming days are sure to be long ones."

Rye nodded. "I'll be right there."

He waved a hand. "I'll go save that cockeyed sailor from your sister. She's hidden his boots and won't go to bed until he guesses where she put them."

Rye directed her attention to the ominous ships once more as Waldron plodded inside. She felt her ears growing hot again, but was interrupted by the sound of a voice at her feet. She leaped back.

"Are you quite finished?" it asked.

The voice came from under the boat's hull. Rye carefully peeked through a large hole. She was shocked to find a man sitting amid a pack of supplies and some loose bedding. He brushed splinters from the coarse white hair that draped his face under a well-worn leather cap.

He looked up at the new holes in his makeshift shelter. "I hope it doesn't rain tonight."

His voice, and the glint in his gray eyes, now seemed familiar.

"Harmless?" she whispered.

"It's a good thing Waldron didn't find me here. I'm afraid he would have practiced his swing on my head." Harmless flashed a grin.

Rye scrambled through the gap and joined him under the hull.

She threw her arms around him and he held her tightly. When she sat back she couldn't contain herself.

"What are you doing here?" she gasped. "And what happened to your hair?"

Harmless lifted his cap with a wink. His long white locks were actually a wig of horse tail sewn into the lining of the hat. He set it on the ground and scratched his own head of dark hair, tied back into a ponytail.

"I arrived last night. I've been masquerading as a shoemaker ever since," he explained, patting a bag of tools.

"So I guess you know that Longchance's ships have followed us here," Rye said.

Harmless nodded grimly. "Those rumors began swirling shortly after you left Drowning. I wouldn't have come otherwise. And now I've seen them offshore myself."

"Can we be certain they'll attack Pest?"

"I don't expect Longchance would commission three warships if he had anything less in mind. Their hulls sit low in the water—loaded with soldiers. His forces in Drowning are down to minimal reserves." Harmless narrowed his eyes, deep in thought. "It's an incredible risk to commit so many men in this way, and the timing is most peculiar. Constable Valant himself commands the lead ship."

"The Constable has come this far?" Rye asked in disbelief. "Are we such a prize?"

"I can't fathom the logic either, and yet, undeniably, here he is."

"They sank the *Slumgullion*," Rye said. "Captain Dent told me so himself. He's at the farmhouse."

Harmless nodded again. "Fortunately, Dent keeps a few spares. He's still got the *Slumgullion Too* . . . or *Slumgullion Thrice*," Harmless added. "I can never tell them apart."

Rye looked at him in surprise.

"Don't let Dent's guise of doddering clown fool you. It masks the shrewdest smuggler on all the seas." Harmless gave her a wink. "I would never have entrusted your safety to anyone less."

Rye's thoughts turned to her uncle and the turmoil in Village Drowning. "What about Bramble? Has he returned to High Isle as well?"

Harmless's eyes darkened. "I come alone. Bramble stayed in Drowning at my request. He's keeping watch on Slinister and the Fork-Tongue Charmers until I return." Harmless raised an eyebrow. "As I'm sure Waldron has told you, Luck Uglies are no longer welcome on Pest."

With the urgency of Dent's news, Rye had forgotten about the mysterious black stones that seemed to follow her wherever she went. If Slinister and the Fork-Tongue Charmers were still in Drowning, it seemed the stone on the sill really must be nothing more than coincidence.

"But the Luck Uglies and Fork-Tongue Charmers are concerns for the High Chieftain," Harmless said. "And right now I choose to be a shoemaker of modest ability. Let's see what I can do about those."

He rolled up his sleeves and pointed at her ragged boots.

"It's been years since your grandfather has seen me, but he was always as keen-eyed as a hawk. It's best that I stay away from *his* shoes."

"He hardly ever wears any," Rye said with a smirk.

Harmless smiled in return. "You won't say anything about my arrival until I can speak with you mother?" he said, with a knowing look.

Rye nodded.

"Good. And how is her mood?"

"Hit or miss," Rye said.

"For the sake of my jaw, let's hope she misses."

Rye giggled as he got to work.

"What's wrong with your feet, by the way?" he asked, looking up. "They smell dreadful."

"Folly smeared mushrooms on them," she said, wiggling her toes. "They glow in the dark, too."

Harmless shook his head. "I don't understand the games children play these days."

23 Kiss of the Shellycoats

After a night filled with the sounds of wind and rain, Rye and her friends woke to fair skies the next morning. It wasn't long before a winding caravan of wagons pulled by shaggy ponies arrived from the crushed-shell path. They were followed by a large group of Belongers on foot—Fishers and Dunners, mostly children joined by their elderly relatives. The Crofter children already lived in the hills and would meet the rest of the Belongers at Westwatch. Rooster had set out with Padge to join Hendry and his family at the Tarvish farm.

Knockmany wasted little time in organizing the caravan for the trip through the hills. The hike would be long and steep, and he loaded the youngest and oldest Belongers onto the wagons to make the first run to Westwatch.

Rye found her mother by the old fishing boat. She was surprised but glad to see Abby sitting with a certain white-haired shoemaker in its shadows. Rye didn't know when Harmless had gotten around to finding Abby, but it was the first time she could remember seeing them share a private moment.

Harmless eyed the crowd congregated around the farm. "I'm glad to see someone was able to bring them to their senses." He flashed Rye an impressed look.

"News of brash action travels fast in small places," Abby said, catching Rye's eye as well. She hadn't scolded Rye, or said anything much about her solution to the Pull. Rye couldn't tell if her mother was proud or exasperated.

"You're quite certain your father didn't hear me at your window last night?" Harmless asked Abby.

"He had a long day in Wick," Abby said, flicking a glance toward the farmhouse. "And he sleeps heavy."

"Just like old times," Harmless said.

Abby narrowed an eye in return, although Rye thought she saw the tightest of smirks at the corner of her lips. Maybe she wasn't entirely unhappy to see him.

"What do we do now?" Rye asked.

"You, Folly, Quinn, and the other children will get to Westwatch," Harmless said. "The Belongers will stay in Wick until Valant plays his hand. I don't think they will have long to wait."

He gestured for Rye's spyglass.

"They've been offshore for days," Harmless said, raising the spyglass to his eye. "With crews that size, supplies will run short quickly. The seas are as fair as one could hope for . . . and I believe they will come under cover of darkness. If I had to guess, it will be tonight."

Harmless lowered the spyglass and handed it back to Rye.

"Waldron's already in Wick. I'll go there myself and stay out of sight until we see what the night might bring," he said. "The Belongers are a hardy lot—I don't doubt their skills or ferociousness once the fight is brought to them. I worry about their numbers, though. Longchance's forces may be overwhelming. If Wick falls, any Belongers who remain will retreat to Westwatch."

"You can come with us," Abby said quietly.

Harmless shook his head. "I owe the Belongers this much. If not for me, neither the Constable nor Longchance's soldiers would be here at all."

Rye chewed her lip and clenched her itching toes inside her mended boots. The burden wasn't just Harmless's. They'd all come to Wick for safety, and only succeeded in putting the entire isle in jeopardy.

"The more distance between you and Wick, the safer you will be," Harmless said, rising to his feet. "All that I can buy you now is time."

They all sat in silence. Harmless placed a warm palm on Rye's head. He removed it, and for the first time she'd ever seen, brushed his fingertips across her mother's cheek.

Abby stood and put her hand on his arm as he turned to leave. "Will you not say good-bye to Lottie? Knockmany is helping her onto the wagons."

Harmless looked back. "I'm not saying good-bye. I'll see you all at Westwatch." He gave her a tight smile and his gray eyes flickered. "Even if I have to drag a dozen soldiers on my back to make it."

And with those words he was gone, disappearing quickly down the crushed-shell path. Abby's face was a mask that couldn't hide the concern in her eyes as she turned to Rye, Folly, and Quinn.

"I'm seeing Lottie and the little ones to Westwatch," she said. "I've a good mind to bring you three with the wee ones to keep you out of trouble . . . but I've thought better of it." She raised an eyebrow. "Knockmany and I will be back this afternoon for you and the older children. Be ready to leave on those wagons—there's no time to waste."

She hitched her dress up from under her heels and made for the crowd gathered by the sheep pens. Rye pushed up from the ground and hurried after her.

"Mama, we can't hide in the hills!" she called. "You can't abandon Wick. This is our fault—the Constable is here because of *us*."

Abby turned in surprise, her eyes flaring. She stepped back toward Rye. Rye swallowed hard. *Uh-oh.*

But Abby's voice was measured as she crouched in front of Rye. "Riley, my darling, I do not go to the hills to run from a fight. Just as I didn't abandon our home on Mud Puddle Lane because I feared the Earl or any soldier. Perhaps there is something you should finally know."

She placed her hands on Rye's shoulders.

"If I am hard on you, it is not because your maddening behavior reminds me of your father," she said. "It is because it reminds me of myself."

Rye just blinked. Had she misheard her mother?

"I, too, was young once. And your mischief pales compared to the follies of my youth. I didn't leave this island as some lovesick maiden. I followed your father to join him. Not only as his bride, but as a Luck Ugly."

Rye was stunned. She opened her mouth but no words came out.

"There have never been women in the Luck Uglies' ranks, but I meant to change that. It was Bramble who was promised to your father—I was not part of that bargain. And although it was I who insisted on leaving, Waldron and Bramble have never forgiven him. Why do you think your father and uncle refuse to speak except when forced? Why do you think your father cannot let Waldron lay eyes on him?"

Abby's grip softened on Rye's shoulders.

"I left this island with every intention to don the Luck Uglies mask and cowl. But motherhood changes your priorities, my love."

Abby stood up and smoothed the folds of her dress. Her eyes were intense but not angry.

"So, no, it is not my nature to run from a fight," she said. "But my fight is for you and Lottie now. Nothing else. That is where *my* battle lies."

Abby pressed her lips to the top of Rye's head.

"You are braver than most men and women three times your age," she whispered. "But sometimes a hero's work is as unexciting as hitching wagons and packing supplies. The best thing we can do now is get the children of Wick somewhere safe."

Rye rejoined her friends, squinting at the horizon where Longchance's warships rocked offshore like patient wolves.

Instead of her ears burning, now her toes did. She knew Abby spoke the truth. Surely there were many preparations to be made. But what good would a well-packed wagon do when those ships came to Wick?

Rye stuffed her fingers into her boots, trying to soothe toes that felt like they were being gnawed by rats. Angrily, she pulled them off and scratched furiously with her fingernails.

"Stop that," Folly said. "You're going to make it worse."

Folly took a small tin from her pocket and spread some of her mushroom concoction between Rye's toes. Rye cringed.

Quinn looked glumly at the hills. "Where are the Shellycoats when the island needs them?" he muttered.

Rye furrowed her brow as Folly applied what was left of the ointment. Folly must have assumed it was the sting of the balm, but it was really an idea taking hold.

"What do you suppose Shellycoats look like?" Rye asked.

Quinn raised an eyebrow. "I don't know . . . has anyone actually seen one?"

Rye dabbed her fingers into Folly's tin. She examined her finger.

"Folly, can you get more of these mushrooms?"

"Sure," Folly said. "They're all over the island."

Rye chewed her lip as she thought. "How much of

your paste will a mushroom make?"

"Plenty. A little mushroom goes a long way. Why?"

"Quinn, let's start picking," Rye said, leaping to her feet. "Folly, you get to mixing—make as much as you can. Then we need to spread it over everything. A rock here, a tree there—we'll go all along the stone walls. Not all in one place, though. We want to give the illusion of numbers."

"Numbers of what?" Quinn asked, reaching over and plucking a stray mushroom from the ground. He examined it in his fingers.

"Shellycoats," Rye said with a grin. "Who are as superstitious as Belongers?"

Quinn shrugged his shoulders. "Toddlers?"

"Sailors. Surely, they've heard the legends of Pest, although I doubt any of Longchance's men have ever set foot here. Let's make them think that they have more than just the Belongers to worry about."

Folly and Quinn looked at each other in surprise.

"It may not work . . . but at least it's something," Rye said. "You gave me the idea, Quinn. Now Folly just needs to provide the magic."

Folly hesitated. "I wish I hadn't left my Alchemist's Bone back in Drowning," she said, pursing her lips.

"You don't need it," Quinn said. "You already made the balm without it."

Folly grinned as they both jumped to their feet.

Rye straightened up at the sound of wheels in the distance. Several wagons set off up a hill.

"My mother will be back for us soon enough," she said. "But if we get the Belonger children to help, there may be time."

After several hours, with the assistance of the other children, they'd managed to fill numerous large buckets and cook pots with Folly's mushroom balm. They began to paint it onto rocks and fence posts. The concoction was gray under the light of the afternoon's waning sun. It wouldn't begin to glow until after dark.

Rye wiped her brow and took a break from their toils in the grazing fields. She climbed atop the fishing boat to check on the warships, raising the spyglass. The ships were close enough now that she could scan the decks. She could make out the grim faces of the crew, all of whom were busy preparing the ships for battle. When she turned her spyglass to the lead ship, the sight caused her to lurch back. At the ship's bow was a man in a leather war helmet topped with a crimson hat. On his belt was a coiled red whip.

Constable Valant.

His hard eyes bore down on her through her spyglass. Although it was impossible for him to see her from that distance, Rye had the unnerving feeling that the

Constable was the one doing the watching. She quickly lowered the lens.

But even more unsettling was the sight of the third ship. There, with her naked eye, she could see it moving away from the other two. Away from Wick Harbor. Rye didn't know whether it was heading for the stretch of beach beneath the cliff, or maybe the Wailing Cave. Captain Dent had said the Wailing Cave was the only other navigable port for heavy ships on Pest. Regardless of where it laid anchor, it would be somewhere the Belongers weren't expecting. And if Longchance's soldiers reached High Isle from another port, they could circle around and surround Wick, trapping the Belongers against the harbor.

Rye jumped from the hull and ran to Folly and Quinn.

"This one looks like your father," Folly was saying with a chuckle, pointing to a boulder smeared with a crooked smiley face.

Quinn frowned as he examined a fencepost painted into the shape of a stick figure. "These things aren't going to fool anyone."

"One of the ships has broken away from the others!" Rye called. "They're trying to take Wick by surprise!"

Folly and Quinn turned in alarm.

"We need to warn the Belongers," Rye said. "So they'll be ready to meet them."

"We haven't gotten very far with our Shellycoats," Folly said, dispirited.

"This isn't going to work," Quinn added. "Even when they're glowing, they'll just look like green rocks and trees."

"I'll go to Wick myself," Rye said. "You stay here and do as much as you can."

Folly looked at the sun. "It's getting late. Your mother should be here any minute. I'm surprised it's taken her so long."

"Pigshanks," Rye cursed, and bit her lip. The hills must have slowed her and Knockmany down, but they wouldn't be gone much longer. "She won't leave without me," Rye said finally. "I'll get back as soon as I can."

Quinn scanned the hills. Out of habit, he removed the Strategist's Sticks from his pocket and rolled the little stickman between his fingers. "I've got an idea in the meantime," he said, brightening. He turned to Folly. "We'll need Hendry, though."

He grabbed a bucket with each hand. "Let's go, Folly. Gather some of the others and load up a pony. There's no time to waste."

"Meet back here at the farmhouse," Folly called to Rye as she and Quinn hurried off. "If your mother's back before you, not even the Shellycoats will be able to protect you from her."

Rye glanced out over the cliff one last time before

running for Wick. The ships were moving rapidly with the wind. Pest had run out of time.

She was too hurried to notice the uneasy mist stirring on the surface of the water. The Salt had begun to rise.

Rye pushed through the crowd of Belongers, searching for Waldron, Harmless, or even Rooster's father. Unsuccessful, she ran up an embankment between two village houses, scuttling up the craggy hillside to get a better view of the sea.

Dull shadows of a gray twilight settled over Wick even though night had not yet fallen. The eastern horizon was now entirely obscured by the gloom of the Salt, the bruised sky an impenetrable curtain that draped the tops of the waves. Rye extended her spyglass. The ships were nowhere to be seen!

Rye flushed with hope. Perhaps the Salt had done its job. She lowered her spyglass and called out to the skies.

"Yes! Thank you, Shellycoats!"

She saw a twinkle of light amid the fog, then another, as if they were answering her. Then the lights began to form the outline of a shape. Two shapes.

Rye's face fell.

The warships emerged from the Salt, lanterns blazing from the decks and portholes, lights strung from the masts so as to light their way through the darkness.

Somehow they had found their way through.

The lead ship was the smaller of the two but still massive. So close now that even with her naked eye she could see the flag of the House of Longchance flying atop its tallest mast. She put the spyglass back to her eye.

Its figurehead ran the full length of the bowsprit. The dense black elm was carved into the form of an outstretched forearm and clenched fist, an eel-like hagfish coiled around its wooden wrist. Valant clutched the rails atop the highest deck, studying Wick with simmering eyes under his crimson hat.

Rye heard a familiar, booming voice. It was Waldron's, barking orders to men at the catapult on the nearest seawall. She hurried down the embankment and along the wall amid a flurry of Belongers, the burly men and women too preoccupied to take notice of her. She stopped, out of breath.

"Waldron—" Rye said, grabbing his thick hand.

"Riley!" he cried, his voice awash with anger and surprise.

"The third ship," Rye gasped. "It's not out in the harbor. It's gone north. I think they mean to land elsewhere on the isle."

Waldron's face changed and Rye knew he understood exactly what that meant. He grabbed a Fisher by the shoulder and shouted in his ear. The Fisher nodded and hurried off.

"You've done well, Riley," Waldron said, placing his enormous palms on each of her cheeks. "We'll send men to the eastern shore. But now you must be off. Get back to the farm without delay."

Rye just nodded without debate. He pulled her tight, kissed her atop her head so hard she thought she might get lost in his fiery beard, and gave her a not-so-gentle push to send her on her way.

She turned and started back across the rocks toward Wick, but that was when the first flaming missile from Longchance's ships crashed into the seawall.

Rye spun at the sound. She gasped as she saw Waldron fall to his knees, then lost sight of him behind the smoke.

24
The Uninvited

The ships' projectiles created more smoke than fire, disorienting Rye as well as the Belongers. The haze made her lungs heave and her eyes water. With the distraction, the larger warship rammed through the barricade of fishing boats, scattering the smaller vessels that now piled harmlessly against its hull like driftwood. The huge ship moved as far into the harbor as it dared, just to the opening between two seawalls. Any nearer and it would risk grounding itself.

Valant's warship, with its clenched-fist bowsprit,

trailed just behind it. As the smoke cleared, Rye saw that the harbor had filled with longboats and skiffs launched from the closest ship. Longchance's soldiers scrambled out onto docks, stretches of beach, and the seawalls themselves, pushing forward wherever armed Belongers weren't waiting to meet them.

Rye heard the clash of swords and axes. The roar of battle rang in her ears. She sprinted through the confusion along the seawall, calling for Waldron. Ahead, a team of Longchance soldiers pressed themselves against the catapult until it tumbled down the rocks and into the harbor. She thought she heard someone yell her name, but when she turned toward the voice, she was knocked off her feet. A soldier stood over her, a sharp cutlass in his hand and a crazed grimace on his face. Rye threw her hands up to protect herself.

As the soldier raised his blade, a heavy wooden staff caved in his helmet, sending him toppling into the water below.

Waldron extended a large hand. "Let's get to shore," he said. "This wall's no place for an old man and a young lady."

They huddled close together to steady themselves as they hurried over the uneven boulders. But soon their path was blocked by a thick company of men in Longchance tartan. Rye looked to Waldron for an answer but jolted in pain before he could reply.

"Ow," Rye shouted, and buried her fingertips into her hair. It felt like her scalp was being seared by tiny, ferocious mites.

Nearby, Longchance's men took up what looked like a painful, twitching dance. Rye realized that the Fiddlers on the opposite seawall had launched their burning sand from the other catapult. The soldiers had taken the brunt of it and were now desperately digging into the seams of their light armor trying to get it out.

"Fiddlers!" Waldron cried, to no one in particular. "Wait until *we're* off the walls!"

Of course, no one at the other catapult could hear him. Rye pulled the hood of her coat over her head while the Fiddlers reloaded. At least they'd cleared a path through the soldiers.

Rye and Waldron rushed down the seawall as fast as Waldron's old legs would allow him. He swatted away another soldier with his staff but tried to avoid the intensifying skirmishes. Rye suspected her grandfather wouldn't have shied from the fight if he wasn't seeing her to safety. But when they somehow found themselves on Wick's main road unscathed, Waldron had reached the limits of his energy. Rye helped him into the shadows of a dead-end alleyway between two houses. The battle had now reached the streets of Wick. Masses of

Belongers and soldiers stretched before them, just an arm's length from where they sat catching their breath. It wouldn't be safe to stay idle for long.

Rye looked out at the harbor just as the Fiddlers launched a flaming cask from the catapult on the westernmost seawall. She watched hopefully as the cask hurtled through the darkened sky toward the lead warship, but cringed as it sailed over its bow and landed with an uneventful splash in the harbor just beyond it. The cask sizzled and smoked as it bobbed on the surface. Rye clenched her fists in frustration.

"Waldron, the soldiers are gaining ground."

Waldron's face was grim. Rye saw him try to regain to his feet, but his chest was still heaving and she knew that they would never be able to navigate their way through the mobs in the street.

"Wait here," she said, and darted from the alleyway before he could protest.

Rye ran to the road, ducking between the slashing and pummeling of Belongers and soldiers. She scanned the streets and alleyways for a clear path or shortcut that might lead them to safety, but every time she saw an opening it quickly filled with soldiers and grappling bodies.

A second cask launched from the Fishers' catapult, the burning, twisted rag that served as its wick dangling behind it like a tail. This time its path remained true, and the cask crashed through one of the warship's masts. The cask and broken mast, together with its heavy sail, tumbled to the ship's deck with a great crash. But the Fishers' initial cheers stopped abruptly. The rag had fallen out during its flight and the cask did not ignite.

Longchance's men overran the seawall as the Fishers attempted to roll another cask into the enormous contraption, and the Belongers were forced to abandon the remaining catapult and flee for the shore.

Rye realized that there would be no further launches. The situation in Wick was growing bleaker. Not wanting to leave Waldron any longer, she hurried back to the alleyway.

Waldron was gone.

"Pigshanks," Rye cursed, and spun around, calling for him. Her heart sank as the masses grew thicker around her, bodies closing in on all sides.

It was then that Rye noticed a flurry of activity on the recently abandoned seawall. A cluster of Belongers streamed behind a solitary figure as he fought his way through Longchance's troops. Despite the impossible odds, soldiers seemed to fall in their path as the small group advanced down the rocks. Rye squinted. Their leader's white hair flowed behind him, two short swords flashing in his hands.

Harmless!

Her father sent two soldiers into the water. He ducked the strike of a third and flung himself at another who stepped in front of him. By the time they'd run their gauntlet, only Harmless and two Belongers remained, but at least they'd made it safely to the catapult. Rye didn't think the three men would be enough to load another cask into position, but her jaw dropped when she realized what Harmless had in mind.

Harmless sheathed his swords and climbed into the basket of the catapult. From his belt he removed a flask and examined it. He took a long swig, followed by a deep breath, and settled himself as his companions readied the trigger. He raised his hand and then dropped it by way of a signal. The catapult lurched up and forward.

Rye craned her neck and gawked as Harmless hurtled awkwardly through the air. She held her breath, fearful that she would see her father bashed on the rocks or splattered against the side of the hull. But good fortune was with him, and the mainsail swallowed him up. Like an enormous nightshirt falling from a clothesline, it billowed and tumbled to the deck, trapping several stunned sailors beneath it.

Rye dashed to the harbor's edge for a better look. The downed sail rustled and fluttered as bodies struggled to free themselves. Then she spotted Harmless—staggered but apparently unbroken—a sword in one hand, the flask still in the other. Rye clapped her hands in relief.

Harmless ran to a jib—one of the sails stretching from the bowsprit to the foremast—and paused to take a mouthful of spirits from his flask. But instead of swallowing, he sparked something in front of his mouth and spit forth a plume of fire, setting the sail ablaze.

The ship's crew rushed to the burning sail, trying to contain the blaze. Harmless weaved through their ranks, pausing at the base of the mainmast. Rye saw him take hold of a pulley, slash at a rope in the rigging, and quickly take flight again—rocketing high up the mast. He perched there for a moment, pausing to examine the scene below him.

Then, cocking his head back, he filled his cheeks with one last swig from the flask and pitched it aside. With a final roar, he bellowed a stream of fire into the sails all around him.

The intense light of the blazing sailcloth illuminated the entire harbor. Even the soldiers on dry ground seemed to freeze at the spectacle, unsure of what to do. Harmless peered through the smoke, watching the terrified crew struggle to extinguish the flames below. Unfortunately, there was now no way down through the inferno of burning canvas. His white wig smoldered and his cloak glowed red with sparks.

On his toes, he carefully maneuvered to the farthest end of the yardarm. Then he placed a hand on his singed cap, measured his jump, and plunged off, hurtling downward like a rock until he hit the harbor with a heavy splash and disappeared beneath the surface.

Rye couldn't believe her eyes. Harmless had managed to disable the enormous vessel. She hoped he hadn't drowned in the process.

Still, the conflict in Wick raged on. The Belongers were able to hold their ground while the soldiers turned to the threat on their ship, but the village teetered on the verge of being overrun. Valant's warship loomed in the harbor now, and she saw its crew ready more boats for launch. The Belongers would never be able to fend off more reinforcements. She feared the time had come for everyone to abandon Wick and make their retreat.

Clouds shifted overhead and the Salt made twilight look more like nightfall across the island. Rye had no idea how long she'd been trapped in the assault on the village. She turned toward the hills, hoping her mother and friends were well on their way to Westwatch.

Then she had to blink, for surely her eyes were playing tricks on her.

In the darkness of the hills, everywhere she looked,

eerie green lights dotted the highlands. There were so many, they all couldn't possibly be of Folly and Quinn's doing.

Suddenly an explosion boomed like a clap of thunder from a far-off peak. Rye jumped at the sound. For an instant, the Belongers and Longchance's men alike paused and peered into the distance. There was another loud boom, followed by several more all over High Isle. Their echoes rumbled throughout the valleys.

And then, as if on cue, the glowing orbs were in motion, charging down from the hilltops. It was as if the island itself had awakened. Rye watched, mouth agape. She knew of no potion that could make rocks and trees come to life.

"Shellycoats!" a Belonger howled in joy. "They've risen to protect the island!"

Longchance's soldiers all cast their eyes upward, staring in disbelief. An army of glowing shapes even larger than the Belongers' and soldiers' combined forces raced down the slopes and hillocks, on their way to Wick. It only took the first soldier to step back toward the harbor before the others joined in retreat.

Emboldened, the Belongers pushed forward, driving the soldiers to the edge of rocks and piers. The Belongers had already set fire to the soldiers' longboats, so no return to their ship was possible. Many of the soldiers splashed into the water to swim for it but, weighed down by their cumbersome helmets and gauntlets, they were swept away by the currents. Faced with the choice of drowning or being slaughtered by unseen spirits, others threw down their weapons. The survival instinct spread quickly, and soon the soldiers were casting aside their arms and throwing up their hands in surrender to the advancing Belongers.

Rye quickly extended her spyglass and directed it toward the remaining ship. Valant was at the bow over the clenched-fist bowsprit, a grim look on his face as his crew awaited their orders. He seemed to weigh the new development carefully. Finally, he turned and marched from the bow and Rye lost sight of him.

Rye looked back at the village and the seawalls, where the Belongers now stood watch with pointed weapons over the surrendered soldiers. They remained at the ready, waiting for the assault from the second warship. Valant's ship loomed on the water. The next wave of longboats might be launched at any moment. It began to move; its enormous hull was creeping broadside, repositioning itself. Rye held her breath.

Yet, instead of launching another attack, it began to ease away. Could it be? Yes, it was retreating. Rye braced herself, waiting for whatever surprise Valant might have in store for them. But the warship headed for the darkness of the sea, leaving the harbor and sailing for open water, where the only surprise waiting was an enormous jagged shoal hidden just beneath the surface. The ship lurched to a stop and its towering masts tilted at an irregular angle. It squatted lower in the waves, slowly at first, then rapidly as its hull took on water.

The Belongers thrust their cudgels and swords in the air when they realized what was happening, and Wick echoed in cheers even louder than the explosions that had set the Shellycoats in motion.

The lanterns of the Constable's ship went dark as it vanished beneath the waves, the ocean swallowing the massive vessel so completely it was as if it had never existed at all.

In the aftermath of the failed assault, Rye finally found Waldron, who was safe and speaking with some of the village elders. A Belonger rushed to meet them. He gasped and buckled over, as if he'd just run a great distance, but his face was beaming.

"The Salt has claimed the third ship on the reefs south of the Wailing Cave," he reported breathlessly. "Fishers are on hand to greet any Uninvited who try to paddle to shore."

She was even further relieved to catch a glimpse of the wet, flowing white hair of a shoemaker, who just nodded before drawing his cloak and disappearing into the shadows. Exhausted, Rye stumbled out of the village and headed for the farm. She hoped she might find Folly and Quinn at the farmhouse, where they'd arranged to meet. Her mother was likely there too, and Rye hoped Abby would understand why she'd rushed off to Wick.

The footpath was dark and it was only when she rounded a bend that it occurred to her that she had not previously ventured out into the hills after dark.

She stopped short and caught her breath. Ahead, blocking the path in front of her were a dozen glowing green beasts. They were four legged and stocky, shorter than Rye. She could see their breath in the night air.

"Shellycoats," Rye whispered to herself.

Rye might have fled back to Wick, but surely they had already seen her. If they meant her harm, running would do no good. She swallowed hard and crept forward carefully.

The closest Shellycoat turned. It licked its lips with a long tongue. Rye paused, stood up straight in alarm, and then squinted through the darkness. She began to laugh so hard she had to put her hands on her knees to keep from falling over.

A flock of disoriented sheep blinked back at her. Their wool was matted with glowing paste, and they must have wondered what could possibly have been so funny.

25

What the Wind Brings, the Tide Takes Away

The morning dawned bright. Small toes greeted Rye's face when she finally woke. They were Lottie's—her sister was wedged between Rye and Abby in the small bed, sleeping head-to-foot. Rye slipped out of her mother's arms, stepping carefully over Folly and Quinn, who dozed in blankets on the floor. They'd all taken comfort in each other's company at the end of a harrowing night.

Rye opened the farmhouse door, pushing her way through a large flock of wayward sheep who'd finally stopped glowing. She climbed atop the hull of the fishing boat and anxiously surveyed the horizon, but quickly realized that Pest's victory had not been imagined. She extended her spyglass.

The flooded wreck of the warship that had attempted to circumnavigate the harbor was now hung up on a jagged archipelago to the northeast. Seabirds circled it before darting in and out of the ship's hold to loot any remaining provisions. Turning her attention to Wick Harbor, she could see the burned and broken masts of the warship seized by the Belongers. There was no sign at all of the ship with the clenched-fist bowsprit. The Constable's vessel must have come to rest on the ocean floor, and she could see the growing evidence of its demise strewn across a sandy beach below her. The tide washed ashore a steady stream of planks, shredded sails, and other flotsam.

Rye lowered the spyglass and peeked down through a large hole in the fishing boat's hull. Harmless's blankets were empty.

"Did you like my explosions?" Folly's voice called. She rubbed her blue eyes awake as she worked her way past the sheep.

"My ears are still ringing," Quinn mumbled behind her, scratching his scattershot hair.

Rye nodded enthusiastically. "That was you, Folly? How did you do it?"

Folly waved a hand as if it was nothing, but couldn't conceal her grin. "Explosions are old hat. Sometimes I make them without even trying."

"I was nearly stampeded by those sheep," Quinn said. "I don't think I'll wear wool pants ever again."

One of them bleated at him.

"Don't listen to his grousing. It was all his idea," Folly said, turning to Quinn. "I think those Strategist's Sticks are finally rubbing off on you."

"How did you ever get so many sheep pasted in time?" she asked.

"The Tarvishes helped," Quinn said. "Lots of Tarvishes."

"Turns out Hendry has even more brothers than me," Folly added. "Plus cousins all over the island."

"Your mother, too," Quinn said. "She found us on her way back from Westwatch."

"Here are more!" a voice called from the edge of the farm.

It was none other than Hendry. He hurried forward, wading hip-deep into the flock of sheep. Rooster, Padge, and a shaggy herding dog were right behind him.

"We've been rounding them up since daybreak," he said, out of breath.

Rye greeted her new friends with a wide grin. "You all helped save Pest. That's even better than winning the Pull." She gave Hendry an apologetic shrug. "Sorry about that, by the way. I know this was supposed to be the Crofters' year."

Hendry flashed a mock scowl. "There's always next year," he grumbled, then smirked back.

"Told you no one was going to win," Padge said to Rooster. She paused and tapped her finger to her chin. "Then again, maybe everyone did."

"Truth be told, I hope we've seen the last of those ropes too," Hendry said. He put his hands on his hips, and turned his attention to the matted and sticky-looking sheep with a heavy sigh. "It'll take me all summer to get that mushroom goop out of the wool."

"We can help," Rye volunteered cheerfully.

"Yes . . . at least until we get home," Folly said, her voice drifting off.

Rye looked at Quinn. His eyes drifted to the ground. And for the first time it occurred to her—while her best friends and all of her family happened to be right there on Pest, Folly and Quinn had been torn away from their own families. She never stopped to think how hard that might be on them. In fact, right now the Dead Fish Inn might be home to a new brother or sister Folly had never even met.

And they weren't the only ones far from home.

"What will happen to the captured soldiers?" Rye asked Hendry.

"Your grandfather and the clan elders are meeting at Cutty House today to discuss it," Hendry said, pointing a thumb in the direction of Wick. "In the past, I'm sure we would have marooned them on the Lower Isles." He cocked an eyebrow. "Would have kept Black Annis fat and happy for a year. But now I'm not sure. They did surrender, after all, and without their armor and weapons they aren't the most fearsome-looking lot. Reluctant sailors at best."

Rye remembered Longchance's men she'd seen the night before. They were rough around the edges, but their eyes betrayed an underlying sadness. Their faces reminded her of Drowning itself. She suspected most didn't want to come to Pest any more than the Belongers wanted to have them. A pang of guilt jabbed at her gut.

"Nobody's sure why the Uninvited chose to return to Pest after all these years," Hendry said. "But whatever the reason, I don't think Long Pants will have much of a fleet left to trouble Pest again."

Folly and Quinn giggled.

"Longchance," Rye corrected.

"Him either," Hendry said with a wink.

Rye, Folly, and Quinn arrived at the sandy beach under the cliff just as the tide was heading out, leaving in its wake seaweed, scuttling crabs, and an assortment of wreckage from the sunken warships. Hendry, Rooster, and Padge had stayed in the fields to herd the scattered sheep. Quinn rushed forward excitedly.

"There's sure to be a souvenir around here," he said. "Spread out and help me look."

A crowd of Belongers combed the beaches themselves. On an island with scarce resources, flotsam was as valuable as treasure, and they eagerly gathered scraps of metal and wood that could be used to fashion hooks and repair fences. A party of Fishers patrolled the shore, keeping an eye out for any sopping Uninvited who might swim in with the debris.

Rye spotted a familiar figure a short distance down the beach—a man with a leather cap and white hair singed black at the ends.

She trudged across the sand to join him. Harmless stared out at the sea.

"You asked me once if I was ready to learn how to fly," she said. "Was that what you had in mind?"

He shook his head with a smile. "Last night's flight was a first. And one I hope never to repeat." He arched his back and stretched until his joints cracked in protest. "I may have knocked a few misaligned bones back into place, though."

"Will you now reveal yourself to Waldron?" Rye asked. "To the Belongers? Shouldn't they know that the

High Chieftain of the Luck Uglies came to their aid, without asking for any price in return?"

"Does it really matter?" he asked with a tilt of his head. "Might Waldron forgive me for my past transgressions? Perhaps. But this is not my home . . . I will never be a Belonger." He gave Rye a sad smile. "Even I cannot deny that Pest will be a better place without the Luck Uglies."

"So what happens next?" she said. "When can we return to Drowning?"

"It's difficult to say. Longchance will be furious once he receives word of this disaster. The loss of so many men and ships leaves him more vulnerable than ever. Trouble still brews there . . . perhaps even more so now."

Rye caught sight of Folly and Quinn hurrying toward them before he could continue.

"And here we have two other heroes of the day," Harmless said warmly. "I believe High Isle has never seen two more important sheepherders."

Quinn eagerly showed them something in his hand. "Look what I found!"

Rye squinted at the strange item Quinn had plucked from the beach. A slimy blue puddle in the shape of a bell rested in his palm, long opaque strings dangling down between his fingers.

"Quinn," Harmless said, "you should probably put that down."

"What? Why? Ow!" Quinn shook his hand frantically and the blue creature dropped to the ground, its long transparent tentacles wriggling in the sand.

He looked down at his wrist. The skin was red and swollen as if he'd been lashed by a whip.

"A jellyfish," Harmless said, pursing his lips. "Their sting is terribly painful, but not lethal. It will leave a scar, though, if you don't treat it right away."

"With what?" Quinn screeched, dancing in pain.

"The saliva of some animals will soothe the sting."

"Which animals?" Quinn asked suspiciously.

"Well, sheep are said to be best—you might be able to find one or two around here."

"No," Quinn said, shaking his head. "No more sheep!"

"Come on, Quinn," Folly coaxed. "Let's go get you licked."

Folly hurried Quinn back up the shore.

Harmless returned his gaze to the sea, his eyes narrowing. "Folly and Quinn deserve to go home, but a strange tide now stretches from here to the Shale. The Luck Uglies will undoubtedly notice that Longchance is weakened, and I fear old ambitions may fuel hasty actions. Castles built on weak foundations soon crumble on their builders."

Rye wasn't certain what castle Harmless was talking about, or whether the builder was Harmless, Slinister, or someone else entirely. But she suspected it must be the Fork-Tongue Charmers that weighed heavy on his mind.

"I need to return to Drowning first to seal the cracks," Harmless said. "And pave the way for you and your friends."

"Will Slinister and the Fork-Tongue Charmers listen? Are they even Luck Uglies anymore?" Rye asked.

"Once a Luck Ugly, always a Luck Ugly," Harmless replied. "Until the day you take your last breath."

"But what about your differences?" Rye asked. What she really wanted to know was what Harmless had taken from Slinister. What caused the rift that now threatened to divide a brotherhood that had survived in secret for generations? And so, finally, she just asked.

"What did you take from him?" Rye said. "What have you hidden from Slinister Varlet?"

Harmless looked at her somberly. He might have asked her how she knew, or made her rehash the details of what Slinister had told her. But Rye had never known Harmless to dwell over irrelevant questions. Since she had met him, her father had always done his best to answer her honestly. Sometimes those answers were cryptic, but the truth always lay nestled somewhere within his words.

"Family," he said simply.

Rye was confused. "But Slinister is an orphan."

"And, as a Fork-Tongue Charmer, he chose to forego raising a family of his own. For all the joy it might bring, he saw it only as a weakness." Harmless smiled at her fondly, as if to assure her that he harbored no regrets himself. "So the Luck Uglies are the only real family Slinister has ever known."

Rye already knew that, except for the High Chieftain, whose title passed by birth, children were rare among the Luck Uglies. She listened intently.

"As you know, my father and I were forging a new path for the Luck Uglies. We agreed that we would rid the Shale of the Bog Noblins if our crimes would be pardoned—so that our heirs might one day walk outside the shadows and lead normal lives."

Harmless traced a line in the sand with the heel of his boot.

"Slinister was furious. To him, every step the Luck Uglies took away from the shadows was a threat to the family he holds so dear. He too believed we should defeat the Bog Noblins. But rather than destroy them, he aspired to conquer them. Turn them into our own army against not only the House of Longchance but all of our enemies, so that all of the Shale might fly the Ragged Clover."

Harmless completed his drawing in the sand. It

looked like an upside down letter *Y*.

"When the Earl broke our bargain and banished us, it was Slinister and the Fork-Tongue Charmers who burned the village to the ground, ensuring that the Luck Uglies would be cast back into the shadows once again." Harmless paused. "As I once told you, not all Luck Uglies are cut from the same cloth."

Rye was silent. It explained a question she had often pondered—why the Luck Uglies would have lashed out at Village Drowning one last time, ruining all of the good Harmless and her grandfather had worked for.

Her eyes fell to the marks Harmless had made in the sand. A forked tongue? Or perhaps a fork in the road?

"Just give it up," she snapped. She stomped his drawing until it was just a blur.

"Give what up?" Harmless asked, raising an eyebrow.

"The High Chieftain's Crest," Rye said. "You're back now. What about *our* family? You, Mama, Lottie—we can all go somewhere far away. Together. Somewhere the Earl or Slinister can't bother us anymore. Give the Crest to another Luck Ugly. Why must it be your problem forever?"

Harmless gave her a tight smile.

"Because I assumed that burden and it is part of me now," he said quietly. "It's the skin I wear."

Harmless put his hand to his chest, unbuttoning the

top buttons of his shirt. Pulling the material aside, he revealed a tattoo Rye had seen but never taken particular notice of before.

Over his heart was an elaborate knot-work outline in the shape of a shield. Inside its boundaries was a black four-leaf clover and crossed swords. The Ragged Clover.

"Some choices cannot be undone," he said.

Rye was quiet. Maybe there was no such thing as easy answers.

Harmless softened.

"Don't worry, Riley. I won't rush off to Drowning lightly. You should head back to Abby and Lottie. Tell your mother I am well after the battle in Wick and that I'll come see her as soon as I can."

Harmless gently touched her cheek with his palm before trudging off down the beach. There was a weariness to his gait that she'd never noticed before. Rye watched him until the tide washed away his footsteps in the sand. She kicked away a jellyfish that had wrapped its tentacles around her boot.

That night the farmhouse lanterns stayed lit well into the early-morning hours. Waldron returned late from Wick and shared news of the Belongers' grand plans to rebuild the fishing fleet, reinforce the seawalls, and restore Westwatch. Captain Dent regaled the children with colorful stories of distant ports. Abby cooked more food than they could eat, and when they had all finished, the table erupted with grateful belches. Even Waldron joined in, giving Abby the loudest "thank-you" Rye had ever heard. They hadn't seen Knockmany since morning, so Rye left a full plate for him outside his empty potting shed.

Finally, after everyone had gathered outside to help Lottie catch dragonflies to fill Newtie's former cage, Rye and her friends settled into their blankets. Rye found herself counting the thatch in the ceiling even while her friends fell into deep slumber. Thoughts of Drowning weighed heavy on her mind. She wished Harmless could have joined them all for supper—who knew when they might have the opportunity again? She imagined he must be cold and hungry under the fishing boat, and would make a point to bring him something to eat at first light. She passed the hours restlessly, and when her coughs and heavy sighs failed to wake Folly or Quinn to keep her company, she allowed herself to drift in and out of sleep until the sky out her window glowed with pre-dawn light.

Rye snuck out of the farmhouse, careful not to wake Waldron or her mother, and dropped to her hands and knees beside the fishing boat.

"Harmless," she whispered. "Harmless, are you there?"

But when she looked under the hull, his makeshift camp was gone.

Rye sprang to her feet, calling for him as loud as she dared. Had he already left? Why would he go without saying good-bye? Then her eyes fell on the small dark shapes that looked to have been carefully arranged all over the hull. She reached down and picked one up.

A smooth, black stone. Dozens of them.

"The Wailing Cave," Rye whispered to herself. She was certain these stones were some sort of message. Maybe Harmless wanted her to meet him there. It was a port after all, albeit a secret one. Maybe he wanted her to come with him. Whatever the message, she needed to hurry before it was too late. She set off up the crushed-shell path right away.

Rye gave the strings of shells a stiff shake as she peered down the cliff above the Wailing Cave. She didn't necessarily believe in Shellycoats, but wouldn't refuse their help should they have any to offer. Fortunately, the tides cooperated as she descended into the cave itself. She rushed into the grotto, stomping over the polished black stones littering the ground at her feet. The first rays of morning light now beamed down from a crevice high above, reflecting off the glass-like pool of water. Breaking the surface were six stepping stones, each spaced apart by the length of a man's stride. They led to a larger rock at the pool's center just big enough to make an enticing seat.

Rye stopped short and caught her breath. The seat was occupied. Rye had expected she might find someone here. Hopefully Harmless. But no Luck Ugly was waiting for her.

Constable Valant smiled out at her wickedly from under his battered crimson hat, its flat-topped crown dented and its brim stained with salt.

26
Under the Crimson Hat

"You!" Rye called out in shock. "What are you doing here? Your ship was sunk."

"Yes, very tragic," Constable Valant said flatly. "But I already know that, of course. After all, I'm the one who scuttled it."

Rye couldn't believe her ears. "You sank you own ship?"

"Well, yes. Once it became clear we wouldn't take the Isle without a struggle, I couldn't let all those soldiers sail back to Drowning. They'll serve my purposes just as well at the bottom of the sea as they would on Pest." Valant clasped his hands over his worn leather vest.

Rye took a step backward. "I don't understand. And I don't know why you're here. Does the Earl value me so much he's willing to conquer an entire island?"

Valant shook his head. "The Earl values power and stature. With a little coaxing, I convinced him I could deliver not only your family but also this slippery *prize* none of his noble neighbors could seem to keep their fingers on." He said *prize* with a roll of his eyes and a flourish of his hands to indicate the island.

"Where's your father?" the Constable asked, peering over her shoulder. "Hasn't he come with you? Surely, after all those stones, he didn't let you come alone?"

It was Rye's turn to be dubious. "You? You're the one who's been leaving stones for me?" She drew the one from her pocket and held it between her fingers.

"Yes, in a manner of speaking," the Constable said. "Although they weren't so much for your benefit as for your father's. Haven't you shown them to him?"

Rye shook her head. "No."

"What?" The Constable threw up his hands as if someone had spit in his soup. "Well, that ruins the whole effect. Don't children share everything with their parents?"

"You obviously don't have children," Rye said.

"Obviously."

"If you think you'll drag me back to Longchance, I won't make it easy for you," she said, summoning her courage.

"Really, Rye O'Chanter," the Constable said with amusement. "You still haven't put it all together?"

He stooped over and seemed to contemplate his reflection in the pool of water. He ran his hand through the waxed, fingerlike spikes of his beard and rubbed the stubble under his nose. The Constable rolled up the cuffs of his sleeves and, for the first time, Rye noticed a swirl of green tattoos ending at his wrists. He drew a sharp knife from a sheath at his hip.

Rye took another step away.

Valant pressed the blade to his skin and began to neaten his beard, scraping away the stubble that dotted his upper lip while peering into the reflecting pool. "Ouch," he said, nicking himself. "I'll be glad when I can be rid of this garish chin wig." He cast his eyes on the blade.

Rye turned to run the way she came, but a small, snarling creature blocked the tunnel in front of her. Its gray wrists and ankles were in shackles, tethered to the end of a long chain. Its nose twitched in her direction and it dug at the stones with fingers that ended at stubby knuckles instead of claws. Saliva soaked the rust-orange hair that hung from his distended jaws.

This time Spidercreep wore no muzzle over his teeth.

Rye hadn't even noticed her choker, its pale blue glow matching the reflection from the water. She finally understood why Spidercreep didn't seem to fear her runestones, either now or in the Spoke. He hadn't seen them. Spidercreep had no eyes, only hollow sockets.

Rye whirled back around.

The Constable smiled. "How about now? Any idea what's going on?" he asked.

He held the knife close to his mouth, then licked it with his tongue. It was forked, the two ends moistening the blade like wriggling eels.

And by then Rye understood. The man in front of her had never been a real constable at all.

Slinister Varlet resumed shaving with the wet blade.

Rye put a hand against the cave wall to stop it from whirling. It didn't help. It wasn't the cave but her head that was spinning. The Constable—that is, the man masquerading as a constable—just examined his reflection with a smirk over his elaborately whiskered chin. She blurted out the first of many questions that came into her mind.

"How did you come by this Bog Noblin?"

"I found him and raised him myself. He's a pygmy . . . a dwarf version, I suppose." Slinister continued to groom his beard. "For his sake, it's good that I did. His own kind do not suffer weaklings. They would not have spared him."

Rye ran the stone in her hand over the cave wall as she steadied herself, the final messages of so many sons of Pest etched around her fingers.

"I did eventually have to declaw him. Despite my best efforts to train him, Spidercreep just couldn't keep his hands to himself. But his lack of sight makes his nose perfect for hunting." Slinister returned his knife to its sheath and looked up. He removed a scrap of material from his pocket—the torn swatch of elbow from Rye's coat. "One sniff, and he was able to lead me to you as soon as I arrived on Pest."

Slinister removed his ruined crimson hat and set it on the rock. It bore not only the damage from the sea but also a hole from the kiss of her mother's arrow. With both hands, he carefully eased his leather helmet from his head.

His scalp was shaven except along the top, where his long, sand-brown hair was plaited into a single, thick braid that now fell down the back of his neck. A deep, pink groove of an old wound ran like a ravine over one ear. The rest of his scalp was etched with a lattice of green tattoos, flicking back across his skull like fiendish tongues.

Having shed the skin of a constable, Slinister looked as wild, bleak, and imposing as Pest itself.

He followed her eyes to his head. "Tell me you've ever seen a more impressive scar than this one," he said, running a finger over the pink groove.

Harmless may have had more scars, but this was certainly the largest she had ever seen. "How did you get that?" she asked.

"An axe." He smiled, and cocked an eye. "Swung by none other than your very own father."

Rye was taken aback. "So that's why you despise him so."

Slinister burst into a laugh. "Of course not. I can hardly blame him. After all, I would have buried one in his own skull had I been a step faster. But that's all within the realm of fair play. I despise your father for what he took from me."

Rye had tired of Slinister's game. She had no interest in his riddles. Harmless had already told her what he took—or at least what Slinister perceived as a theft. "You think he stole the Luck Uglies from you?" she asked hotly.

But this time Slinister did not reply in riddle. His

words were blunt. "No, Rye. What he stole was a greater treasure than that. The only thing of value on these isles—the treasure of the Sea Rover King."

Rye's face fell. *That's* what this was really about? The years of hatred. The fighting. For treasure? She felt a great fatigue wash over her.

"I don't know anything about that," Rye said, shaking her head. Maybe she shouldn't be surprised that all of this was over greed. "I don't know where it is."

"But I think you do, Rye." He pushed himself up from the rock. "I told you once that I dreamed of you. Why was that?" Slinister's eyes had gone wide. Without the red-rimmed sockets of his mask, she saw that they were flecked green like the sea and as sharp as splintered jewels. "I am of the Lower Isles. Born with a gift to perceive that which flows just below the currents of our consciousness. The Belongers would tell you it's some dark witchery. But I've come to know it's just a heightened awareness. A stronger intuition."

Slinister stepped into the reflecting pool. He didn't bother with the stepping stones.

"That Sight grows stronger when I'm around others who share it. It's at its strongest here on Pest."

Rye retreated backward.

"I've seen what I'm searching for, Rye—I've dreamed it. I have seen *you* in a place—somewhere cold and hard, a place battered by the sea. And that treasure is right there with you—right under your nose. So tell me, where is it?"

"I don't know," Rye said hurriedly.

"Yes, you do," he hissed.

"I don't," Rye said. But it was making sense now. There was only one place Harmless kept secret from all others.

"Tell me," Slinister demanded, and splashed through the water menacingly. Sand stirred and clouded the glassy pool.

"I've never seen any treasure."

"But you know where it is."

Now she did. It could only be in one place. But Rye wouldn't give him the satisfaction.

"No," she said, her eyes flaring back.

"This close now," Slinister simmered, "you must realize that I won't stop. Tell me, or everyone you know and cherish will suffer the consequences. Your family, your friends. I know where they all are right now."

Rye's chest tightened. Her mother and Lottie. Folly and Quinn. Waldron now too. They were worth more than any amount of treasure. Whether Slinister could deliver on his threat she did not know. But if someone like Harmless called Slinister dangerous, did she really want to take that chance?

"Tell me!" he boomed, and clutched his leather helmet feverishly in his fists. "If you do, I assure you they shall never be harmed at my hands. If not . . ."

"Grabstone!" Rye yelled, and her words stopped Slinister knee-deep in the water. "It's called Grabstone. South of Drowning at the edge of a shoal. Harmless has kept it a secret from everyone. There's a room there called the Bellwether. If the treasure you seek is at Grabstone, that's where it will be."

Slinister paused, savoring the information he'd sought for so long as if it were a fine meal.

"And I hope you twist an ankle on your way there," Rye added, throwing the black stone as hard as she could. It bounced off Slinister's cheek with a sickly thud and he clutched his hands to his face.

She turned and rushed past Spidercreep into the tunnel before the Bog Noblin could catch her.

Rye tore through the darkened cavern. She followed her own best advice whenever being chased—*don't look back.* If Slinister and Spidercreep were in pursuit, she couldn't hear them over the splash of her own boots. If she could just make it to the mouth of the Wailing Cave, she might be able to call for help. Maybe Folly and Quinn had woken, found the black stones, and figured out where she'd gone.

But as the towering wall of light from the cave

entrance emerged ahead of her, a blow from behind sent her hurtling. She fell forward, bounced off her chest, and landed on her back, sliding across the slick cavern floor like a turtle on its shell. She wheezed to catch her breath. A shape tumbled over her and also hit the ground several yards away. Spidercreep had been unchained and now struggled to regain his feet. He snarled in her direction.

Rye pushed up on an elbow, reached over her shoulder, and slid her cudgel from its sling.

But this time, as she moved to raise it, the cudgel didn't budge. A thick boot stepped on it, pinning it to the ground.

Rye thrust her hand into her own boot for Fair Warning.

"Tut, tut," Slinister said, hovering over her, his fingertips tapping the red whip at his belt. "I assure you that will not end well."

27
Grit

Slinister tossed an anchor and moored the dinghy on a tiny sliver of beach. He'd donned his helmet but not his hat. It didn't matter. Now that Rye had looked behind his ruse, she could never think of him as the Constable again.

"Go on," he said. "I'd rather not have to pitch you over the side too."

He offered a hand to steady her. Rye ignored it, stepped out of the boat, and splashed on to the shore by herself.

The isle was little more than a knobby hill of rocks streaked with bird droppings. Rye could see from one end to the other. The desolate place was devoid of vegetation except for some thatch at the peak of the hilltop and a dead, barkless tree that had been bleached white by the salt and sun. Its petrified limbs clutched at the air like the hand of a drowning man. Tied from one branch, a frayed ship's rope dangled and swayed in the breeze.

In the distance, numerous small islands and sea stacks dotted the waves like a giant's stepping stones across the ocean. Slinister's personal sloop—one he'd apparently used to secretly shuttle himself back and forth from the warships to High Isle—bobbed in the waves offshore. Rye was relieved he'd left Spidercreep back on it.

"What is this place?" she yelled.

"It's called the Isle of Grit," Slinister said, balancing himself in the dinghy. "I've charted all the Lower Isles and only recently rediscovered it myself. Be warned, it gets even smaller at high tide. You'll want to spend the night at the base of that tree." He pointed to the top of the hill. "And should a storm roll in, well, you might consider climbing it."

Gray-green clouds rolled across the sky like bruises, bringing with them the nip of the wind. Rye pulled her coat tight around her. She was so livid, there was no curse she could hurl foul enough to make her feel any better.

"You're leaving me to starve on a pile of barnacles? You should have just fed me to your monster."

She jumped as something landed at her feet. She ducked as Slinister threw two more objects toward her. She was surprised to see her spyglass, cudgel, and Fair Warning lying in the sand. She looked up at Slinister in confusion. With both hands, he heaved a heavy pack from the boat and hurled it past the reach of the waves. It landed with a thud.

"What's this?" Rye asked, kicking it with her boot.

"A week's worth of provisions. Maybe longer if you use them wisely. There's dried fish and water, flint for fire, some blankets."

Rye was dumbfounded. "You wish to drag out my suffering?"

Slinister seemed genuinely surprised. "I don't wish to see you suffer, Rye O'Chanter. In fact, I'd prefer to not see you harmed at all. You're an unusual girl. Overly excitable and unbearably nettlesome—that's for certain." Rye just frowned back at him. "And yet one with traits I admire, as hard as that may be to believe."

She narrowed a skeptical eye.

"But I need you out of the way, on this forsaken spit,

to be sure I get what I *do* want."

"I told you about Grabstone," Rye called. "What more is there?"

"Indeed you did—and I remain thankful. Rest assured that, as promised, your mother and sister shall meet no harm. But I need just one more thing from you. That is your influence."

"Look at me," Rye screamed, throwing her arms in the air. "I have no influence."

"Oh, but you do. In fact, I suspect you have the greatest influence of all. Your father is a formidable man. He and I play a dangerous game, and there can be only one winner. You, Rye O'Chanter, are my trump—my security, if you will. I'll arrange to meet him in Drowning, and if all else goes sour, it will be you who saves my skin."

"Why would I do that?"

"*Why* implies some say in the matter. The question you mean to ask is *how*? And that is by putting him in an impossible position. I am the only living soul who knows your whereabouts. I'll make that clear to your father. Should the High Chieftain seek to give me an inglorious demise . . ." Slinister just shrugged and cast his gaze to the sea stacks around them. "The ocean is vast and unmerciful. How long do you think it would take him to find you?"

Rye looked down at the supplies. How many days could she possibly last? She remained silent, her fury building.

Slinister pulled in his anchor. Rye rushed to the edge of beach.

"I hope he laughs at your game and cuts you down where you stand!" Rye yelled.

Slinister took up the oars and squinted through the low-hanging sun. "Then I will suffer the consequences of a bad wager." He paused and placed his elbows on his knees as he met her angry gaze. "But you and I both know that won't happen."

He offered Rye a smile that was neither cold nor sinister, and for that reason it unnerved her even more. "If I had a daughter of my own, even a monster such as I would admit that there's really no choice at all."

Rye unclenched her fists and her shoulders fell. She knew what Slinister said was true.

"You'll see me again, Slinister Varlet," Rye said as he rowed out into the surf, although her voice was more flat than menacing. At that moment, she wanted desperately to believe it.

"Careful what you wish for," he called back. "Ugly luck seems to follow wherever I tread."

The tide rose quickly as darkness descended, and Rye struggled with the flint, some dry thatch, and a few branches she'd broken loose from the lifeless tree. She finally managed to light a pathetic, smoky fire. Huddling over it, she was at least able to warm her hands. Rye sifted through her provisions, nibbling a few bites of salted fish and allowing herself a mouthful of water. They did little to quiet the rumble in her gut. With few tasks left to occupy her thoughts, hopelessness crept forth to fill the void. Rye's nose tingled, then the rest of her face, and try as she might to compose herself she feared that tears were only a moment away. But she was startled by the rustle of wings, and a large, dusky brown gull landed at the base of the tree. It cocked its head and eyed Rye's pack.

"These are mine, Bonxie," Rye said, remembering the name she'd heard a Fisher call a similar bird that had pilfered his nets. "Go catch a fish."

The gull waddled and strutted around the island as if he were lord of a tiny manor, but didn't fly away.

Rye wrapped herself in blankets, leaving only a slit for her eyes, and stared up at the starry, cloudless sky. The moon was a waning crescent overhead. She doubted she would make it to see another Black Moon. She asked Bonxie if he had any suggestions. He was too busy preening his feathers to offer any useful advice.

Rye spoke with the bird well into the night. She told him of Drowning and her little cottage on Mud Puddle Lane. She described the sweet smells of her mother's

Silvermas porridge and the sticky-sweet scent of Lottie's hair as they dozed in their shared bed. She recalled the warmth of Shady's coat as he napped in her lap. Bonxie listened from a branch but had few stories of his own to share.

She wondered why he lingered but found his presence strangely comforting. Still, she knew better than to blindly trust a friendly face. She carefully folded up her pack of supplies and tucked it under her head as a pillow, where she was sure to be woken by any opportunistic beak that tried to sample her rations.

"I'm going to sleep now," she said. "Don't peck my eyes out."

That night her dreams were foggy and turbulent. Rye woke up with a start. It was dark on Grit, her fire smoldering out. The ocean roared all around her. She closed her eyes tightly.

When she next awoke, light met her eyes. Blinking, she glanced around for Bonxie. With the tide out to sea, Grit was as large now as she had seen it, but it still took only a moment to walk its edges. She was sorry to find that the gull had left the island. At least he'd listened to her about the eye pecking. Rye looked out at the rocks and sea stacks that dotted the water, larger now and black with seaweed. It reminded her of Grabstone, of the hidden path she and Harmless had taken to and from the tide pools.

Then she saw him. Bonxie was perched on a rock not far from the shore. He peered into the lapping waves beneath him, then jabbed his head underwater. His beak came up empty. The bird hopped across several smaller stones on his webbed feet until he found a new perch where he could try again. This time he emerged triumphantly with a tiny crab in his beak. Rye let out a cheer of encouragement. He unfurled his wings and flew low across the water to another rock far in the distance, where he sat and enjoyed his breakfast.

Rye considered the deserted isle around her. She imagined another day of waiting, trying to light a fire, and hoping that a storm wouldn't blow in and leave her clinging to the tree. She surveyed the chain of rocks stretching out into the ocean. Far off on the horizon was a much larger island. She had no idea if it was High Isle or just another of the lower settlements, but it was undoubtedly more substantial than Grit. Maybe, if she could just get a bit closer . . .

Rye remembered what Harmless had told her once: *There's always a path, Riley. You just need the courage to take the first step.*

She thought hard over a decision she knew she might have only one chance to make. Then she quickly lightened the pack, leaving inside only as many supplies as she could easily carry, and threw it over her shoulders. She rolled up her leggings, pulled off her boots, and held them under one arm. In her other hand she clutched her cudgel, and set out for the nearest stone.

Rye was not the strongest swimmer and told herself she would only wade where the water was no higher than her waist. Using her cudgel as a measuring stick, she made for a remote rock before discovering that the churning waves were too deep. She backtracked and tried a different course. Despite her best measurements, swells sometimes rolled through and soaked her up to her chest. She held her boots high above her head and pressed forward. Where the chains of sea stones dead-ended into open ocean, she doubled back, all the while taking herself farther and farther away from her starting point.

After what must have been several hours, Rye realized that she could now barely see the fingers of the Isle of Grit's tree. But the larger island had hardly moved on the horizon. Perhaps she could travel back to Grit to wait out the rising tide and retrace her steps come morning.

Rye looked down as swirling waves bathed her pink feet and legs. Her toes were now so numb she could barely feel them at all. The tide was advancing fast. Several of the rocks along her path had already disappeared beneath the surface. Rye's heart pounded at the thought of being stranded in open water. Not far from where she stood, a taller crag jutted out from the sea. If she could reach it, it would afford her a better view and she just might be able to plot a new course for her return to Grit.

She plunged forward up to her knees, then her hips, mindful only of the short distance between herself and the crag. But just as she was nearly there, a hard swell struck her face and her feet left the bottom. Rye spun in a churn of foam, her pack tearing free from her shoulders. She was aware that she should cast away her boots and cudgel, but she held on to them stubbornly, kicking her legs and stroking her cudgel through the water like an oar. Her feet touched stone and she clambered out of the surf.

Rye dumped her sopping boots onto a rocky shelf barely wide enough to sit on. She examined her anklet, an iron lattice against her frigid, red skin. Harmless had called it the Anklet of the Shadowbender, and said it would help her bend the laws of darkness and light. She'd suspected it was just puffery at the time, and now she was convinced. While Folly and Quinn seemed inspired by their gifts, she'd only managed to run recklessly from one trouble to the next. She pressed her back against the crown of the slippery crag. A dusky brown gull flew overhead. It could have been Bonxie. This served her right—taking suggestions from a bird.

"Pigshanks!" Rye cursed.

She angrily thrust her head back, the way she sometimes banged it against her bedroom wall in frustration. The thud on the back of her skull did not hurt nearly as much as the deafening clang in her ears. Rye spun around and almost slipped back into the water.

Bolted to the crag was a large, tarnished ship's bell and frame, so green with grime that she thought it was part of the rock itself. She couldn't believe her eyes.

Whispers of fog blew in as Rye pulled her knees tight and watched the white caps snapping around her. Then she did the only thing she could—she rang the bell. Endlessly. Until her head ached and her shoulder burned to the point where she could lift it no more.

Rye scanned the horizon but saw no boat or ship that might hear her. She pulled her damp coat up over her ears to dull the din, changed position, and rang with her other arm. When it, too, cramped, she lay on her back and rocked the bell with her feet.

She finally gave up when the water rose so high that she had to wrap her arms around the bell to keep the tide from dragging her away. The fog was so dense it obscured everything around her. She had rung for so long that she still heard the clang of the ship's bell in her ears. But instead of fading, the volume grew.

Somewhere nearby, a ship was returning her call.

Rye peered through the fog. Could it be? She rang

the tarnished bell one last time, and the glowing light of a lantern cut through the fog like a beacon.

"Goomurnin-fi-seas?" a familiar voice called from the boat rails.

"I-fairwins-t'ya," Rye said in a whisper—the loudest sound her dry throat could muster.

Rye had never been so happy to find herself belly-up on damp, worm-riddled timbers. The deck of the small vessel shifted beneath her with the waves, and three and a half pairs of eyes looked down on her in anticipation and relief. The half pair belonged to Captain Dent—the old smuggler's good eye blinked with surprise.

Folly helped Rye sit up and Quinn threw a dry blanket over her shoulders. Knockmany put a leathery palm on her back. It was the most affection Rye had ever seen him display. She noticed the freebooters' green flag atop a single mast, but the boat was much smaller than the *Slumgullion*. There was no other crew.

"How did you find me?" Rye asked between chattering teeth.

"We saw the stones on the fishing boat," Quinn said. "When you and Harmless were nowhere to be found, we figured you must have seen them too—and followed them back to the Wailing Cave."

"We found your message on the wall," Folly said.

In desperation, Rye had used the black stone to hastily scrawl R-Y-E while leaning against the grotto. She feared that no one would ever see it.

"And this," Folly added, showing her Slinister's battered crimson hat. "We weren't sure what had happened, but we knew it couldn't be good."

"Slinister and Constable Valant are one and the same," Rye explained hurriedly, then turned back to her question. "But how did you know I was on Grit?"

"I'd like to say it was m' keen instincts," Knockmany said. "But the truth is a strange li'l girl insisted you'd be found on a rock in the middle o' the sea."

"Padge," Folly clarified.

"When you've lived on Pest long as I have," Knockmany said, "you learn to heed the hunches of strange li'l girls."

Rye was stunned. "She knew to send you *here*?" Padge's intuition must be stronger than she could have ever imagined.

"Not exactly. All she said was that you were on a Lower Isle," Quinn replied.

"Dent and I were packing for a voyage anyway," Knockmany interrupted. "So we set out for the Lower Isles right away. Abigail, Waldron, and the Belongers are searching High Isle. Your stubborn friends here insisted on joining us." He grunted, glancing at Folly and Quinn. "We were nearby and heard your signal. It seems luck was with us all today."

Rye took note of Knockmany's stoic expression. She didn't care if you wore horseshoes on your feet and ate nothing but clovers for a month—nobody was that lucky.

"Dent and I can't delay our trip any longer," Knockmany said hastily, before Rye could question him further. "We'll see you three to Wick then be on our way."

"You're sailing to Village Drowning?" Rye asked suspiciously.

Quinn and Folly exchanged glances. Knockmany hadn't said anything about Drowning.

He seemed to be taken off guard by Rye's query. "Perhaps . . . if the wind takes us there."

"You're bringing Gristle with you?" Rye asked.

Knockmany followed Rye's nod to the wicker basket on the deck of the boat. Gristle's shaggy head watched them all with a wary glare.

"Just for a little company," he said dismissively.

"What's wrong with Captain Dent?" Rye asked.

"He's terrible company," Knockmany said.

Dent huffed. Folly and Quinn looked to Rye for answers. What was going on that they did not yet understand? Rye had only just put it together herself.

Rye stared Knockmany hard in the eye. “Take us with you,” she said finally.

“No, no, lass,” he said. “I can’t do that.”

“Harmless is in danger,” Rye said.

“Sorry, lass. You mus’ stay here.”

“Please, Knockmany.”

He shook his head with finality.

“*Please*,” she implored. “You have no choice. I’m calling in my favor.”

She thrust out her hand.

Rye clutched a piece of damp fabric between her trembling fingers. It was the Ragged Clover Bramble had given her.

“You know what this means, don’t you?” Rye asked.

Knockmany let out a heavy sigh. He took the fabric from her and scrutinized it carefully. “Aye, lass, indeed I do.”

He was silent for a long while.

“My brother’s promise is my own,” he said finally. “Each Luck Ugly shall honor a brother’s favor as if he promised it himself.”

Knockmany cocked an unhappy eye. “I’ll fulfill my duty . . . but I don’t like it one bit.”

28
The Bellwether

The sun set over the western horizon, bathing Pest's green hillsides in a golden light. The sea was gentle; its whitecaps played rather than pounded. Seabirds hurtled toward their nests in the cliffs. A flock of razorbills made for the boat and flew low over Rye's head before exploding scattershot into the sky, as if bidding them farewell.

"How long did you know he was a Luck Ugly?" Folly whispered. She and Quinn had joined Rye at the stern and watched the harbor disappear behind them.

Rye smiled at her. "Not until I handed him the Ragged Clover."

It was the truth. She had only just pieced it together, even though the clues had been there all along. Harmless's words to her mother before they departed for Drowning—that there was only one Luck Ugly he could trust, and she'd know where to find him. Knockmany's coincidental discovery of them on the beach, almost as if he'd been waiting for someone. His unusual knowledge of Bog Noblins and the thick-maned "pet" that bore a striking resemblance to the O'Chanters' own Gloaming Beast. And finally, the old Belonger's sudden voyage to Drowning that just happened to coincide with Harmless's departure and the troubles back home.

Knockmany had sent word to Abby and Waldron with a fisherman they'd come across on his way back into port. Rye felt awful sending a message that way, as her mother must be mad with worry. But she couldn't take the chance that Abby would insist on keeping her on Pest. For she knew that Harmless would never accept that she was safe until he could be absolutely certain. He would bend to Slinister's will unless he saw her with his own eyes.

"Sorry you never found a souvenir," Rye said to Quinn.

"At least I've gotten over my seasickness," he said with a shrug.

Rye looked back out over the stern. She had only been on Pest for a blink of an eye, and yet it felt like she was leaving somewhere dear to her heart. She hoped she would return someday to see Waldron and Padge and their new friends again. She wanted to sit on the cliffs, smell the lavender in the air, and watch the whims of the sea without the threat of warships on the horizon.

Knockmany joined them at the rail. He mentioned to Folly and Quinn that Captain Dent was ladling out the night's meal, and they took his cue to find the Captain belowdecks. Rye noticed that he carried Slinister's crimson hat.

"I knew yer other grandfather too," he said after some time. Rye looked up eagerly. Except for the occasional legend, no one, not even Harmless, spoke much of Grimshaw the Black.

"Thirty-five years by the prior High Chieftain's side an' another fi'teen here wit' Waldron, I suppose I know yer ancestors better'n anyone. Maybe it should be no surprise how you've turned out." There was fondness in Knockmany's usual gruff tone.

"Does Waldron know you are . . ." She caught herself midsentence. "Does he know what you are?"

"He'd have run me out long ago if he did,"

Knockmany said with a coarse laugh, and like a sudden shift in the breeze, she noticed that his Mumbley-Speak accent was gone.

"What have you been doing here then?"

"When your father left Pest . . . with Abigail . . . he knew it would crush Waldron. Gray asked me to stay to keep an eye on him, help him out if I could."

"That's a lot to ask of someone," Rye said.

"I left High Isle when I was just a wee babe, spent my best years far away. But deep down I'm a Belonger, and I was happy to end my days on Pest. Most Luck Uglies think I turned up my toes long ago."

"But you're leaving now," Rye said.

"These are important times—the brotherhood has reached a fork in the road. Even an old graybeard like me needs to have his say. Besides, Waldron is a new man . . . your unexpected visit has done more for him than I could ever hope to." He gave her a wink. "I'll be back someday."

"What awaits us in Drowning?" Rye asked.

Knockmany just shook his head. He didn't know either.

"Knockmany," Rye said after a moment. "Padge told you I'd be on a rock in the middle of the sea. But of all the Lower Isles, why did you come to Grit? I know better than to believe mere luck is to thank."

Knockmany's face turned grim and he glanced down at the hat in his hands. "Because it was I, many years ago, who marooned Slinister Varlet on that very same isle."

Rye's eyes went wide.

"I was the one tasked with selecting those sons of Pest who would join the Luck Uglies' ranks," Knockmany explained. "It was always a boy on the verge of manhood, one willing to forego all bonds of family and leave Pest forever. Once my decision was made, I summoned them by leaving a black stone from the Wailing Cave."

Rye's hand went to her pocket, but the stone she'd hurled at Slinister was long gone.

"Slinister sought out the cave on his own. But willingness wasn't enough," Knockmany said. "The mettle of each candidate needed to be tested. After they arrived at the Wailing Cave I would sail them to the Isle of Grit, blindfolded and in silence, where the prospect was provided enough provisions to last one week. They were not told when, or if, I would ever return."

Rye's mind raced at the possibilities. Had Slinister intended to replicate the test on her?

"The Isle of Grit has a way of revealing the true nature of men, of which I found there were three types." Knockmany extended one finger. "First, there were those who waited out the week—who endured through weather, deprivation, and the unknown. For them, rescue came at the end of their seventh night."

He extended a second finger.

"Far too many were of the second sort. Those were the ones who fell into a despair from which there was no return."

Rye cringed. How many ghosts had she spent the night with on that little isle?

"And what of the third?" Rye asked.

"Those were the rarest kind. The ones so strong-willed, so foolhardy, you might say, that they believed they could do the impossible—walk across the ocean."

"But that *is* impossible. I found out myself."

Knockmany raised a silver eyebrow.

"Of course it is. And for the most part, those who tried now rest at the bottom of these waters. But," Knockmany added, eyeing her carefully, "for anyone fearless enough to brave the watery maze, *and* clever enough to walk the stepping stones as far as they could possibly take him, a bell awaited." Knockmany gave her a wry smile. "I was never far away—waiting for the bell. If anyone sounded it, I would come rescue him, whether he'd endured a week or a day on the Isle of Grit."

Rye shook her head. "Slinister said he needed me on

that island. How could he make such a mistake, leaving me there if he knew there was another way off?"

Knockmany cast his gaze to the water for a long while before answering.

"Because Slinister Varlet never found the bell," Knockmany said slowly, and with a flick of his wrist, pitched the crimson hat far into the sea. He turned, and his weather-lined face studied Rye, as if seeing her with new eyes.

"No one did. Until you."

Unfortunately, Rye and her friends would leave the fair seas behind them in Pest. The voyage back to Drowning was turbulent, the ocean so fierce that they found themselves huddled belowdecks, and poor Quinn discovered that he had not yet cured his seasickness after all. They all locked arms so that they wouldn't tumble as the small ship climbed and plunged over huge, rolling waves, bilge water swirling around their ankles.

Finally, after days that felt like months, they reached the mouth of River Drowning on a starry night. Rye would have gladly gotten out and swum through the darkness if it meant reaching dry ground sooner, but Knockmany told her not yet, and passed a gold grommet to a shrimper anchored nearby. The villager pulled in his nets and sailed upstream. When he returned it was with the news that all was quiet.

Only after receiving the fisherman's message did Dent brave the river. The sloop skulked silently through the pre-dawn glow, passing the hard-packed sand of Slatternly Flats. Ahead, Rye saw familiar lights atop the bridge over the River Drowning. Candles glowed in the windows along the banks and she knew they were at the Shambles. To her relief, it was in better condition than when they'd left it.

Folly shifted nervously as they all watched from the boat's rails.

"I wonder if they even noticed I was gone," she said under her breath.

A lantern flared on the dock. A small crowd had gathered, waiting.

Rye grew alarmed. "Soldiers?"

Quinn peered ahead. "Just an army of Floods," he said, then his face went pale. "And one Quartermast."

Rye looked to Knockmany.

"I thought they could use a warm welcome," he said out the side of his mouth.

As the boat eased into the slip, Rye saw the white-blond mops of Folly's parents and eight brothers. Faye Flood's belly was still enormous, looking as if it might pop at any moment. Rye smiled. They weren't too late.

Rye tugged Folly's arm before she could climb out

of the boat. "Folly," she whispered quickly, "if you see my uncle Bramble, tell him that Slinister and the Constable are one and the same. And tell him how to get to Grabstone."

"Why?" Folly asked. "Aren't you coming?"

Rye glanced at Knockmany out of the corner of her eye and gave her the slightest shake of her head.

Folly hesitated, then climbed out of the boat, taking a few careful steps forward. Faye flung her arms open, and Folly ran as fast as she could to meet them. The entire family surrounded her, and Rye saw beaming grins and damp eyes, even from the twins.

Angus Quartermast didn't wait for Quinn. The hefty blacksmith lumbered down the dock.

"Uh-oh," Quinn said.

When Angus reached him, he plucked Quinn from the boat. Angus squeezed him so tight that Quinn's eyes bulged, but his voice was joyful when he just said "My boy" over and over. Quinn blushed and gave Rye a tiny wave as Angus carried him away in his thick arms.

Knockmany tossed his satchel onto the dock, carefully setting Gristle's basket beside it. Although he had honored the Ragged Clover and granted Rye's request, she knew that the favor would not include allowing her to rush off in search of Harmless. He was sure to stash her in the Dead Fish Inn or lock her away somewhere she'd be of no use at all. So when Knockmany turned and extended his hand to help her down from the deck, she made sure that she was already gone.

Rye disappeared into the shadows under the wharves and piers and was halfway down the embankment, on her way to the only place she could think of where she might find Harmless.

And quite possibly Slinister Varlet.

The carved-stone hags stared down at her as she approached the towering mansion. Their lifeless eyes and lips seemed to smile in greeting. She flung open the doors to the entry hall—Grabstone wasn't the type of place that required locks.

Some spare cloaks hung on hooks, all of them dry. She climbed the stairs to the main room. An empty plate and cup sat at the table but no fire burned in the fireplace. She carefully poked a finger into the ashes. They were warm to the touch.

"Harmless?" she called out, and waited. But there was no reply. Her face fell. "Slinister?" she tried with trepidation. Fortunately, that brought no response either.

A kettle rested on the stone hearth. Rye tested the copper with her thumb and found it cold. Liquid swished inside. Rye poured the water into the empty cup on the table. But instead of herbs, the tea smelled stale and fishy. She opened the kettle's top. Three round black orbs sat inside. Submersed in briny water, their needle-like spikes jutted out in all directions. Midnight sea urchins. Rye thrust the kettle next to the cup on the table and stepped away. There was no telling what might happen if someone drank that.

The sea urchins appeared to be alive. They couldn't have been in there since she'd left Grabstone.

A noise caught Rye's attention. She cocked her head. Muffled voices echoed down from the stairways above her.

"Harmless?" she called in a hushed whisper. "Harmless, are you here?"

She carefully climbed the stairs toward the bedchambers, calling quietly as she went.

Rye stopped at her former room and peeked inside. It was exactly as she'd left it, empty but for her unmade bed and a collection of trinkets piled in the corners.

The louder of two voices was clearer now, coming from still higher overhead. It was familiar, heated and raw. She cast her eyes up the last flight of stairs to the Bellwether.

Her heart raced.

The door to the Bellwether was open!

Rye crouched on the steps, not daring to climb any closer. She recognized the voice now; it belonged to Slinister.

Were Slinister and Harmless arguing?

Their words were scattered, difficult to piece together.

"After all the years I have searched," Slinister bellowed, his tone anguished, "won't you join me? I've gathered resources . . . everything we need."

"I've no more appetite for what you offer," came the reply. The voice didn't belong to Harmless. It was a woman's lilt, but old and gritty, like sand stuck in the folds of your ears.

"I've just sailed from Pest," Slinister implored. "I spared them for now, but when I return it will not be to build some noble's trading post. I'll bring an army that will raze the isle into dust . . . and fulfill your greatest wish."

"Those were the words of a desperate woman," the voice said wearily.

"But that is what you promised!"

"Those words alone had no power," she said. "Only a wrathful son who clung to them could give them truth."

"You scorn me."

"I have never thought of you with anything but a warm heart."

"Then stay in this tower and rot in your warmth!" Slinister railed. "I'll not return here again."

"Is vengeance really all we have to share?"

But Slinister did not reply. Instead, Rye heard his heavy boots on the stairs. She darted inside her room and pressed herself against the wall.

Slinister's broad frame filled the stairway just outside her door. His elaborate braid fell down his back and the skin of his shaved skull was pink with anger. Rye gasped as he turned and looked back over his shoulder, but his gaze was up at the Bellwether. His jewel-like eyes were dull, his face crestfallen. He turned and hurried down the stairs without further words.

Rye found herself shaking, unnerved by the ragged emotion in his voice. She wanted to follow him but feared this time he might not spare her. Her concern turned to the other voice in the Bellwether. She waited until Grabstone was silent, then continued cautiously up the stairs. The Bellwether's door remained open.

She stepped into the unfamiliar room and came to a halt. Several gulls stopped pecking at the breadcrumbs strewn across the floorboards. More fluttered in from the windows, cocking their heads nervously as if just returning home after a storm.

Harmless was not in the Bellwether.

But someone else was.

A small, withered woman sat hunched on a stool. Her white hair dangled in long stringy snarls past her creased and weathered face. Her earlobes hung low and the folds of her neck seemed to melt into her frock. Any eyebrows she once had must have fallen away with age. But when she raised a keen eye, it glinted like sea glass.

"What a nice surprise, child," the woman said. "I've been wondering when you'd finally get around to visiting me."

29 Treasures

Rye opened her mouth but no words escaped her lips.

The woman raised a gnarled twig of finger and beckoned. "Don't just stand there slack-jawed like a hatchling. Come in."

Rye didn't move. She glanced over her shoulder to the stairs.

"He's gone. You have nothing to fear." The old woman patted a rickety-looking stool next to her own. "*Come,*" she said more firmly, "before my beaked companions are frightened away again."

Rye took a careful step forward and sat down.

"You haven't brought me a treat in weeks," the woman said, and tapped the petrified remains of a stale crust against the floor. The birds hopped after the crumbs. "My friends enjoyed your bread. Alas, I don't have the tools to eat it myself."

She grinned wide, displaying her empty gray gums. Rye pursed her lips. Maybe she should have offered Harmless's snail stew.

Rye looked around the small circular room. The expanse of windows on all sides afforded the extraordinary view she'd always imagined. But the space was empty except for the two stools and a bed of old blankets rumpled in a corner. The Bellwether was surely no treasure trove. If Harmless had hidden Slinister's treasure at Grabstone, it wasn't here.

"The man who came here," Rye said. "Did he harm you?"

"We spoke for a long while. He has quite a temper, that boy." She clucked her tongue. "There's a rage in him that has yet to cool. But no, he did no real harm."

"He came seeking treasure—" Rye began, but her voice failed her. Slinister's words suddenly ran through her head. His answer when she had first asked him what Harmless had taken from him:

Something I have never seen nor touched but that

made me who I am. Something that remains mine and only mine, whether I live or die, and that even the High Chieftain cannot deny.

Slinister had been speaking about his own mother.

"Black Annis," Rye whispered.

"None of my friends call me that, duckling. Just Annis will do."

Rye shook her head. "When Slinister spoke of treasure . . . I thought he meant gold, or riches."

Annis raised a fold of skin where an eyebrow once was. "And yet, don't our greatest treasures shine brighter than any coins or jewels?"

Waldron's story of Black Annis's curse flooded back to Rye, and she pushed herself up in alarm. The startled gulls fluttered their wings.

"Are you a witch?" Rye asked, her voice rising.

"Don't get your knees in a wobble, young lady," Annis said firmly, but not unkindly. "And no name-calling please—I assure you I know far uglier slurs than you. I am no witch."

She pressed her colorless lips into a thread of a smile. "I was but a simple island girl with the clarity of Sight. I wasn't the only one—perhaps I was just more outspoken than most."

"Sight?" Rye repeated. She had heard Slinister speak of it in the Wailing Cave.

"Longsight. Intuition. Perception. Call it what you will. You've got a touch of it yourself. Someone in your line was a Low Islander, I can see it around your eyes." Annis swirled her finger in the air, gesturing at Rye's face. "Your gram, or great-grammy. The gift has been known to skip a generation."

Rye thought of Padge, her distant cousin with the uncanny knack for divining information from her dreams.

Annis let out a long and deep sigh. "But Slinister's Sight flowed directly from me. It's strong in him—undiluted. Sight can be a cruel gift. Unfiltered, it can drive one to madness."

Rye's confusion grew. "I don't understand. You were banished . . . do you live here in the Bellwether?"

"I have for a short while, yes. Ten years. Twelve. Maybe fifteen. A blink of an eye, really."

"That doesn't sound like a short while," Rye said. "How old *are* you?"

"That's an impolite question to ask a lady," Annis said with a scowl. "Even a withered old relic like me."

Rye's face fell, ashamed at her bad manners. Annis chuckled.

"Pigshanks, child, I'm just pulling your braids. I'm as old as the sea . . . but that doesn't make me nearly as interesting as you seem to think." She leaned forward, her keen eyes flickering green, then blue, as they dug into Rye. "I'm here because your father, that young fellow you call Harmless, brought me here."

Rye swallowed hard. "You're his prisoner?"

Annis snickered and slapped her hands on the bony thighs beneath her frock. "Don't be pigeon-headed," she said. "The Bellwether's door locks from my side, not his. He brought me here to honor a bargain made long ago."

"A bargain with who?"

A fond looked passed over Annis's face, and Rye saw a glimpse of the young woman she must have once been.

"He called himself the Sea Rover King. He was *my* treasure, and I his. He had many enemies, some of whom might find a way to seek vengeance upon him even after he'd hoisted his final sail. If anything happened to him, Harmless agreed to watch out for me . . . as if I needed the help."

She waved her hand, shooing away a memory like a fly. "Alas, men like that never live long enough. I wasn't at all happy when your father took me from my little isle. I was perfectly content sitting by the water and dreaming. But he meant well, and I suppose he thought he was protecting Pest, too, by keeping my whereabouts secret from my boy." Annis's eyes flickered green with mischief. "After all, you can never be too careful when it comes to curses." She let out a girlish chuckle. "I'll get around to forgiving him . . . one of these days."

Rye bit her lip. Annis might forgive Harmless, but she doubted Slinister ever would.

"Slinister means to do great harm to my father," she said. "I overheard some of what he told you. Did he say any more about his plans?"

Annis sucked her gums. She opened palms that looked as fragile as late-autumn leaves. "Some things must remain private between a mother and son, even if they are merely strangers to each other. But I will share this much, for you to do with as you choose. Slinister has persuaded your father to meet him this evening at nightfall." Her hard gaze now held Rye's. "But with him, he brings a storm."

"Where?" Rye asked urgently.

"At the farthest edge of the Shale. At the place where the forest meets the bogs."

Rye was relieved—that wasn't far from Mud Puddle Lane. She could make it if she hurried. But an important question still lingered.

"You didn't leave with Slinister," Rye said. "Will you not join your own son after all these years?"

Annis smiled sadly. "That I shall sleep on, and see what my dreams tell me." She shook her head, tangled white knots of hair now darkening her face. "A cruel gift indeed," she muttered to herself.

There was a noise below them. Both Rye and Annis turned toward the stairs.

"Riley!" a man's voice called.

Rye made for the door. "Harmless?"

"Wait," Annis said.

"I have to warn him."

"Child, be careful. All is not what it may first seem."

But Rye wasn't listening. She ran from the Bellwether and rushed down the steps. She tore into the main room. A cloaked man had his back to her.

"Harmless!" Rye cried.

The man spun around, a grin spreading across his face.

"Bramble?"

Bramble stepped forward and put his hands on her shoulders. "Aye, my fair niece. Long time no see."

Bramble seemed tired, frayed. He was even more unshaven than usual.

"How did you find me here?"

"Frothy told me where you were headed," he said.

"Folly."

"I was at the Dead Fish Inn when your friends and Knockmany arrived. She was able to give me an idea of how to get here. Fortunately, I caught sight of you when you started for that shoal—you really need to look over your shoulder more often, by the way. In any event, it was lucky I did, otherwise I might never have found this place."

Bramble stepped away from her and wandered around the room, examining the sprawling views.

"It's quite the hideaway your father has here," he commented with an impressed nod.

"Have you seen him?" Rye asked. "He's in danger. Slinister has lured him into a trap."

"I know, Riley," he said gravely. "He most certainly *is* in danger. I wish you had stayed on Pest."

Bramble stopped and placed both palms against the glass of a window. He stared out at the shoreline. There was a rustling behind Rye and she turned to see Shortstraw ambling down one of the flights of stairs.

"So you must know about Slinister?" Rye asked, turning back to Bramble. "He's pretending to be the Constable. I mean, they are one and the same."

Bramble nodded. "So I discovered while you were all away. Slinister sheds his skin more deftly than an adder."

"He just left here. Did you see him on the shoal?"

Bramble gritted his teeth as he scanned the water. "He may have come by boat. I've always known Slinister to be an expert seaman—and I've known him longer than most."

He dropped himself into a chair, as if a great weight rested on his shoulders.

"He's planning a meeting tonight and—" Rye caught herself and raised an eyebrow. "Wait, you've known him longer than most?"

Bramble nodded. "Since I was just a boy on Pest."

"You knew him on High Isle?"

Bramble waved his fingers in the air and sighed. "It's a long and winding story," he said, and his eyes caught sight of the cup and kettle on the table. "Probably best told over tea."

He picked up the cup Rye had poured and pressed it to his lips.

"Bramble!" Rye yelled. "That's midnight sea urchin!"

Bramble's face looked stricken and he jumped to his feet. Shortstraw jolted. Bramble spat the liquid into the fireplace. He coughed and sputtered, trying to get every drop of saliva out of his mouth. He stuck out his tongue as far as he could and wiped it with the folds of his cloak, then spit again to get rid of the lint.

When he was satisfied that he had expelled the toxins from his mouth, he wiped his forehead with the back of his hand and slumped against the wall.

"That certainly wouldn't have been the most glorious way to pawn the clogs," he said, flashing Rye a relieved grin.

Rye's mouth was dry now too. All the color had drained from her face.

"Don't worry, I'm none the worse for wear . . ." Bramble began to say, but caught himself when he realized what had actually caused her alarm.

Rye took a step back.

She had seen Bramble's tongue.

It was split down the middle and forked like a snake's.

30
A Fork-Tongue Charmer

"Riley," Bramble said urgently, "allow me to explain."

"You're a Fork-Tongue Charmer!" she cried.

"Riley," he said, taking a step closer. "Please wait."

Rye backed against the far wall. Bramble stood between her and the stairway.

"Stay back," she said.

"Riley," he said, more sternly, "you must listen to me."

"I'm leaving," she said. "You keep away."

"You can't," he said, closer now. There were only inches between them.

Rye tried to dart around him, but his fingers bit into her shoulder.

"Stop!" he demanded.

Rye's hand found her cudgel. Before she realized what she was doing, it was free from its sling, and without thinking, she swung it. The blow was straight and true—like Waldron had taught her—and it found its mark in the fleshy muscle just above Bramble's knee. He broke his grip and crumpled to the floor.

Rye ran past him. Shortstraw screeched in protest, but she glared and pointed her cudgel at him, too. The monkey whimpered and retreated to a corner.

"Don't leave here," Bramble said, his face masked with pain as he reached out for her.

"Don't you come any closer," Rye said, shaking the cudgel. But Bramble was in no position to pursue her.

Rye rushed down the stairs, ignoring his further pleas. She made her away across the shoal as quickly as she dared. This time she looked over her shoulder frequently, but neither Bramble nor Shortstraw followed. Rye's ears burned hotter than ever before. How could her own uncle be an enemy of her father? How could he have turned his back on them?

And yet, now it all seemed clear. Harmless and Bramble had always been cold to each other. Her mother herself had told Rye that her departure from Pest was the start of a rift between the two that had never been mended. If Bramble had known Slinister since he was a boy, it made sense he'd become a Fork-Tongue Charmer.

Rye made it back to the stable behind the fisherman's shanty. She set out quickly on the pony she'd ridden from the Shambles, making her way toward the village along the beach but cutting a wide swath around Drowning itself.

It was dusk when she paused at the far end of Mud Puddle Lane. She could see lanterns flickering in cottage windows and smell smoke from their chimneys. She wondered if Quinn was sitting down to a long overdue supper with his father. Amid the cluster of cottages, she noticed that one house remained dark, its chimney cold. The O'Chanters' cottage hadn't been warmed in a long time. So close to her home, and yet Rye felt more lost than ever before. Her mother and sister were across the sea, her uncle had betrayed them, and her father seemed to harbor a knot of secrets she might never untangle.

She turned the pony and headed for the forest, its hooves splashing through the damp turf. Here the edges of the bogs had poisoned what was once forest floor, and the dead husks of needleless pine trees rose around her like looming skeletons. The pony carefully stepped over the fallen branches and jagged trunks that now littered the ground.

Rye stopped when they neared a dense wall of towering trees stretching north as far as her eye could see. The bogs were quiet. So were the shadows of Beyond the Shale, which spread across the ground like pools of spilled ink. She'd hoped to spot Harmless coming by way of Mud Puddle Lane so that she might warn him before he wandered into Slinister's trap. Better yet, maybe he wouldn't come at all. But her journey from Grabstone had taken longer than she'd expected, and she feared he had already made his way to their meeting spot.

She climbed down from the pony, giving him a pat and encouraging him to find his way back to the village.

Something caught her eye. Her choker was glowing. The blue was just a pale flicker, but its light unmistakable. If Spidercreep was near, that meant Slinister would be too. And Harmless couldn't be far behind.

My choker will lead me to him, Rye told herself.

When she reached the edge of Beyond the Shale, she could do little more than crane her neck and gawk. The pines towered above her. The lowest branches had long since died and shed their needles. Now the jagged remains of the limbs had been carved into spikes as sharp as spears, forming an impenetrable barrier. Rye couldn't tell if they were designed to keep the forest's denizens in or the villagers out.

She checked her choker. The glow was stronger.

Rye took a deep breath. She had never ventured into Beyond the Shale. Not even at its edges. With her thumb, she tested the razor-sharp tip of a branch that jutted out at eye level. There was only one way to get through. Carefully.

She made her way methodically through the dense maze of jagged limbs, stepping over one lethal spike, ducking her head under another, contorting herself to slip between two tightly packed trunks. For once, being small and lean was an advantage. After traveling some distance, Rye stepped through a ridge of trees and was able to stand at normal height. The spiked branches still surrounded her, but she found herself in a narrow, branchless corridor that wended through the forest.

"It *is* a maze," Rye whispered. "And I've found a path."

Her choker grew brighter as she hurried carefully but quickly now, unobstructed by the meddlesome limbs. The leaves and debris crunched under her feet, and as Rye's runestones began to glow with even greater intensity, she spotted shimmering lights in a clearing ahead. Before she could rush forward, a hand clutched her arm.

The boy named Hyde glared at her menacingly

with his narrow-set eyes, the enormous mottled dog by his side.

Even if Rye thought she could outrun Hyde, she knew the dog would catch her before she got far. Their struggle was brief. Hyde took her cudgel, bound her wrists behind her, and gagged her with leather straps that tasted like they'd been cut from an old saddle. If nothing else, she was confident he would take her to Slinister . . . and Harmless. But instead, he dragged Rye to the edge of the circular clearing and deposited her out of sight at the base of several thick pines. Hyde watched her carefully. The dog sat on its haunches and eyed her too.

From her seat in the shadows, she saw that dozens of lanterns hung in varying heights from the jagged branches that ringed the clearing. The area itself was dotted with enormous stumps—remnants of the huge old trees that must have been felled by hand to create the open space.

Slinister strode from the trees in his leather helmet and full constable attire. He led Spidercreep on a length of chain, the Bog Noblin's jaws encased in an elaborate iron muzzle. It must have been the same device Spidercreep had worn when she'd encountered him in the Spoke.

On a stump, someone was waiting. A man sat with

his elbows on his knees, eyes on Slinister. His eyelids were heavy, but they betrayed no alarm.

Harmless!

Rye squirmed on the ground helplessly. Hyde nudged her still with a boot.

"Good evening, High Chieftain," Slinister said, taking one end of Spidercreep's chain and fastening it to a thick iron post nailed into one of the other stumps.

"If I'd known you'd taken a bride, I would have sent a gift," Harmless said. He eyed Spidercreep with a look that conveyed more pity than anger.

Rye noticed that Harmless's own choker was glowing bright in Spidercreep's presence.

The two men regarded each other in silence.

"So, *Valant* is it now?" Harmless said finally. "It has a rather regal ring to it."

"I'm glad you approve."

"It's much nicer than Slinister—about time you finally let go of childhood taunts."

"It's not easy recasting oneself," Slinister said. "But we are who we say we are."

He removed his battered leather helmet and placed it on a stump at his side. The deep, shiny scar on his head reflected the lantern light. Again, without the ornamental trappings, his whole persona seemed to change.

"For ten years I have been reinventing myself as a

lawman. An enforcer of rules and order, by any means necessary." He flashed a smile and ran a palm down his thick braid that now fell loose. "It helps to look the part."

"You look like death," Harmless said.

"You should know. Last time you saw me, I believe you introduced me to your axe."

"Days fondly remembered," Harmless said. "Perhaps I'll reacquaint you."

Rye didn't like the direction of the conversation. Hyde's attention was focused on the clearing, so she fidgeted her legs, trying to gauge how fast she might climb to her feet. The dog let out a low growl, and she froze.

"Yes, the good old days," Slinister repeated. "I, too, long for them. This lawman business has grown tiresome."

"And when you robbed the Mud Sleigh, breaking our bargain with Good Harper," Harmless said, "was that Valant the lawman or Slinister the Luck Ugly?"

"Killpenny rode under the protection of our reputation for ten years without paying for it. As I see it, I was just collecting our past-due commission."

"You put a nail in our coffins with every bargain you break," Harmless said.

Slinister shrugged. "Grand plans require resources. Last autumn, when you sounded the Call to Drowning, it presented a most interesting . . . opportunity."

"Opportunity?" Harmless asked.

Slinister nodded. "Yes. There are pressing developments to be discussed. Matters that affect all the Luck Uglies."

"And what might those be?" Harmless asked.

"You would know if you weren't spending all your time playing watchdog for your family, or taking holidays at your little hideaway." Slinister's tone was bitter. "Grabstone, you call it?"

"So you've learned of Grabstone," Harmless said gravely.

"Yes, a lovely girl told me all about it."

Harmless's eyes flared.

Rye could hardly contain herself any longer. She might not be faster than a dog, but she only had to make it far enough for Harmless to see her.

"I really gave her no choice," Slinister continued.

Harmless rose menacingly from the stump at Slinister's words. Slinister raised a cautionary finger, his other hand resting on the hilt of the blade at his side. "Stop and think," he warned. "Think long and hard before you take your next step."

Rye sprang to her feet. Before Hyde or the dog could react she tore from the trees as fast as her legs would take her.

"At the moment, your daughter is on a very small rock in a very large—"

Slinister's voice came to a dead stop.

Rye could only call out a muffled cry as she ran to Harmless. He pulled her in tight. She couldn't hug him either since her hands were still bound, but he removed the leather strap from her teeth.

"He stranded me on an island . . . he said you couldn't hurt him because then I'd be stuck there forever . . . but it's all right because I'm here now," she said breathlessly. Her eyes flared and she turned to Slinister.

Slinister wasn't wearing the white ash of the Fork-Tongue Charmers, but the color drained from his face as if a ghost had just rasped in his ear. Incredulous, he looked to Hyde, who stood with the dog at the edge of the treeline.

"Rye O'Chanter," Slinister said slowly. "I am speechless."

"I told you you would see me again," Rye said defiantly.

"Yes," Slinister said quietly. "And I told *you*, bad luck follows wherever I tread." He shook his head. Slinister seemed more stunned than angry.

Harmless's rage was beyond words, but the two swords at his back spoke for him, hissing as he drew them from their sheaths. He seemed to catch himself before he advanced toward Slinister, tilting his neck as if listening. Rye heard something too. Hooves. Horses.

"Our guests have arrived early," Slinister said, repositioning his leather helmet over his skull. He twisted his face and seemed to push back whatever emotion had left him so flustered. "You'll appreciate this part, Gray," he said in a near whisper.

An armored soldier on horseback appeared from a break in the trees. He was followed by a parade of mounted troops, each of the warhorses adorned in black-and-blue tartan saddle blankets. There were so many soldiers they were able to form a tight ring around the entire clearing.

"I told him to bring every man he could spare," Slinister explained to Harmless. "In case you had any surprises in store." He glanced at Rye. "Although, it appears your well of surprises has finally run dry."

Harmless sized up the soldiers warily but didn't move from his position at Rye's side.

With the area now secured, Rye saw a final horse and rider emerge from the trees. The man in the saddle was framed tall and harsh, like the jagged pines rising high above them. He guided his umber-colored stallion around the perimeter twice, surveying the surroundings with hard coal eyes. His dark hair was tied in an elaborate knot atop his head. The long ends of his mustache were plaited and dangled down past his chin like the barbels of a catfish. The last time Rye had seen him, he'd worn a similarly adorned beard. That was right before Harmless cut it off and promised to feed it to the Bog Noblins.

The rider was Earl Morningwig Longchance.

He directed his steed to the center of the stumps, where Slinister greeted him with a broad smile. Hyde followed closely behind. Spidercreep had become aware of the new arrivals and sniffed the air anxiously. The stillness of the forest was now broken up by the snorts of nervous horses, the scuffling of their hooves, and the gentle clank of riders' armor.

Longchance stared down at Harmless from high atop his mount. Harmless and Rye were alone and surrounded by soldiers, and yet Longchance still maintained a healthy distance.

"I'm glad you found us," Slinister said. "I hope my directions through the forest weren't too difficult to follow."

"You've really done it, Valant," Longchance cooed. "Not only have you won me an island, you've delivered to me the most notorious outlaw in all the Shale. It has been a banner week for you. Your reputation is well earned."

Slinister bowed with a flourish.

Rye glanced at Harmless. Slinister had told the Earl he'd been victorious on Pest.

"And he is alone?" Longchance asked, casting a wary eye to the shadows of the trees.

"He is." Slinister seemed to hesitate. "Except for her, that is."

"That's delightful, Valant," Longchance said dryly. He drew his horse back as if it might step in something unseemly. "You know how I adore children. Now we'll need to get rid of her, too."

Longchance gave Harmless the smuggest of grins. "I told you not long ago that your days were numbered," he said. "Turns out I was right."

Harmless didn't blink or say anything in reply.

"Unchain your little monster, Valant," Longchance said, turning to Slinister and Spidercreep. "Let's feed them to it and be done."

Harmless took a step forward. The soldiers quickly stirred and Longchance drew his long sword from its ornamental sheath at his hip. He pointed it over Harmless's head, toward Rye.

"One more step and she goes first," Longchance spat.

"Morningwig," Harmless said, his tone severe, "you don't know who you are dealing with. This is no constable. Think of me what you may but this treacherous snake will have your throat before the night is out."

Slinister opened his mouth in mock offense. "Hurtful words," he said.

"The lies of a condemned man," Longchance shot back at Harmless. "I'd expect nothing less from a conniving criminal such as you. Go on, feed him to the beast."

"In front of his own daughter?" Slinister asked, and Rye thought she heard a tone of disdain in his voice. "I serve at your pleasure, but alas, Spidercreep is just a runt better suited to hunting and tracking than any real destruction. He doesn't even have eyes or claws."

"Oh, for the sake of the Shale, I'll do it myself," Longchance said, dropping down from his horse. He took two lumbering steps forward, like a crane wading through the shallows, then hesitated. He glanced at Harmless's blades, then his own sword, and called out, "Soldiers, disarm him."

"But . . . ," Slinister said, putting up his hands and quickly stepping between Longchance and Harmless. "Perhaps something bigger than Spidercreep will do the trick."

Only then did Rye see the ominous shadows emerge from the trees. Her stomach twisted in horror. If she had been able to find her voice, she would have screamed out loud. All around the perimeter, massive gray forms stepped from the forest. In the lantern light, Rye saw the knots of red-orange hair, the misshapen faces pierced with fish hooks and metal bolts. Her nose filled with the stench of the bogs.

The soldiers barely had time to turn and defend themselves. It took only minutes for the Bog Noblins to vanquish every last one of them, leaving just a few terrified horses galloping frantically around the clearing.

31
Revenge of Slinister Varlet

Harmless threw himself on top of Rye to shield her. He cut the bonds at her wrists with a sword and pulled her body close to his own.

Slinister and Hyde anxiously surveyed the carnage around them. They were all surrounded by more Bog Noblins than Rye could count. None of them were as small as Spidercreep, who had wrapped himself in a terrified ball behind his stump. These beasts were thick and hulking, each at least three heads taller than a man. But when Rye saw Slinister's face, he wore a look of quiet satisfaction.

Longchance stood dumbstruck, his sword dangling limp in his hand.

One of the largest of the Bog Noblins lurched for him, its jaws and long plaited beard slick with the remains of a soldier. Before the beast could take the Earl, a red coil wrapped around Longchance's neck like a tentacle and pulled him back. It was Slinister's whip. He put his foot into Longchance's leg and dropped him to his knees, then stepped between him and the Bog Noblin.

Slinister stood straight and stared up at the Bog Noblin's hard, malicious eyes.

"Not this one," he commanded.

The Bog Noblin growled and ducked down, his protruding chin and upturned nose just inches from Slinister's spiked beard.

"NOT this one," Slinister commanded again. "I still need him."

The Bog Noblin glowered, as if waiting for Slinister to back down. He didn't. Reluctantly, the creature took a step away.

"Slinister," Harmless called. "What have you done?"

Rye's eyes flicked around the clearing. The ring of monsters seemed to inch closer. Their shadows now dimmed the lantern lights strung from the trees.

"Only what we should have done long ago, Gray," Slinister said. "I've brought the House of Longchance to its knees. Two-thirds of his forces are lost at sea or prisoners on Pest."

"What?" Longchance demanded from the ground.

"Hush." Slinister tightened the whip around his throat and gave him a rough tug that made the Earl gasp. He turned his attention back to Harmless. "Most of the rest are now lying around us. And I have my own army now—not only the Fork-Tongue Charmers, but a legion of beasts. Quite an important development, wouldn't you say?"

From the trees, chalky, hooded faces appeared, their eye sockets and lips black. Fork-Tongue Charmers masking themselves with ash. The Charmers and Noblins eyed each other uneasily but did not attack.

"What did you promise them?" Harmless asked gravely. "What did it take to get the Bog Noblins to agree to assist you?"

"Not as much as you might expect," Slinister said with a tight smile. "I promised them the one that their kind sometimes calls *the Nightmare. The Painsmith.* You haven't heard those names in a long time but you remember them, I'm certain. I promised them *you.*"

Rye's face fell.

"And here you are." Slinister waved his hand at the Bog Noblins. "This is the clan of the Dreadwater."

Harmless eyed the Bog Noblins as they circled

closer around them. He crouched and pressed Rye tighter behind his arms.

"Now you *do* have a few options here," Slinister said conspiratorially. "You can let them take you, but we both know that wouldn't be your nature. You can stay and fight them, but frankly, look at the numbers. That's a fight even you know you'll lose." He tapped the spiked beard on his chin. "Or you can run. Into the forest and never look back." He looked at Rye, and she thought she recognized a hint of regret in his eyes. "Take Rye with you, of course. It was never my intention that she become part of this, but the best laid plans are sometimes thwarted by the unwitting. Maybe you can outpace them for a day or even a week."

Slinister's lips curled and any sign of regret was now replaced by self-satisfaction.

"But regardless, when I signal the Call for the next Black Moon, you won't be here to answer it. The High Chieftain failing to answer the Call? That's unheard of. That's another important development that all the Luck Uglies will need to discuss."

And there was the final piece of the puzzle, Rye thought. Slinister had masked himself as a constable to earn the Earl's trust. He'd convinced Longchance to commission a fleet of warships to sack the Isle of Pest, diverting the Earl's soldiers from Drowning and using them as pawns in his own game of revenge. But when it became clear that Pest would not fall easily, he sabotaged the fleet to achieve an even greater ambition—the House of Longchance laid crippled at his feet.

And now, finally, with no High Chieftain, Slinister could wrench control of the Luck Uglies for himself.

Slinister extended an open palm toward Harmless and called to the large Bog Noblin that had approached him. "Go on, claim your prize."

"Wait," a voice called out.

An ashen-faced Charmer hobbled from among the others at the edge of the forest. Rye bristled at the familiar, pale blue eyes behind the ash.

Bramble paused when he reached Slinister. He was winded and limped noticeably. Harmless regarded him with dark eyes.

"Let me take my niece," he said to Slinister. "Don't condemn her to her father's fate."

Rye was so furious she thought she might spit on her uncle's boots. She should have taken her cudgel to his head.

Slinister's sea-flecked gaze found Rye, then retreated. His face betrayed indecision, as if he was battling against some old, dark turmoil that raged far away.

Had Slinister hoped to spare her all along? Would he have returned to find her on the Isle of Grit himself?

"Go on," he told Bramble quietly. "Be quick about it, before I change my mind."

Bramble stepped over to Harmless and looked down at him with cold eyes. Harmless just stared back, and Rye couldn't tell if he was angry or disappointed.

"Come," Bramble said, and extended a hand to Rye.

Rye just glared out from behind Harmless's arms without budging. Harmless tried to push her forward but Rye struggled against him.

"No, I won't leave you."

"COME!" Bramble barked, and grabbed her hand roughly. Rye yanked herself free but felt something in her palm. She opened her hand to see what Bramble had given her.

The leather band was strung with runestones like her own. She knew it well. It was a collar.

"Keep it," Bramble whispered, "to remember him."

Rye looked to her uncle in confusion.

Dead leaves rustled as a thick, black shape exploded across the clearing. It bounded to the nearest Bog Noblin and lurched at it with such fury that the massive creature dropped to one knee. Rye couldn't believe her eyes. It was Shady!

But Shady wasn't alone. Another Gloaming Beast was at his side, springing at the Bog Noblin's throat, embedding its nails and claws. This Gloaming Beast was the color of smoke. Gristle.

The Bog Noblins suddenly turned on the Fork-Tongue Charmers.

"This is not my doing!" Slinister called out urgently. "We've been betrayed!"

But the rest of the Dreadwater were not listening, and the Fork-Tongue Charmers had no choice but to draw their weapons and defend themselves against the Bog Noblins' wrath.

Bramble extended a hand and pulled Harmless to his feet. He looked around at the chaos. The Gloaming Beasts had quickly brought down another Bog Noblin but too many remained. Horses fled madly. The Fork-Tongue Charmers held their own for the time being, but they would not be able to hold off an entire clan.

"The numbers are all wrong," Bramble said. "Even with the Gloaming Beasts, this one won't end our way." He looked to Harmless for an answer.

"Get Riley out of the forest," Harmless said. "That's all we can hope for now."

Rye could hear them speaking, but their words only made her feel even more helpless. She spotted Hyde slowly inching away from a Bog Noblin, his back to her. She charged forward and snagged her cudgel from his belt. He turned quickly. Rye raised the cudgel over her shoulder. She didn't know whether the blow would be for Hyde or the Bog Noblin, but someone grabbed her arm and pulled her away before she could swing. It was Bramble.

"Bramble, I'm . . ."

"Not now, niece," he said. Limping, he rushed her toward a horse.

In the confusion, Rye saw Slinister ferociously cut down a Bog Noblin. He escaped to the shelter of the trees, dragging Longchance roughly behind him. Shady and Gristle preoccupied several more, but the rest of the Bog Noblins now bore down on Rye and Bramble. Bramble stopped and turned to protect her, his sword drawn as one rushed at them.

Harmless threw himself across its back, his arms and twin swords wrapped around the beast's neck. The creature stopped, craned its head, and clamped its jaws down on Harmless's arm. The sword in Harmless's bitten hand dropped to the ground. Before the monster could do further damage, Harmless buried his remaining sword home, and rode the beast down as it slumped to the forest floor.

Harmless rolled to the side and stumbled to his feet. Bramble had no time to help him as he sprang to fend off another attack.

Rye's jaw fell open. The Bog Noblins were too numerous. They were overrun. She saw Harmless look at his arm, hanging limp at his side. He'd been severely injured. His wolflike eyes flashed at the destruction around him.

When his gaze found Rye's, she gasped. Rye shook her head and mouthed "no."

Harmless's eyes were telling her good-bye.

"NO!" she yelled.

Harmless grabbed the sleeve of his lifeless arm and shook it, the splatter from his wound creating a trail on the dead leaves. Then, clutching it to his side, he stumbled toward Longchance's own warhorse.

"No, Harmless!" Rye cried as she stepped toward him. "Don't go!"

But he had already pulled himself onto the horse. He tugged its reins so that the animal whinnied and reared on its hind legs. The Bog Noblins spotted him, just as Rye knew he'd intended. Slumped on the horse's neck, Harmless kicked his heels, and the stallion tore off into the trees, just ahead of the first Bog Noblin, who plunged into the forest after him. Rye lost count as five, six, seven more Bog Noblins followed.

Rye ran to where they'd disappeared, but someone grabbed her collar from behind. She gasped and pulled free momentarily, but a menacing Fork-Tongue Charmer lurched for her again. He tightened his hand around her throat. Rye coughed as she struggled to break free.

A swift blow jolted the Charmer's head and his grip went slack. His eyes rolled back and he sprawled at her feet. A cloaked figure stepped over him, its fists still clenched and at the ready. When the Charmer didn't move, the figure turned to Rye, its hooked beak and hollow eyes staring out from its hood. The Luck Ugly placed its studded leather gauntlets on her shoulders.

A mouth of scrap-metal teeth opened and a familiar voice rasped in her ear. "Easy, lass. It's time for you to go."

"Knockmany?" she said.

He lifted an arm and pulled her into his cloak like the folds of wing. The next thing she knew, she was boosted onto the back of a horse and felt someone climb on behind her.

Rye craned her head to look back at the far end of the clearing and the darkness of the forest beyond.

"Harmless," she whispered.

She saw now that Knockmany had not joined her. The old man stepped back into the fray, felling one Bog Noblin, then another, with blades and bare hands, until so many surrounded him that his black cloak finally crumpled into a heap. He disappeared under their flail of claws.

"Keep your head down," the man behind her said. A hand gently pressed her face against the horse's mane.

"Just stay still and this old girl will do all the work." It was Bramble's voice.

The horse tore forward. It plunged into the trees and Rye pinched her eyes tight as jagged branches leaped at her. They rushed through thorns and thickets. It seemed they would be impaled by the jagged spikes of the tree limbs at any moment. But when she opened her eyes, she saw that the horse was careening left and right, hurdling one branch and narrowly threading through tight, invisible passageways.

She dared to glance behind them one last time, but saw no one following. No Luck Uglies or Fork-Tongue Charmers. No Bog Noblins or Gloaming Beasts. No Knockmany.

And no Harmless.

All that lay behind them was the dark, wooded labyrinth of Beyond the Shale.

32 The Toll

Rye skipped across the barnacle-pocked rocks. The mild ocean breeze carried with it early hints of summer, and Rye breathed deeply, enjoying the salt air. But the nagging tickle in her chest left her coughing, reminding her that she was not fully mended. She paused and put her hands on her knees.

"Rye, are you coming?" Folly called from up ahead.

Quinn looked back over his shoulder expectantly, teetering on his heels just above the waves.

Rye smiled at the sound of her friends' voices and

hurried forward. Grabstone awaited them.

They entered under the watchful eyes of its carved-stone guardians, but were greeted inside by the warm smell of familiar cooking. They eagerly joined Bramble, Lottie, and Shortstraw at the dining table.

"How was your walk?" Abby called from the fireplace. "You took it easy, I hope."

"Of course," Rye fibbed.

"Hmmm," Abby grunted skeptically, and stirred her pots.

Abby and Lottie had arrived from Pest shortly after Rye's rescue from the Bog Noblins. Abby quickly tracked Rye down at the Dead Fish Inn, where a fever had kept her in bed for days. As soon as Rye was well enough to be moved, Abby brought them to Grabstone. It seemed to be safest for everyone. Rye wasn't concerned that Slinister would return there. He had already found what he sought, for better or worse. Whatever his future plans, she didn't think they involved Rye, her mother, or sister any longer.

Bramble played a card game he called Running the Black while the children waited for their meal. He showed them three Hooks cards, two red Ladies and one black Liar, and told them to "follow the black" as he shuffled the cards' positions on the table, their identical backsides up. Each time, they picked the wrong one. Shortstraw perched on the back of his chair and plucked at Bramble's hair with his leathery little fingers. Bramble didn't seem to mind.

"Are you done corrupting the children?" Abby interrupted with mock annoyance, and set bowls of porridge in front of each of them.

"This bunch is already incorrigible," Bramble said, pushing himself up from the table. "I'm afraid it's about time for Shortstraw and me to say farewell anyway."

"Nothing to eat before you go?" Abby asked, pointing to a bowl.

Shortstraw jabbered excitedly.

"We'll eat on the way," Bramble said, and the monkey grumbled in protest. "I've stayed to see you settled, but I've lingered too long for all of our necks." He teased Shortstraw with a tickle under his chin. "I won't be able to stay a step ahead of the Fork-Tongue Charmers forever, and I'm probably the one person Slinister Varlet would most like to get his hands on right now, next to . . ." Bramble glanced at Rye and Lottie and seemed to catch himself. "Let's just say I would make a good consolation prize."

Rye already knew that nobody in Drowning had seen or heard from Harmless since he disappeared into the forest Beyond the Shale. Even the rumormongers around the Dead Fish Inn had come up empty. All of the Luck Uglies—and Fork-Tongue Charmers—had receded into the shadows. How they might settle their differences remained a mystery.

"Will you make your way back to Pest?" Abby asked.

Bramble shook his head and Rye noticed a far-off look in his pale blue eyes. "There's a village south of Trowbridge that isn't home to any Fork-Tongue Charmers that I know of. It may be just the place for me to disappear for a while."

Rye watched Bramble gather his pack. He still moved with a limp. Since their last unfortunate encounter around this very same table, he had shared with her the truth—the story he'd tried to explain before she hobbled him. Bramble had indeed been a Fork-Tongue Charmer long ago, before the Earl drove the Luck Uglies from Drowning. But over time he'd seen the error in his ways. He and Harmless disagreed on many things, and might never to see eye to eye. But they were not enemies. Bramble had stayed close to the Fork-Tongue Charmers at Harmless's own request, and it was Bramble who had learned of Slinister's plans in the forest. If not for his and Knockmany's quick thinking, Rye might never have made it out from Beyond the Shale.

She felt a deep pang of sadness as she thought of Knockmany. He had been a loyal friend to both of her grandfathers and, from what Bramble had told her, a legend even among the Luck Uglies themselves. She wished he'd gotten the opportunity to return home to Pest.

Rye got up and hugged Bramble tightly.

"Remember," he whispered in her ear, "the old scars of the body don't always reflect what dwells in a person's heart."

He pulled up a handful of his black hair in his fist and tilted his head so she could see the back of his neck. There, on his skin, was an ugly pink scar shaped like Slinister's Fork-Tongue inkwork she'd seen at Thorn Quill's: the remains of a brand that must have been painfully scraped away over time.

"I'm sorry, Bramble," she whispered back.

"Don't be, niece," he said kindly. "You're as ferocious as your mother when protecting what's dear to you." He stepped out of her embrace and gave her a wink. "That's not the worst trait in the world."

"I'm just glad I still need more practice with the cudgel," Rye said.

"Don't fret, with a little time I'll be dancing as well as I ever have."

"You never dance," Abby said.

Bramble gave Abby a kiss on her cheek. "Stay out of sight and send word if you hear anything," Rye heard him say.

"Be sure to follow your own advice," Abby told

Bramble as he mussed Lottie's hair. Lottie pinched his nose.

"Shortstraw, say good-bye to your cousins," he instructed.

Shortstraw screeched grumpily, turned, and slapped himself on the bottom with both hands.

"Don't mind him . . . the warm weather makes him irritable." Bramble patted himself on the shoulder and Shortstraw climbed up to his usual perch.

"Good-bye, Quinn. Be well, Fuzzy," he called as he headed down the stairs. Folly gave him a mock scowl, but Rye saw Bramble flash her a little wink as he disappeared.

Abby ladled out a bowl of porridge for herself and joined the children at the table. For a fleeting moment, things seemed almost normal—Rye, Abby, and Lottie sitting around the dinner table with her two best friends. Just like they had done so many times on Mud Puddle Lane. Rye looked around at Grabstone. Maybe home wasn't about *where* you were, but rather *who* you were with.

Abby had poured her cranberry wine earlier than usual and set her drink on the table. It reminded Rye that Harmless wasn't the only one they were missing. No furry black face found its way into Abby's cup.

"Have you seen him again, Quinn?" Rye asked. "Any more signs of Shady?"

Quinn paused and thought. "I think so, although it's hard to be sure. Some nights, right around dusk, I see two shapes creeping around the forest's edge. One's black, the other's gray. They could be cats . . . or Gloaming Beasts. Every time I've tried to get a closer look, they disappear."

Rye would bet it was Shady and Gristle. Her hand went to her pocket, where she no longer kept a black stone but a well-worn leather collar. Shady might be gone, but at least he wasn't alone. Hopefully he was happy.

"And Newtie?" Lottie asked excitedly.

Quinn glanced at Abby and Rye.

"Yes, Lottie," Quinn fibbed. "I think I saw a very happy dragon swimming in the river."

Lottie smiled and ate her porridge without a single protest or bang of her spoon.

"Well, I'm glad Angus has finally let you out of the cottage again," Abby said to Quinn.

Quinn nodded. "Me too. He settled down after he realized I was none the worse for wear. Well, except for this." Quinn showed them the back of his hand, which was adorned with a swirling pink scar from the jellyfish's sting. "And my crooked toe where a sheep stepped on me . . ."

Rye laughed. "So you did bring home souvenirs!"

After all, she thought, weren't scars just reminders of the places you'd been?

Quinn smiled. "I suppose you're right."

"And what about your news?" Abby said, turning to Folly. "How is little Fox? We want to hear all about him."

Fox Flood was Folly's newest sibling. Rye couldn't wait to meet him. For Folly's sake, Rye was secretly glad that Faye Flood had delivered yet another boy. Folly might not be the youngest anymore, but she was still the only girl.

Folly glowered. "He's loud . . . and fussy. When he's not screaming, he's sleeping or soiling linens. Besides that, he doesn't do much of anything at all."

Rye looked at her in surprise. Then she saw Folly's lips pucker as if she were trying to stifle an expression. It was a smile. Before long, a huge grin spread across Folly's face.

"But his hair is so soft and he smells really good. When he falls asleep on your shoulder, you don't want to move for hours."

"It's true," Quinn said with a nod and a shrug. "It's happened to me too."

That thought put a grin on all of their faces.

Rye waved cheerfully as she watched Folly and Quinn leave Grabstone, but underneath her smile she held a heavy heart. Her friends said they would return to visit soon, but what Rye knew, and Folly and Quinn didn't, was that Bramble wasn't the only one saying good-bye that day. Abby had already told Rye as much, and it took all of Rye's willpower to keep it from them.

No one in Drowning had seen or heard from the Earl since the disastrous night in the forest. No Longchance soldiers patrolled the streets. If Slinister re-emerged, who knew what he might have in store for the village, or his enemies? Worse, if the Bog Noblins resurfaced, neither noble nor Luck Ugly would be there to give the villagers a fighting chance. Abby was taking Rye and Lottie away. She'd told Rye it was better if nobody—not even Folly and Quinn—knew where they were going next. Abby had even kept it from Bramble, for fear he might try to stop them.

Rye balanced a cup of tea as she climbed the steep, winding stairway. She'd told her mother she was going for a short rest, but when she reached her bedchamber she kept going. Rye was the only one who knew they weren't alone at Grabstone. The door to the Bellwether still remained sealed at all times. Except, that is, whenever Rye ventured up the stairs with an extra cup of tea or bowl of stew, and found the door miraculously cracked—as if she had been expected.

Rye slumped down in the rickety stool and looked out at the sweeping views around her.

"Thank you for the tea, duckling," Annis said, slurping from her cup.

Annis's white hair was combed straight and shone like fishing line in the sunlight. Rye was glad she'd appreciated the hairbrush Rye had brought her.

"We're going away for a while," Rye volunteered.

"I know," Annis replied with a nod.

Somehow, Rye wasn't surprised.

"Have the birds brought you any news?" she asked hopefully.

"Plenty. There's some bad weather brewing to the south, and I understand this will be a fine season for summer squash. But if you mean news of your Harmless, I'm afraid there is none."

Rye frowned and stared at the wormholes in the floorboards.

She looked up after a moment. "Do you think he's . . . alive?"

Annis frowned and stared into the dark hollow of her cup. She swirled its shallow contents into a little whirlpool as she contemplated the question. She sucked her gums.

"I would guess so. For the time being."

"And what about Slinister?" Rye asked.

Annis thought for a moment before answering. "You find yours, I'll find mine, and what we do with them is a problem for another day."

Rye picked her fingernails. "Is there really anything *we* can do . . . to change the way this will end for them?"

Annis watched Rye carefully. "You can always change the ending," she said.

Rye looked at her with a spark of hope.

"You just have to be willing to pay the toll."

Rye swallowed. "What's the toll?" she asked quietly.

Annis shrugged. "Not for me to say. But you'll know it when the payment comes due."

She reached out and handed Rye her cup. Rye pushed herself up from the stool and turned to leave the Bellwether.

"Riley," Annis said, and Rye paused at the door. It was the first time Annis had called her by her given name. "It may get worse before it gets better."

Rye's shoulders slumped. Then she noticed a twinkle of sea glass in the old woman's eye.

"But it *will* get better," Annis added. "Of that, you can be sure."

EPILOGUE
Beyond the Shale

Rye knew she was near the door even before she saw it. The Spoke had been warm and damp throughout her trek, but now the air had gone cold and stale. The hair stood up on the back of her neck, not due to the drop in temperature, but because of what lay ahead. Deep claw marks laced the face of the iron door behind thick coiled chains and dozens of locks. A small eye-level grate betrayed no hint of what was behind it, but Rye already knew. It was the door to Beyond the Shale.

She pulled her sealskin coat tight at the neck and adjusted the pack on her shoulder. Her cudgel hung across her back. She reached back and ran her fingers over it nervously.

Rye was no stranger to this place. She had been here before. The last time she had unlocked the door at Harmless's instruction, but hadn't ventured through it. He had told her that for many, the door was the start of a one way journey. Rye swallowed hard. She now stood on the verge of what could be just such a trip.

But this time she wasn't alone. Rye looked over her shoulder.

Abby's jaw was steady under the hood of her scarlet cloak. She had slung her crossbow across her back and a satchel at her hip. For the first time Rye could recall, her mother had foregone a dress and now wore leggings like Rye's. Her tall black boots extended to her knees. Even Lottie was uncharacteristically somber. She stood close by Abby's side and had insisted on carrying her own pack. Mona Monster was stuffed into her belt. Lottie puffed her cheeks and watched the fog of her breath rise from her nostrils.

They all stared at the locks.

"Go on, Riley," Abby said. "You're the only one who's done this before."

"Do you have the first piece of the puzzle lock?" Rye asked.

"No," Abby replied, shaking her head.

Rye raised her eyebrows in surprise.

"But you do." Abby reached into Rye's hair. She removed her hair clip, snapped off the back clasp, and placed the rest in Rye's palm.

Rye carefully examined the hair clip retrieved from the remains of the Willow's Wares. The one Waldron had given to her mother before her. Rye noticed now that the dragonfly was uncharacteristically fearsome. Unlike the colorful ones that populated Pest, this dragonfly was menacing—the color of an angry sky before a storm.

Rye looked to Abby with wonder.

"When your father commissioned the new locks to be placed upon this door, he wanted to be sure that only an O'Chanter could open it." Abby shrugged. "Sometimes the best hiding place is the one in plain sight."

Rye nervously rubbed the dragonfly between her fingers. She turned back to the door and considered the numerous locks strung along the chains. Deciding on one, she reached out and carefully placed a finger on it. She quickly pulled her hand away. It was frigid to the touch. Rye glanced back at Abby. Her mother gave her a reassuring nod.

"Go on, Riley," Abby said. "It's time to find your father. We won't wait for ten years again."

Rye reached out, grasped the lock more fully in her hand, and twisted it to examine the open puzzle slot at its base. She positioned the dragonfly and began to slide it into the slot. She cracked an anxious smile, looking at Abby and Lottie, who had pressed around her. She couldn't believe it—she'd found the correct lock on the first try.

Rye slid the dragonfly piece into the lock smoothly. The bolt slid open and the first lock fell away. But instead of opening up to reveal the next puzzle piece as it had done last time, another lock clicked and dropped, then the next. Rye's eyes darted as the locks popped and fell onto the tunnel floor, until finally the last one opened and the heavy chains tumbled to the ground with a loud clatter. Rye sprang back so the coils wouldn't smash her toes.

Abby pulled Rye and Lottie close. They all held their breath as they stared at the unbound door in front of them. Nothing rushed forth to attack them. No force seemed to draw them in. The door just loomed, daring them to open it.

"It looks like luck may be on our side today," Rye whispered.

"It always is, my love," Abby whispered back.

With Abby's gentle prompting, they inched closer. Finally, Rye reached out and pressed her palm against the door.

The next step, they all took together.

The End

A Seafarer's Guide to Mumbley-Speak and Other High Isle Chatter

Belonger: If you or your kin were born on Pest, be it High or Lower Isles, you'll always be welcomed back to Wick with a pair of dry boots and a good-natured cuff. Of course, most Belongers never leave at all. Belonger children are taught early on that there's no finer life than one built on a hard day's work and a generous helping of herring by the fire. Besides, everyone knows that a big, frightening world lies beyond the sea.

Brannigan: Worse than a brouhaha but not quite as violent as a donnybrook. At best, this type of loud disagreement might leave you with a headache. At worst, well, a cudgel to the head is not out of the question.

Climbing Boy: Climbing boys scale the cliffs of Pest to harvest eggs from the seabirds' nests. It's dangerous work—a pecked hand being the least of a climbing boy's problems. But who doesn't enjoy fresh eggs with their morning stout?

Freebooters: Not to be confused with sea rovers, pirates, or corsairs, freebooters don't plunder the loot of others, they simply help move it. These smugglers are as guileful as they are swift, and for the right price, there's no cargo they can't see safely from one port to another.

Goomurnin-fi-seas: The traditional Pest greeting exchanged between Belongers. Regardless of whether or not you're having a good morning or if the seas are truly fine, the appropriate response is "*I-fairwins-t'ya.*" Because, really, we're just trying to be nice—nobody wants to hear about your troubles.

High Isle: The Isle of Pest is actually a chain of windswept islands off the coast of the Shale. High Isle, the largest and most populated, is home to the more sophisticated and worldly of the Belongers. Popular High Isle leisure activities include sheep races, the boulder toss, and rope pulls.

Intuitives: The Low Islanders whisper that once every several generations, an Intuitive may be born into a Lower Isle family where Longsight runs in the blood. Intuitives are almost always women because, let's face it, men's idea of intuition amounts to guessing what's for supper. Of course, Low Islanders have also been known to tinkle in their own boots to keep their feet warm, so most folks take what they say with a grain of salt.

Jack-in-Irons: The most famous of all legendary giants, Jack-in-Irons was said to inhabit Pest long before the arrival of mankind. Guilty of offending a powerful hag, he was bound in shackles and cursed to stack rocks on High Isle for the remainder of his days. Either that or he was just bored. An island can seem like a small place for curious children, never mind a giant.

Longsight or Sight: When used properly, this gift—or some would say curse—can help you become a wise guide, leader, and sage. Use it improperly and you'll just sound like a great big know-it-all. The prideful Belongers don't like being told what to do under the best of circumstances, and have been known to react poorly when told what they *will* do. For that reason, most Intuitives have learned to keep their big mouths shut.

Lower Isles: The hundreds of tiny islands east of High Isle are wild and weather-beaten, much like their isolated pockets of inhabitants. Old superstitions are prevalent among the Low Islanders, and their populations are rumored to include descendants of shipwrecked sea rovers, witches, and even giants. The worst punishment in Pest is to be marooned on the most remote of the Lower Isles, where if the winds and wild boars don't get you, the hag Black Annis will.

Luck Uglies and Other Fork-Tongue Charmers: Again with these questions? Told you before—no idea who you're talking about.

The Pull: The Belongers are masters of democracy. The last clan pulled into the harbor each spring governs Pest for the following year. What, your political system is so much better?

The Salt: A bookish Uninvited once tried to explain that the Salt was the result of condensed water droplets suspended in the air. The Belongers recognized his crazy ramblings for what they really were—the wicked wordsmithery of a sorcerer—and promptly marooned him on the Lower Isles.

Shellycoats: If a favorite wool sock goes missing from the wash, or your rowboat springs a leak, you can bet one of these mischievous spirits is to blame. When kept appeased by small tokens of affection, these should be the worst of the little imps' tricks. However, a Belonger who scorns the Shellycoats can find himself hopelessly lost in the mires at dusk or, worse, bring the full rage of the sea upon his village.

Uninvited: History has proven to the Belongers that the Uninvited traveler packs his satchel with nothing but trouble. The Belongers may knock heads like rams among themselves, but they all agree that any Uninvited should swim right back to whatever dry-footed hollow he came from.

Turn the page for a sneak peek at the epic finale to the Luck Uglies series!

1

H Is for Harmless

Rye O'Chanter crept through a dense maze of leafless branches sharp enough to skewer her. The towering pines in this stretch of wood were charred black like victims of a great fire, yet they hadn't been burned. It was as if the dark soul of the forest had poisoned the ground itself and bled into their roots, staining the trees forever.

Rye's nose twitched at the smell of a cook fire wafting from the small clearing ahead. She was confident that she'd visited this spot once before and found it empty, but she'd need to check more closely to be certain. The forest Beyond the Shale hid countless invisible secrets, its rolling hills and dense stands of pine and hemlock disguising hollows you might pass right by without a second glance. She understood now how the Luck Uglies, and others like them, might disappear into the forest for months, years, or even forever.

Rye listened carefully as she dug a rotting toadstool from the ground and rubbed it over her sealskin coat. The leather was already caked with the remains of smashed birds' eggs, mud from a beaver dam, and dung from some unknown animal. The stains hadn't gotten there by accident. If her friends Folly and Quinn could see her now, they would think Rye had gone daft, but the mixture of forest smells served to mask her own scent. Beyond the Shale was teeming with keen but unseen noses, too many of which might come calling if they caught wind of a human.

Satisfied that the small camp was unoccupied—at least for the moment—Rye stepped forward to inspect it. A tent made from animal hide housed a fur bedroll. Several small pots were arranged around the remains of a fire and the blade of a hand axe lay embedded in a fallen log. Rye's excitement grew. These were the types of supplies that could be packed and transported in a hurry—just the type of camp her quarry was likely to make.

She circled the clearing, pausing when she found the familiar trunk of a thick pine. There was her symbol in the bark: a circle with a capital letter *R* inside. It beamed white from dried sap that had filled the hollowed letter like a scab. She'd carved dozens of these in recent months. It meant Rye had searched this spot before and found it empty. But now there was another marking next to her own. The bark was still raw, as if recently cut.

A letter *H*.

She didn't blink, for fear she might reopen her eyes and find they were playing tricks on her. She was hunting for her father—the man she called Harmless.

Rye tried to temper her excitement as she glanced up at the sliver of sky peeking through the limbs high above, the muted sun hanging low behind the trees. The long days of summer were now gone, and roaming after dusk was far too dangerous. She bit her lip. Could she afford to wait to see if it was Harmless who returned to this camp? No, but she *could* leave a message of her own and come back at first light.

Rye removed the knife called Fair Warning from the sheath in her oversized boot and began to carve the stubborn bark.

"The sap in these trees is no good for sugaring," a coarse voice called out behind her.

Rye spun at the sound. A man appeared from the trees on the opposite side of the clearing, his footfalls nearly silent. A hunter's bow was slung over his shoulder and he dragged the carcass of a red stag behind him. His gaunt cheeks and wary eyes reflected the face of someone who'd spent many days alone in the forest. Unfortunately, it was a face she didn't recognize.

Rye's first instinct was to flee, but it occurred to her that this huntsman might have useful information. Here, in the lightly traveled reaches north of the Shale, information was more valuable than gold grommets. She sheathed Fair Warning, backed away a safe distance, then stopped, confident she could outrun the stranger if need be.

"Do you speak, child?" the huntsman asked when she offered no reply. "Are you a Feraling?" He eyed the grime that covered her coat.

Feralings were humans who lived in isolation Beyond the Shale. Reclusive and untamed, they'd adapted to the way of the wood in order to survive. In all of Rye's recent travels, she'd met only one.

"I'm no Feraling," she said. "And I'm not looking for sap."

The huntsman raised an eyebrow. "You do speak . . .

and with a Drowning accent, if I'm not mistaken." He sucked a tooth behind a rough beard.

"That's right," Rye said. "And if you know Village Drowning, then you're no Feraling either."

The huntsman abandoned the stag, pulled the hand axe from the log, and plodded to the tree she'd carved. He jabbed the bark with the axe head as he stooped and examined it.

"Letters *R* and . . . *H*. What do they stand for?" he asked, casting a suspicious glance at her.

When he looked back, Rye had removed her cudgel from the sling over her shoulder.

"*R* is for Rye," she replied. "And *H* is for Harmless. That's who I'm looking for. But make no mistake, he's not harmless at all." She tightened her grip. "And neither am I."

The huntsman chuckled. "Put your twig away," he scoffed.

Her *twig* was a High Isle cudgel, a dangerous weapon made from the hardest blackthorn in all the Shale. If the huntsman was as well traveled as he was road worn, he would have known it. Rye didn't put it down.

"Have you come across anyone in these woods lately?" she asked, gesturing her cudgel toward the trees. "A man maybe? Traveling alone?"

"Travelers are rare in the forest, as are young girls.

And yet, strangely enough, both have wandered into my camp in recent days." The huntsman studied her carefully before speaking again. "There *was* a man. Appeared like a ghost—startled me while I fixed my supper. He was cordial enough but didn't linger."

That sounded like Harmless, Rye thought.

"Did you notice anything else about him?" she asked. "Was he wearing an unusual necklace? Like this?" With her thumb, Rye hooked the runestone choker she wore around her neck so that the huntsman could see it.

She saw a flash of recognition in his eyes, then they shifted, as if calculating something. "It's possible, although I don't have a keen eye for jewelry," he said coolly. But his expression had already betrayed his real answer.

"When did he leave?" Rye demanded. "Do you remember which way he went?"

"I do," he replied, his face expressionless. "He was heading south along the Wend. But the rest of the details have already been bought and paid for."

Rye narrowed her eyes, unsure of what he meant.

"Several other travelers arrived the following day. They too had an interest in this man you call Harmless."

"Who were they?" Rye asked sharply.

The huntsman shrugged. "They wore no crest or colors. They weren't overly friendly—but at least they paid well for my answers to their questions. Well enough that I'll be able to spend my winter in the warm bed of a roadhouse instead of shivering in a tent. Can you offer the same?"

Rye's ears burned. "I have no coins."

"But if you are looking for this Harmless, he must be of value to you." He rubbed two grimy fingers through his beard. "Perhaps, you, in turn, are of value to him?" he asked, his voice darkening. "Or maybe . . . to those others who seek him?"

Rye took a step away.

"Now, now," the huntsman said. "Why not have a seat and join me without a fuss? I spend my days tracking fleet-footed creatures through this forest. If you run, I'll surely catch you. And then you'll have to spend the night in a sack with the rest of the game. I've got one right over there that's just about your size."

But Rye wasn't listening. She turned and ran, darting into the trees. She was no novice when it came to being chased and, if need be, she could bite much harder than some frightened hare. But just as she reached full stride, her legs kicked up and her body lurched skyward. The forest floor spun below and the blood rushed to her head. Rye craned her neck and peered up at the nearly invisible line strung over a limb. A snare had caught her around one boot and she now dangled upside down, several feet above the ground.

The huntsman shook his head as if to say *I told you so* and retrieved a thick burlap sack from his supplies.

Rye still grasped her cudgel and shook it threateningly in his direction. She doubted her effort was particularly menacing as she spun slowly and helplessly in a tiny circle at the end of the snare. She desperately wiggled her foot in her oversize boot, which only made her rotate even faster.

When the huntsman came back into view he was at the edge of the clearing, his axe raised in one hand, the burlap sack ready in the other.

A looming figure loped from the shadows opposite them, covering the space in two long-legged bounds. Rye sucked in her breath with such alarm that the huntsman paused to look behind him. A huge clawed hand sent him sprawling.

Rye thrashed her whole body, sending herself spinning furiously. She saw the blur of the massive beast. It regarded the huntsman's motionless body with bulging eyes set on top of its misshapen head. From its elongated jaws hung a plaited, rust-orange beard tied at the end with a child's bootlace. It snuffed at the air with a long, pig-like nose and, to Rye's great relief, briefly turned its attention toward the stag. Rye's own nose filled with the stench of the bogs.

She was no stranger to beasts of this kind. It was a Bog Noblin.

With one final tug, her foot slipped free from her boot with a cascade of damp straw stuffing. For once it had come in handy to wear her father's old boots that were three sizes too large. She met the ground head-first, the impact knocking the wind from her lungs.

The Bog Noblin looked up from its prize. First one bulging eye turned to meet her gaze, then the other. Hunched over the stag, its gray skin hung in folds from its broad, bony shoulders and ribs. Its floppy ears were pierced with an assortment of metal hooks, and around its neck dangled a crude necklace strung with the blackened remains of human feet. The Bog Noblin sniffed the air in her direction and stood to its full height.

Rye pushed herself up from the dirt. She only hesitated long enough to draw Fair Warning and cut her boot down from the snare.

Tucking it under her arm, she rushed deeper into the forest without looking back, her runestone choker cutting through the shadows with a pale blue glow.

The Hollow

Rye scurried under, over, and around razor-sharp branches. She squeezed through the narrowest gaps she could find in the thicket, forging a path impossible for anyone larger than a young girl to follow. She didn't stop to catch her breath until she'd reached the edge of a narrow stream. The afternoon's dying light disappeared behind her.

Rye put her hands on her knees, examining her flushed reflection in the clear water. Where her brown hair wasn't stuck to the sweat on her forehead, it fell to her shoulders now, longer than she'd ever grown it before. Normally, by summer's end, Rye's face glowed like a creamy pecan after long days helping her mother in the garden. But life Beyond the Shale was one of perennial shade, and her cheeks still maintained last winter's pallor. At the moment, she was just relieved to see that her choker was no longer glowing either. Its runestones only stirred when Bog Noblins were near.

She stood up straight, water flickering silently at her feet. The stream was called the Rill. It flowed like a silver thread around a mossy glade and looped back into itself, hollowing the glade out from the rest of the dense forest. The Hollow was dominated by an enormous old oak tree, its thick roots engorged like veins bulging from the ground. A spiral staircase of knotted wood planks snaked around the oak's massive trunk, leading to a series of landings and ramshackle buildings embraced in its boughs. Rope bridges slumped like clotheslines between the main house and several smaller, overgrown cottages nestled in the tree's outstretched limbs.

A stocky, horned figure barely taller than Rye hurried forward, a handmade platform of intertwined rowan branches tucked under his arm.

"Miss Riley," the barrel-shaped man called breathlessly. "Where in the Shale have you been? It's practically nightfall!" He laid the makeshift bridge across the stream at her feet.

"It's all right, Mr. Nettle," she said. "I made it back, didn't I?"

Mr. Nettle lifted the bridge as soon as Rye crossed, his ferret-like eyes glancing at the shadows on the other side.

"Without an eyelash to spare," he replied, sniffing the air.

Mr. Nettle's curled horns were, in fact, part of the fur-lined mountain goat's skull that he wore on his head like a hat. His cheeks were buried beneath a curly beard the color of dried pine needles, and the hair on the backs of his hands and knuckles seemed as thick as the scruff on his neck. He wore a rather formal vest and coat that looked to have been quite regal at one time, but his trousers were made of raw, crimped wool that gave him the vague look of a woolly ram from the waist down. Despite his wild appearance, Mr. Nettle wasn't part animal or beast. He was a Feraling—a native forest dweller—the only one Rye had encountered in all of her months Beyond the Shale.

"I found a message from Harmless—at least, I *think* it was from him," Rye explained breathlessly. "There was a huntsman who said he saw him too, or someone who sounded like Harmless anyway."

"Perhaps that's who I smell," Mr. Nettle said, his

wary eyes still on the looming forest.

"I doubt it," Rye said. Her eyes followed Mr. Nettle's gaze across the Rill. "There's also a Bog Noblin out there, and he stinks worse than most anything on two legs or four."

Mr. Nettle turned to her in alarm. "A Noblin this far from the bogs?" he asked. "Just one?"

"That's all I saw."

"Traveling alone . . ." He furrowed his brow. "Even stranger. You're quite certain that's what it was?"

Rye nodded. "Trust me. I've seen more than my fair share."

Mr. Nettle pulled a curly lock of beard between his teeth with his tongue and began to chew. "Well, if he's foolish enough to linger, he may never make it back to whatever dank moor he crawled from. Worse beasts than Bog Noblins prowl these woods . . ."

"Is my mother back?" Rye interrupted, glancing up at the tree house high above them.

"Yes, she returned not long—"

Rye didn't wait for Mr. Nettle to finish. She raced past him, stomping up the spiral steps so fast she nearly made herself dizzy.

Abby O'Chanter raised her thin, dark eyebrows as she listened to Rye's story, looking up from her scavenged cook pot as she scraped the night's meager meal into wooden bowls. She placed one of them on the round stump of a sawed-off bough that served as their table, in front of Rye's little sister, Lottie. The youngest O'Chanter had donned Mr. Nettle's skullcap and now looked like she had grown horns from her ears.

"The letter *H* was fresh, couldn't have been more than a few days old," Rye emphasized after completing the tale. "And the way the huntsman described the traveler—it *had* to be Harmless."

Rye watched her mother carefully and waited for her reaction. Surely Abby would be as excited as she was. After nearly five months in the forest, the most they had heard of Harmless were vague rumors from wayward travelers. But now he had left them a message. Based on what the huntsman had said, he was not only alive, but nearby—not more than a day or two away.

"And the other men in search of your father?" Abby asked. "Did the huntsman have more to say about them? We haven't come across anyone in weeks."

"Just that they weren't very friendly," Rye said, recalling his words. "They don't sound like the type of travelers we'd care to run across."

Abby fell silent. Mr. Nettle watched quietly from his stump next to the sawed-off bough, the only sound the crunch of Lottie's small jaws. She chewed. And chewed some more. Supper consisted of tough meat and bland, boiled roots. Food of any sort was difficult to come by Beyond the Shale, where small game was elusive and the edible plants bitter.

"Tomorrow we can all set out together to search for Harmless," Rye added, grabbing her mother's elbow enthusiastically. "With luck, we'll find him before anyone else does."